MW00593445

Chaucer for Children

A Golden Key

Mrs. H. R. Haweis

TABLE OF CONTENTS

FOREWORDS TO THE SECOND EDITION.

IN revising Chaucer for Children for a New Edition, I have fully availed myself of the help and counsel of my numerous reviewers and correspondents, without weighting the book, which is really designed for children, with a number of new facts, and theories springing from the new facts, such as I have incorporated in my Book for older readers, Chaucer for Schools.

Curious discoveries are still being made, and will continue to be, thanks to the labours of men like Mr. F. J. Furnivall, and many other able and industrious scholars, encouraged by the steadily increasing public interest in Chaucer.

I must express my sincere thanks and gratification for the reception this book has met with from the press generally, and from many eminent critics in particular; and last, not least, from those to whom I devoted my pleasant toil, the children of England.

M. E. HAWEIS.

FOREWORDS.

To the Mother.

A CHAUCER for Children may seem to some an impossible story-book, but it is one which I have been encouraged to put together by noticing how quickly my own little boy learned and understood fragments of early English poetry. I believe that if they had the chance, many other children would do the same.

I think that much of the construction and pronunciation of old English which seems stiff and obscure to grown up people, appears easy to children, whose crude language is in many ways its counterpart.

The narrative in early English poetry is almost always very simply and clearly expressed, with the same kind of repetition of facts and names which, as every mother knows, is what children most require in story-telling. The emphasis[1] which the final E gives to many words is another thing which helps to impress the sentences on the memory, the sense being often shorter than the sound.

It seems but natural that every English child should know something of one who left so deep an impression on his age, and on the English tongue, that he has been called by Occleve "the finder of our fair language." For in his day there was actually no national language, no national literature, English consisting of so many dialects, each having its own literature intelligible to comparatively few; and the Court and educated classes still adhering greatly to Norman-French for both speaking and writing. Chaucer, who wrote for the people, chose the best form of English, which was that spoken at Court, at a time when English was regaining supremacy over French; and the form he adopted laid the foundation of our present National Tongue.

Chaucer is, moreover, a thoroughly religious poet, all his merriest stories having a fair moral; even those which are too coarse for modern taste are rather naïve than injurious; and his pages breathe a genuine faith in God, and a passionate sense of the beauty and harmony of the divine work. The selections I have made are some of the most beautiful portions of Chaucer's most beautiful tales.

I believe that some knowledge of, or at least interest in, the domestic life and manners of the 13th, 14th, and 15th centuries, would materially help young children in their reading of English history. The political life would often be interpreted by the domestic life, and much of that time which to a child's mind forms the dryest portion of history, because so unknown, would then stand out as it really was, glorious and fascinating in its vigour and vivacity, its enthusiasm, and love of beauty and bravery. There is no clearer or safer exponent of the life of the 14th century, as far as he describes it, than Geoffrey Chaucer.

As to the difficulties of understanding Chaucer, they have been greatly overstated. An occasional reference to a glossary is all that is requisite; and, with a little attention to a very simple general rule, anybody with moderate intelligence and an ear for musical rhythm can enjoy the lines.

In the first place, it must be borne in mind that the E at the end of the old English words was usually a syllable, and must be sounded, as Aprillë, swootë, &c.

Note, then, that Chaucer is always rhythmical. Hardly ever is his rhythm a shade wrong, and therefore, roughly speaking, if you pronounce the words so as to preserve the rhythm all will be well. When the final e must be sounded in order to make the rhythm right, sound it, but where it is not needed leave it mute.[2]

Thus:—in the opening lines—

Whan that | April | le with | his schowr | es swoote	when, showers, sweet
The drought | of Marche | hath per | cèd to | the roote	pierced, root
And bath | ud eve | ry veyne | in swich | licour	such, liquor
Of whiche | vertue | engen | drèd is | the flour. (Prologue.)	flower

You see that in those words which I have put in italics the final E must be sounded slightly, for the rhythm's sake.

And sma | le fow | les ma | ken me | lodie	small birds make
That sle | pen al | the night | with o | pen yhe. (Prologue.)	sleep, all

Again, to quote at random—

The bu | sy lark | e mess | ager | of day,	lark, messenger
Salu | eth in | hire song | the mor | we gray. (Knight's Tale.)	saluteth, her, morning

Ful long | e wern | his leg | gus, and | ful lene;	legs, lean
Al like | a staff | ther was | no calf | y-sene. (Prologue—'Reve.')	

or in Chaucer's exquisite greeting of the daisy—

Knelyng | alwey | til it | unclo | sèd was	always
Upon | the sma | le, sof | te, swo | te gras.	
(Legend of Good Women.)	small, soft, sweet

How much of the beauty and natural swing of Chaucer's poetry is lost by translation into modern English, is but too clear when that beauty is once perceived; but I thought some modernization of the old lines would help the child to catch the sense of the original more readily: for my own rendering, I can only make the apology that when I commenced my work I did not know it would be impossible to procure suitable modernized versions by eminent poets. Finding that unattainable, I merely endeavoured to render the old version in modern English as closely as was compatible with sense, and the simplicity needful for a child's mind; and I do not in any degree pretend to have rendered it in poetry.

The beauty of such passages as the death of Arcite is too delicate and evanescent to bear rough handling. But I may here quote some of the lines as an example of the importance of the final e in emphasizing certain words with an almost solemn music.

And with | that word | his spech | e fail | e gan;	speech, fail
For fro | his feete | up to | his brest | was come	
The cold | of deth | that hadde | him o | ver nome;	overtaken
And yet | moreo | ver in | his ar | mes twoo	now, arms
The vi | tal strength | is lost, | and al | agoo.	gone
Only | the in | tellect, | withou | ten more,	without
That dwel | led in | his her | te sik | and sore,	heart, sick
Gan fayl | e when | the her | te felt | e deth. (Knight's Tale.)	began to fail, felt death

There is hardly anything finer than Chaucer's version of the story of these passionate young men, up to the touching close of Arcite's accident and the beautiful patience of death. In life nothing would have reconciled the almost animal fury of the rivals, but at the last such a resignation comes to Arcite that he gives up Emelye to Palamon with a sublime effort of self-sacrifice. Throughout the whole of the Knight's Tale sounds as of rich organ music seem to peal from the page; throughout the Clerk's Tale one seems to hear strains of infinite sadness echoing the strange outrages imposed on patient Grizel. But without attention to the rhythm half the grace and music is lost, and therefore it is all-important that the child be properly taught to preserve it.

I have adhered generally to Morris's text (1866), being both good and popular,[3] only checking it by his Clarendon Press edition, and by Tyrwhitt, Skeat, Bell, &c., when I conceive force is gained, and I have added a running glossary of such words as are not immediately clear, on a level with the line, to disperse any lingering difficulty.

In the pictures I have been careful to preserve the right costumes, colours, and surroundings, for which I have resorted to the MSS. of the time, knowing that a child's mind, unaided by the eye, fails to realize half of what comes through the ear. Children may be encouraged to verify these costumes in the figures upon many tombs and stalls, &c., in old churches, and in old pictures.

In conclusion I must offer my sincere and hearty thanks to many friends for their advice, assistance, and encouragement during my work; amongst them, Mr. A. J. Ellis, Mr. F. J. Furnivall, and Mr. Calderon.

Whatever may be the shortcomings of the book, I cannot but hope that many little ones, while listening to Chaucer's Tales, will soon begin to be interested in the picturesque life of the middle ages, and may thus be led to study and appreciate 'The English Homer'[4] by the pages I have written for my own little boy.

ACCENT OF CHAUCER.

The mother should read to the child a fragment of Chaucer with the correct pronunciation of his day, of which we give an example below, inadequate, of course, but sufficient for the present purpose. The whole subject is fully investigated in the three first parts of the treatise on 'Early English Pronunciation, with special reference to Shakespere and Chaucer,' by Alexander J. Ellis, F.R.S.

The a is, as in the above languages, pronounced as in âne, appeler, &c. E commonly, as in écarté, &c. The final e was probably indistinct, as in German now, habe, werde, &c.—not unlike the a in China: it was lost before a vowel. The final e is still sounded by the French in singing. In old French verse, one finds it as indispensable to the rhythm as in Chaucer,—and as graceful,—hence probably the modern retention of the letter as a syllable in vocal music.

Ou is sounded as the French ou.

I generally as on the Continent, ee: never as we sound it at present.

Ch as in Scotch and German.

I quote the opening lines of the Prologue as the nearest to hand.

Whan that Aprille with his schowres swoote

The drought of Marche hath perced to the roote,
And bathud every veyne in swich licour,
Of which vertue engendred is the flour;
Whan Zephirus eek with his swete breethe
Enspirud hath in every holte and heethe
The tendre croppes, and the yonge sonne
Hath in the Ram his halfe cours i-ronne,
And smale fowles maken melodie,
That slepen al the night with open yhe,
So priketh hem nature in here corages—&c.

Whan that Aprilla with his shōōrĕs sohta
The drŏŏkht of March hath pairsed to the rohta,
And bahthed ev'ry vīn in sweech licōōr,
Of which vairtú enjendrèd is the flōōr;
Whan Zephirŏŏs aik with his swaita braitha
Enspeered hath in ev'ry holt and haitha
The tendra croppes, and the yŏŏnga sŏŏnna
Hath in the Ram his halfa cōōrs i-rŏŏnna,
And smahla fōōles mahken melodee-a,
That slaipen al the nikht with ohpen ee-a,
So pricketh hem nahtúr in heer coràhges, &c.

It will thus be seen that many of Chaucer's lines end with a dissyllable, instead of a single syllable. Sote, rote, brethe, hethe, &c. (having the final e), are words of two syllables; corages is a word of three, àges rhyming with pilgrimages in the next line. It will also be apparent that some lines are lengthened with a syllable too much for strict metre—a licence allowed by the best poets,—which, avoiding as it does any possible approach to a doggrel sound, has a lifting, billowy rhythm, and, in fact, takes the place of a 'turn' in music. A few instances will suffice:—

'And though that I no wepne have in this place.'

'Have here my troth, tomorwe I nyl not fayle,
Withouten wityng of eny other wight.'

'As any raven fether it schon for-blak.'

'A man mot ben a fool other yong or olde.'

I think that any one reading these lines twice over as I have roughly indicated, will find the accent one not difficult to practise; and the perfect rhythm and ring of the lines facilitates matters, as the ear can frequently guide the pronunciation. The lines can scarcely be read too slowly or majestically.

I must not here be understood to imply that difficulties in reading and accentuating Chaucer are chimerical, but only that it is possible to understand and enjoy him without as much difficulty as is commonly supposed. In perusing the whole of Chaucer, there must needs be exceptional readings and accentuation, which in detail only a student of the subject would comprehend or care for.

The rough rule suggested in the preface is a good one, as far as the rhythm goes: as regards the sound, I have given a rough example.

I will quote a fragment again from the Prologue as a second instance:—

Ther was also a nonne, a prioresse,
That of hire smylyng was ful symple and coy;
Hire gretteste ooth nas but by Seynte Loy;
And sche was cleped Madame Eglentyne.
Ful wel sche sang the servise devyne,
Entuned in hire nose ful semyly;
And Frensch sche spak ful faire and fetysly,
Aftur the scole of Stratford atte Bowe,
For Frensch of Parys was to hire unknowe.

Ther was ahlsoa a nŏŏn, a preeoressa,
That of her smeeling was fŏŏl sim-pland cooy;
Heer graitest ohth nas bŏŏt bee Sī-ent Looy,
And shay was cleppèd Màdam Eglanteena.
Fŏŏl well shay sang the servicĕ divinä,
Entúned in heer nohsa fŏŏl saimaly;
And French shai spahk fŏŏl fēr and faitisly,
Ahfter the scohl of Strahtford ahtta Bow-a,
For French of Pahrees was toh her ŏŏn-know-a.

Observe simpland for simple and: simple being pronounced like a word of one syllable. With the common English pronunciation the lines would not scan. 'Vernicle,' 'Christofre,' 'wimple,' 'chilindre,' 'companable,' &c., are further instances of this mute e, and may be read as French words.

CHAUCER THE TALE-TELLER.

I.

DO you like hearing stories? I am going to tell you of some one who lived a very long time ago, and who was a very wise and good man, and who told more wonderful stories than I shall be able to tell you in this little book. But you shall hear some of them, if you will try and understand them, though they are written in a sort of English different from what you are accustomed to speak.

But, in order that you really may understand the stories, I must first tell you something about the man who made them; and also why his language was not the same as yours, although it was English. His name was Chaucer—Geoffrey Chaucer. You must remember his name, for he was so great a man that he has been called the 'Father of English Poetry'—that is, the beginner or inventor of all the poetry that belongs to our England; and when you are grown up, you will often hear of Chaucer and his works.

II.

Chaucer lived in England 500 years ago—a longer time than such a little boy as you can even think of. It is now the year 1876, you know. Well, Chaucer was born about 1340, in the reign of King Edward III. We should quite have forgotten all Chaucer's stories in such a great space of time if he had not written them down in a book. But, happily, he did write them down; and so we can read them just as if he had only told them yesterday.

If you could suddenly spring back into the time when Chaucer lived, what a funny world you would find! Everybody was dressed differently then from what people are now, and lived in quite a different way; and you might think they were very uncomfortable, but they were very happy, because they were accustomed to it all.

People had no carpets in those days in their rooms. Very few people were rich enough to have glass windows. There was no paper on the walls, and very seldom any pictures; and as for spring sofas and arm-chairs, they were unknown. The seats were only benches placed against the wall: sometimes a chair was brought on grand occasions to do honour to a visitor; but it was a rare luxury.

The rooms of most people in those days had blank walls of stone or brick and plaster, painted white or coloured, and here and there—behind the place of honour, perhaps—hung a sort of curtain, like a large picture, made of needlework, called tapestry. You may have seen tapestry hanging in rooms, with men and women and animals worked upon it. That was almost the only covering for walls in Chaucer's time. Now we have a great many other ornaments on them, besides tapestry.

The rooms Chaucer lived in were probably like every one's else. They had bare walls, with a piece of tapestry hung here and there on them—a bare floor, strewn with rushes, which must have looked more like a stable than a sitting-room. But the rushes were better than nothing. They kept the feet warm, as our carpets do, though they were very untidy, and not always very clean.

When Chaucer wanted his dinner or breakfast, he did not go to a big table like that you are used to: the table came to him. A couple of trestles or stands were brought to him, and a board laid across them, and over the board a cloth, and on the cloth were placed all the curious dishes they ate then. There was no such thing as coffee or tea. People had meat, and beer, and wine for breakfast, and dinner, and supper, all alike. They helped themselves from the common dish, and ate with their fingers, as dinner-knives and forks were not invented, and it was thought a sign of special good breeding to have clean hands and nails. Plates there were none. But large flat cakes of bread were used instead; and when the meat was eaten off them, they were given to the poor—for, being full of the gravy that had soaked into them, they were too valuable to throw away. When they had finished eating, the servants came and lifted up the board, and carried it off.

III.

And now for Chaucer himself! How funny you would think he looked, if you could see him sitting in his house! He wore a hood, of a dark colour, with a long tail to it, which in-doors hung down his back, and out of doors was twisted round his head to keep the hood on firm. This tail was called a liripipe.

He did not wear a coat and trousers like your father's, but a sort of gown, called a tunic, or dalmatic, which in one picture of him is grey and loose, with large sleeves, and bright red stockings and black boots; but on great occasions he wore a close-fitting tunic, with a splendid belt and buckle, a dagger, and jewelled garters, and, perhaps, a gold circlet round his hair. How much prettier to wear such bright colours instead of black! men and women dressed in green, and red, and yellow then; and when they walked in the streets, they looked as people look in pictures.

DINNER IN THE OLDEN TIME.

GEOFFREY CHAUCER.

You may see how good and clever Chaucer was by his face; such a wise, thoughtful, pleasant face! He looks very kind, I think, as if he would never say anything harsh or bitter; but sometimes he made fun of people in a merry way. Words of his own, late in life, show that he was rather fat, his face small and fair. In manner he seemed 'elvish,' or shy, with a habit of staring on the ground, 'as if he would find a hair.'

All day he worked hard, and his spare time was given to 'studying and reading alway,' till his head ached and his look became dazed. (House of Fame.)

Chaucer lived, like you, in London. Whether he was born there is not known;[5] but as his father, John Chaucer, was a vintner in Thames Street, London, it is probable that he was. Not much is known about his parents or family, except that his grandfather, Richard Chaucer, was also a vintner; and his mother had an uncle who was a moneyer; so that he came of respectable and well-to-do people, though not noble.[6] Whether he was educated at Oxford or Cambridge, whether he studied for the bar or for the Church, there is no record to show; but

4

there is no doubt that his education was a good one, and that he worked very hard at his books and tasks, otherwise he could not have grown to be the learned and cultivated man he was. We know that he possessed considerable knowledge of the classics, divinity, philosophy, astronomy, as much as was then known of chemistry, and, indeed, most of the sciences. French and Latin he knew as a matter of course, for the better classes used these tongues more than English—Latin for writing, and French for writing and speaking; for, by his translations from the French, he earned, early in life, a 'balade' of compliment from Eustache Deschamps, with the refrain, 'Grant translateur, noble Geoffroi Chaucier.' It is probable, too, that he knew Italian, for, in his later life, we can see how he has been inspired by the great Italian writers, Dante, Petrarch, and Boccaccio.

It has recently been discovered that for a time (certainly in 1357) Geoffrey Chaucer, being then seventeen, was a page[7] in the household of Elizabeth, Countess of Ulster, wife of Lionel, second son of King Edward III.; a position which he could not have held if he had not been a well-born, or at least well-educated, person. A page in those days was very different from what we call a page now—therefore we infer that the Chaucer family had interest at Court; for without that, Geoffrey could never have entered the royal service.

Most gentlemen's sons were educated by becoming pages. They entered the service of noble ladies, who paid them, or sometimes were even paid for receiving them. Thus young men learned courtesy of manners, and all the accomplishments of indoor and outdoor life—riding, the use of arms, &c.—and were very much what an aide-de-camp in the army now is. Chaucer, you see, held a post which many a nobly-born lad must have coveted.

There is a doubtful tradition that Chaucer was intended for a lawyer, and was a member of the Middle Temple (a large building in London, where a great many lawyers live still), and here, as they say, he was once fined two shillings for beating a Franciscan friar in Fleet Street.

If this be true, it must have been rather a severe beating; for two shillings was a far larger sum than it is now—equal to about sixteen shillings of our money. Chaucer was sometimes angry with the friars at later times in life, and deals them some hard hits in his writings with a relish possibly founded on personal experience of some disagreeable friar.

At any rate, Chaucer never got fond of the friars, and thought they were often bad and mischievous men, who did not always act up to what they said. This is called hypocrisy, and is so evil a thing that Chaucer was quite right to be angry with people who were hypocrites.

IV.

Fleet Street still exists, though it was much less crowded with people in Chaucer's day than now. Indeed, the whole of London was very different from our London; and, oh, so much prettier! The streets within the London wall were probably thickly populated, and not over-healthy; but outside the wall, streets such as Fleet Street were more like the streets of some of our suburbs, or rather some foreign towns—the houses irregular, with curious pointed roofs, here and there divided by little gardens, and even green fields. I dare say, when Chaucer walked in the streets, the birds sang over his head, and the hawthorn and primrose bloomed where now the black smoke and dust would soon kill most green things. Thames Street was where Chaucer long lived in London, but, at one time in his life at least, it is certain that he occupied a tenement at Aldgate, which formed part of an old prison; and it is probable that at another he lived in the beautiful Savoy Palace with John of Gaunt, whilst his wife was maid of honour. In 1393, Chaucer was living at Greenwich, near which he had work in 1390— poor and asking his friend Scogan to intercede for him "where it would fructify;" and at the end of his life he had a house in Westminster, said to be nearly on the same spot on which Henry VII.'s Chapel now stands, and close to the Abbey where he is buried.

In those days it was the fashion, when the month of May[8] arrived, for everybody, rich and poor, to get up very early in the morning, to gather boughs of hawthorn and laurel, to deck all the doorways in the street, as a joyful welcoming of the sweet spring time. Chaucer alludes more than once to this beautiful custom. The streets must have been full of fragrance then. He also tells us how he loved to rise up at dawn in the morning, and go into the fresh green fields, to see the daisies open. You have often seen the daisies shut up at night, but I don't suppose you ever saw them opening in the morning; and I am afraid, however early you got up in London, you could not reach the fields quick enough to see that. But you may guess from this how much nearer the country was to the town 500 years ago. There were so many fewer houses built then, that within a walk you could get right into the meadows. You may see that by comparing the two maps I have made for you.

London was also much quieter. There were no railways—such things had never been heard of. There were not even any cabs or carriages. Sometimes a market cart might roll by, but not very often, and then everybody would run out to see what the unaccustomed clatter was all about. People had to walk everywhere, unless they were rich enough to ride on horseback, or lived near the river. In that case, they used to go in barges or boats on the Thames, as far as they could; for, strange as it may seem, even the King had no coach then.

London in the 15th Century.

London in the 19th Century.

I am afraid Geoffrey Chaucer would not recognize that 'dere and swete cityè of London' in the great, smoky, noisy, bustling metropolis we are accustomed to, and I am quite sure he would not recognize the language; and presently I will explain what I meant by saying that though Chaucer spoke and wrote English, it was quite different from what we speak now. You will see, as you go on, how queerly all the words are spelt, so much so that I have had to put a second version side by side with Chaucer's lines, which you will understand more readily; and when I read them to you, you will see how different is the sound. These words were all pronounced slowly, almost with a drawl, while we nowadays have got to talk so fast, that no one who lived then would follow what we say without great difficulty.

V.

Chaucer's connection with the Court makes it probable that he lived during the greater part of his life in London; and it is pleasant to think that this great poet was valued and beloved in his day by the highest powers in the land. He held, at various times, posts in the King's household, which brought him more or less money, such as valet of the King's chamber, the King's esquire, &c.; and he found a fast friend in John of Gaunt, one of the sons of King Edward III.

In 1359 Chaucer became a soldier, and served in the army under this King, in an attack upon France, and was taken prisoner. It is supposed he was detained there about a year; and, being ransomed by Edward, when he came back to England, he married a lady named Philippa. She was probably the younger daughter of Sir Paon de Roet, of Hainault,[9] who came over to England in the retinue of Queen Philippa, who was also of Hainault. These two Philippas, coming from the same place, remained friends during all the Queen's life; for when Chaucer

7

married Philippa de Roet, she was one of the Queen's maids of honour; and, after her marriage, the Queen gave her an annual pension of ten marks[10] (£50), which was continued to her by the King after Queen Philippa died. Some people say Chaucer's wife was also the Queen's god-daughter.[11]

If you would like to know what Chaucer's wife looked like, I will tell you. I do not know what she was like in the face, but I can tell you the fashion of the garb she wore. I like to believe she had long yellow hair, which Chaucer describes so often and so prettily. Chaucer's wife wore one of those funny head-dresses like crowns, or rather like boxes, over a gold net, with her hair braided in a tress, hanging down her back. She had a close green[12] dress, with tight sleeves, reaching right down over the hand, to protect it from the sun and wind; and a very long skirt, falling in folds about her feet, sometimes edged with beautiful white fur, ermine, or a rich grey fur, called vair. The colour of this grey fur was much liked, and when people had light grey eyes, of somewhat the same colour, it was thought very beautiful. Many songs describe pretty ladies with 'eyes of vair.'

When noble persons went to Court, they wore dresses far more splendid than any to be seen now—dresses of all colours, worked in with flowers and branches of gold, sometimes with heraldic devices and strange figures, and perfectly smothered in jewels. No one has pearls, and emeralds, and diamonds sewn on their gowns now; but in the fourteenth century, rich people had the seams of their clothes often covered with gems. The ladies wore close-fitting dresses, with splendid belts, or seints, round their hips, all jewelled; and strings of glittering jewels hung round their necks, and down from the belt, and on the head-dress. People did not wear short sleeves then, but long ones, made sometimes very curiously with streamers hanging from the elbow; a long thin gauze veil, shining with silver and gold; and narrow pointed shoes, much longer than their feet, which, they thought, made the foot look slender. If ladies had not had such long shoes, they would never have showed beneath their long embroidered skirts, and they would always have been stumbling when they walked. It was a very graceful and elegant costume that Chaucer's wife wore; but the laws of England probably forbade her to wear silk, which was reserved for nobles. When she walked out of doors, she had tall clogs to save her pretty shoes from the mud of the rough streets; and when she rode on horseback with the Queen, or her husband Chaucer, she sat on a pillion, and placed her feet on a narrow board called a planchette. Many women rode astride, like the "Wife of Bath" whom Chaucer speaks of.

Now, perhaps, you would like to know whether Chaucer had any little children. We do not know much about Chaucer's children. We know he had a little son called Lewis, because Chaucer wrote a treatise for him when he was ten years old, to teach him how to use an instrument he had given him, called an astrolabe.[13] Chaucer must have been very fond of Lewis, since he took so much trouble for him, and he speaks to him very kindly and lovingly.

As Chaucer was married before 1366, it is likely that he had other children; and some people say he had an elder son, named Thomas, and a daughter Elizabeth.[14]

John of Gaunt, who was Chaucer's patron as I told you, was very kind to Thomas Chaucer, and gave him several posts in the King's household, as he grew up to be a man. And John of Gaunt heard that Elizabeth Chaucer wished to be a nun; and, in 1381, we find that he paid a large sum of money for her noviciate (that is, for her to learn to be a nun) in the Abbey of Barking.

A LADY CROSSING THE STREET IN THE OLDEN TIME.

A nun is a person who does not care for the amusements and pleasures which other people care for—playing, and dancing, and seeing sights and many people; but who prefers to go and live in a house called a nunnery, where she will see hardly any one, and think of nothing but being good, and helping the poor. And, if people think they can be good best in that way, they ought to become nuns. But I think people can be just as good living at home with their friends, without shutting themselves in a nunnery.

10

Now I must leave off telling you about Chaucer's wife and children, and go on to Chaucer himself.

VI.

Chaucer was, as I told you, the friend of one of the sons of the King, Edward III. Not the eldest son, who was, as you know, Edward the Black Prince, the great warrior, nor Lionel, the third son, whom he had served when a boy, but the fourth son, John of Gaunt, who had a great deal of power with the King.

John of Gaunt.

John of Gaunt was the same age as Chaucer.

When John of Gaunt was only 19 (the year that Chaucer went with the army to France), he married a lady called Blanche of Lancaster, and there were famous joustings and great festivities of every kind. In this year, it has been supposed, Chaucer wrote a poem, 'The Parliament of Birds,' to celebrate the wedding. Another long poem, called 'The Court of Love,' is said to have been written by him about this time—at any rate, in very early life.

When Chaucer came back to England, and got married himself, he was still more constantly at Court, and there are many instances recorded of John's attachment to both Chaucer and Philippa all his life. Among others we may notice his gifts to Philippa of certain 'silver-gilt cups with covers,' on the 1st of January in 1380, 1381, and 1382.

It is touching to see how faithful these two friends were to each other, and how long their friendship lasted. The first we hear of it was about 1359, the year when John married Blanche, and for forty years it remained unbroken. Nay, it grew closer and closer, for in 1394, when John of Gaunt and Chaucer were both middle-aged men, John married Philippa's sister (Sir Paon Roet's elder daughter), so that Chaucer became John of Gaunt's brother.[15]

When John of Gaunt was in power he never forgot Chaucer. When he became unpopular it was Chaucer's turn to be faithful to him; and faithful he was, whatever he suffered, and he did suffer for it severely, and became quite poor at times, as you will see. Directly John came into power again up went Chaucer too, and his circumstances improved. There are few friendships so long and so faithful on both sides as this was.[16]

VII.

Chaucer was employed by Edward III. for many years as envoy, which is a very important office. It can only be given to a very wise and shrewd man. This proves the great ability of Chaucer in other things besides making songs and telling stories. He had to go abroad, to France, Italy, and elsewhere, on the King's private missions; and the King gave him money for his services, and promoted him to great honour.

On one occasion (1373) when he was sent to Florence, on an embassy, he is supposed to have seen Petrarch, a great Italian poet and patriot, whose name you must not forget. Petrarch was then living at Arqua, two miles from Padua, a beautiful town in Italy; and though Petrarch was a much older man than Chaucer—more than twenty years older—it seems only natural that these two great men should have tried to see each other; for they had much in common. Both were far-famed poets, and both, in a measure, representatives of the politics, poetry, and culture of their respective countries.

Still, some people think they could never have met, because the journey from Florence to Padua was a most difficult one. Travelling was hard work, and sometimes dangerous, guides being always necessary: you could not get a carriage at any price, for carriages were not invented. In some places there was no means of going direct from city to city at all—not even on horseback—there being actually no roads. So that people had to go on foot or not at all. If they went, there were rocks and rivers to cross, which often delayed travellers a long time.

12

Chaucer, as the King's envoy, must have had attendants, even for safety's sake, with him, and much luggage, and that would of course make travelling more difficult and expensive. He most likely went a great part of the way by sea, in a vessel coasting along the Mediterranean to Genoa and Leghorn, and so by Pisa to Florence: you may trace his route in a map. Doubtless, he had neither the means nor the will to go all the way to Padua on his own account. So you see people hold different opinions about this journey, and no one can be quite sure whether Chaucer did see Petrarch or not.

In 1373 Chaucer wrote his 'Life of St. Cecile;' and about that time, perhaps earlier, the 'Complaint to Pity.'

VIII.

I am not going to tell you everything that the King and John of Gaunt did for Chaucer. You would get tired of hearing about it. I will only say that Chaucer was 'holden in greate credyt,' and probably had a real influence in England; for, connected as he was with John of Gaunt, I dare say he gave him advice and counsel, and John showed the King how shrewd and trustworthy Chaucer was, and persuaded him to give him benefits and money.

John's wife, Blanche of Lancaster, died in 1369, and so did his mother, Queen Philippa. Chaucer wrote a poem called 'The Death of Blanche the Duchess,' in honour of this dead Blanche. John married another wife in the next year, and got still more powerful, and was called King of Castile, in Spain, because his new wife was the daughter of a King of Castile. But all this made no difference in his affection for Chaucer. He always did what he could for Chaucer.

I will give you some instances of this.

Soon after Chaucer's return from his journey to Florence, he received a grant of 'a pitcher of wine' every day 'from the hands of the King's butler.' This seems like a mark of personal friendship more than formal royal bounty; but it was worth a good deal of money a year. Less than two months afterwards he received, through John of Gaunt's goodwill, a place under Government called 'Comptrollership of the Customs' of the Port of London. This was a very important post, and required much care, shrewdness, and vigilance; and the King made it a condition that all the accounts of his office were to be entered in Chaucer's own handwriting—which means, of course, that Chaucer was to be always present, seeing everything done himself, and never leaving the work to be done by anybody else, except when sent abroad by the King's own royal command. Only three days after this, John of Gaunt himself made Chaucer a grant of £10 a year for life, in reward for all the good service rendered by 'nostre bien ame Geffray Chaucer,' and 'nostre bien ame Philippa sa femme,' to himself, his duchess, and to his mother, Queen Philippa, who was dead. This sum of money does not sound much; but it was a great deal in those days, and was fully equal to £100 now.

The very next year the King gave Chaucer the 'custody' of a rich ward (a ward is a person protected or maintained by another while under age), named Edmond Staplegate, of Kent; and when this ward married, Chaucer received a large sum of money (£104 = £1,040).[17]

Then Chaucer's care in the Customs' office detected a dishonest man, who tried to ship wool abroad without paying the lawful duty; this man was fined for his dishonesty, and the money, £71 4s. 6d., was made a present to Chaucer—a sum equal to £700.

So you see it seemed as if John of Gaunt could never do enough for him; because all these things, if not done by John himself, were probably due to his influence with the King.

IX.

The Black Prince died about that time, and Edward III. did not long survive him. He died in 1377. Then the Black Prince's little son, Richard, who was only eleven years old, became King of England; but as he was too young to reign over the country, his three uncles governed for him. These three uncles were John of Gaunt, Duke of Lancaster; the Duke of York; and the Duke of Gloucester.

And all this time Chaucer was very well looked after, you may be sure, for John of Gaunt was then more powerful than the King. Chaucer was still Comptroller of the Customs; and, before long, John gave him a second post of a similar kind, called 'Comptroller of the Petty Customs.'

But all this good luck was not to go on for ever. The people were not so fond of John of Gaunt as Chaucer was, because, in governing them, he was very ambitious and severe. They got angry with everything he did, and with everybody who remained his friend. So, of course, they did not like Chaucer.

This was a very troublous time. The Crown (represented by the King's uncles) wanted one thing, and the great barons wanted another, and the people or lower classes wanted another! These were called the three great opposing parties, and each wanted to have all the power. At last some of the barons sided with the King's party, and others sided with the people; so there were then two opposing parties quarrelling and hating each other. John of Gaunt would have liked to be King himself; but the people were unhappy, and very discontented with his government, and he began to have much less power in the kingdom.

The people knew that John of Gaunt was obliged to go with an army into Portugal, and they began to make plans to get their own way when his back was turned. When he was gone, they said that John of Gaunt did not govern them well, and had given government posts to men who did not do their duty, and neglected their work, and Chaucer was one of them.

Then there was what was called a 'Commission of Inquiry' appointed, which means a body of men who were free to examine and reform everything they chose in the country. Their power was to last a whole year; and these men looked into all that Chaucer had done in the 'Customs' offices. They did not find anything wrong, as far as we know, but still they sent away Chaucer in disgrace, just as if they had. And this made him very poor. It was a harsh thing to do, and unjust, if they were not certain he had been neglecting his work; and John of Gaunt was out of the country, and could not help him now. This was in the year 1386.

A great deal has been said and written about this matter. Some people still believe that Chaucer really did neglect his duties, though the conditions that he should attend to everything himself had been so very strict;[18] that he had probably absented himself, and let things go wrong. But such people forget that these conditions were formally done away with in 1385, when Chaucer was finally released from personal drudgery at the Customs, and allowed to have a deputy, or person under him to do his work.

They forget, too, how Chaucer had plunged into political matters directly afterwards, at a time when party feeling was intensely strong, the people and John of Gaunt being violently opposed to each other; and how Chaucer took up the part of his friend warmly, and sat in the House of Commons as representative of Kent, one of the largest counties of England, on purpose to support the ministers who were on John of Gaunt's side. This alone would be enough to make the opposing party hate Chaucer, and this doubtless was the reason of their dismissing him from both his offices in the Customs as soon as ever they were able, to punish him for his attachment to the Duke of Lancaster's (John of Gaunt's) cause.

Stylus.

But Chaucer never wavered or changed. And his faithfulness to his friend deserves better than the unjust suspicion that his disgrace was warranted by neglect of his duties. Chaucer was too good, and too pious, and too honourable a man to commit any such act. He submitted to his disgrace and his poverty unmoved; and after the death of his wife Philippa, which happened in the following summer, nothing is known of him for several years, except that he was in such distress that he was actually obliged to part with his two pensions for a sum of money in order to pay his debts.

During all the eventful years that followed Edward III.'s death, up to this time, Chaucer had been writing busily, in the midst of his weightier affairs. The 'Complaint of Mars,' 'Boece,' 'Troilus and Cressida,' the 'House of Fame,' and the 'Legend of Good Women,' all of which I hope you will read some day, were written in this period; also some reproachful words to his scrivener, who seems to have written out his poems for him very carelessly. Some persons think that Chaucer's pathetic 'Good Counsel,' and his short 'Balade sent to King Richard,'

15

reflect the disappointment and sadness at his changed lot, which he must have felt; and that, therefore, these poems were written at about the same time.

X.

In 1389 there was another great change in the government. The King, being of age, wished to govern the country without help, and he sent away one of his uncles, who was on the people's side, and asked John of Gaunt to come back to England. John of Gaunt's son was made one of the new ministers. Immediately Chaucer was thought of. He was at once appointed Clerk of the King's Works—an office of some importance—which he was permitted to hold by deputy; and his salary was two shillings per day—that is £36 10s. 0d. a-year, equal to about £370 of our money.

It seems that Chaucer kept this appointment only for two years. Why, we cannot tell.[19] While he held this office (viz., Sept. 1390)a misfortune befell him. Some notorious thieves attacked him, near the 'foule Ok' (foul Oak), and robbed him of £20 (nearly £200 present currency) of the King's money, his horse, and other movables. This was a mishap likely enough to overtake any traveller in those days of bad roads and lonely marshes, for there was no great protection by police or soldiery in ordinary cases. The King's writ, in which he forgives Chaucer this sum of £20, is still extant.

What he did, or how he lived, for some time after his retirement from the King's Works in 1391, is not known; but in 1394, King Richard granted him a pension of £20 (= £200 present currency) per annum for life. This was the year when John of Gaunt married Chaucer's sister-in-law; but, in spite of this rich alliance, I fear Chaucer was still in great distress, for we hear of many small loans which he obtained on this new pension during the next four years, which betray too clearly his difficulties. In 1398, the King granted him letters to protect him against arrest—that is, he wrote letters forbidding the people to whom Chaucer owed money to put him in prison, which they would otherwise have done.

It is sad that during these latter years of his life, the great poet who had done so much, and lived so comfortably, should have grown so poor and harassed. He ought to have been beyond the reach of want. He had had large sums of money; his wife's sister was Duchess of Lancaster; his son[20] was holding grants and offices under John of Gaunt. Perhaps he wasted his money.[21] But we cannot know exactly how it all came about at this distance of time. And one thing shows clearly how much courage and patience Chaucer had; for it was when he was in such want in 1388, two years after he had been turned out of the Customs, that he was busiest with the greatest work of his life, called the Canterbury Tales. Some men would have been too sad after so much disgrace and trouble, to be able to write stories and verses; but I think Chaucer must have felt at peace in his mind—he must have known that he did not deserve all the ill-treatment he got—and had faith that God would bring him through unstained.

XI.

The Canterbury Tales are full of cheerfulness and fun; full of love for the beautiful world, and full of sympathy for all who are in trouble or misery. The beauty of Chaucer's character, and his] deep piety, come out very clearly in these tales, as I think you will see. No one could have sung the 'ditties and songs glad' about birds in the medlar trees, and the soft rain on the 'small sweet grass,' and the 'lily on her stalk green,' and the sweet winds that blow over the country, whose mind was clouded by sordid thoughts, and narrow, selfish aims. No one could have sung so blithely of 'fresh Emily,' and with such good-humoured lenity even of the vulgar, chattering 'Wife of Bath,' whose heart was full of angry feelings towards his fellow-creatures. And no one, who was not in his heart a religious man, could have breathed the words of patience with which Arcite tries to comfort his friend, in their gloomy prison—or the greater patience of poor persecuted Griselda—or the fervent love of truth and honourable dealing, and a good life, which fills so many of his poems—or a hundred other touching prayers and tender words of warning. There was a large-heartedness and liberality about Chaucer's mind, as of one who had mixed cheerfully with all classes, and saw good in all. His tastes were with the noble ranks among whom he had lived; but he had deep sympathy with the poor and oppressed, and could feel kindly even to the coarse and the wicked. He hated none but hypocrites; and he was never tired of praising piety and virtue.

Chaucer wrote a great many short poems, which I have not told you of. Many have been lost or forgotten. Some may come back to us in the course of time and search. All we know of, you will read some day, with the rest of the Canterbury Tales not in this book: a few of these poems I have placed at the end of the volume; and among them one 'To his empty Purse,' written only the year before his death.[22]

There is only a little more I can tell you about Chaucer's life before we begin the stories. We got as far as 1398, when the King gave Chaucer letters of protection from his creditors.

About this time another grant of wine was bestowed on him, equal to about £4 a year, or £40 of our money. In the next year, King Richard, who had not gained the love of his subjects, nor tried to be a good King, was deposed—that is, the people were so angry with him that they said, "You shall not be our King any more;" and they shut him up in a tower, and made his cousin, Henry, King of England. Now this Henry was the son of John of Gaunt, by his first wife, Blanche, and had been very badly treated by his cousin, the King. He was a much better man than Richard, and the people loved him. John of Gaunt did not live to see his son King, for he died while Henry was abroad; and it must have been a real grief to Chaucer, then an old man of sixty,[23] when this long and faithful friend was taken from him.

Still it is pleasant to find that Henry of Lancaster shared his father's friendship for Chaucer. I dare say he had been rocked on Chaucer's knee when a little child, and had played with Chaucer's children. He came back from France, after John of Gaunt's death, and the people made him King, and sent King Richard to the castle of Pomfret (where I am sorry to say he was afterwards murdered).

The new King had not been on the throne four days before he helped Chaucer. John of Gaunt himself could not have done it quicker. He granted him an annuity of £26 13s. 4d. a year, in addition to the other £20 granted by Richard.

The royal bounty was only just in time, for poor old Chaucer did not long survive his old friend,] the Duke of Lancaster. He died about a year after him, when Henry had been King thirteen months.

John of Gaunt was buried in St. Paul's, by the side of his first and best-loved wife, Blanche; Geoffrey Chaucer was buried in Westminster Abbey.

So ended the first, and almost the greatest, English writer, of whom no one has spoken an ill word, and who himself spoke no ill words.

Poet, soldier, statesman, and scholar, 'truly his better ne his pere, in school of my rules could I never find.... In goodness of gentle, manly speech he passeth all other makers.'[24]

17

XII.

And now for Chaucer's 'speech.' How shall I show you its 'goodness,' since it is so difficult to read this old English? Wait a bit. You will soon understand it all, if you take pains at the first beginning. Do not be afraid of the funny spelling, for you must remember that it is not so much that Chaucer spells differently from us, as that we have begun to spell differently from Chaucer. He would think our English quite as funny, and not half so pretty as his own; for the old English, when spoken, sounded very pretty and stately, and not so much like a 'gabble' as ours.

I told you a little while ago, you know, that our talking is much faster than talking was in Chaucer's time; it seems very curious that a language can be so changed in a few hundred years, without people really meaning to change it. But it has changed gradually. Little by little new words have come into use, and others have got 'old-fashioned.' Even the English of one hundred years ago was very unlike our own. But the English of five hundred years ago was, of course, still more unlike.

XIII.

Now, I have put, as I told you, two versions of Chaucer's poetry on the page, side by side. First, the lines as Chaucer made them, and then the same lines in English such as we speak. You can thus look at both, and compare them.

I will also read you the verses in the two ways of pronouncing them, Chaucer's way and our way: but when you have grown a little used to the old-fashioned English, you will soon see how much prettier and more musical it sounds than our modern tongue, and I think you will like it very much. Besides, it is nice to be able to see the words as Chaucer put them, so as to know exactly how he talked.

In Chaucer's time a great deal of French was spoken in England, and it was mixed up with English more than it is now. The sound of old French and old English were something the same, both spoken very slowly, with a kind of drawl, as much as to say—"I am in no hurry. I have all day before me, and if you want to hear what I have got to say, you must wait till I get my words out."

So if you wish to hear Chaucer's stories, you must let him tell them in his own way, and try and understand his funny, pretty language. And if you do not pronounce the words as he meant, you will find the verses will sound quite ugly—some lines being longer than others, and some not even rhyming, and altogether in a jumble.

XIV.

Chaucer himself was very anxious that people should read his words properly, and says in his verses, as if he were speaking to a human being—

And for there is so grete dyversité	great diversity
In Englissh,[25] and in writynge of our tonge,	tongue
So preye I God that non miswrité thee	pray
Ne thee mys-metere for defaute of tonge. (Troilus.)	defect

To mis-metre is to read the metre wrong; and the metre is the length of the line. If you read the length all wrong, it sounds very ugly.

Now, suppose those lines were read in modern English, they would run thus:—

And because there is so great a diversity
In English, and in writing our tongue,
So I pray God that none miswrite thee
Nor mismetre thee through defect of tongue.

How broken and ragged it all sounds! like a gown that is all ragged and jagged, and doesn't fit. It sounds much better to read it properly.

You will find that when Chaucer's words are rightly pronounced, all his lines are of an even length and sound pretty. I don't think he ever fails in this. This is called having a musical ear. Chaucer had a musical ear. Some people who write poetry have not, and their poetry is good for nothing. They might as well try to play the piano without a musical ear; and a pretty mess they would make of that![26]

XV.

When you find any very hard word in Chaucer's verses which you cannot understand, look in the glossary and the modern version beside them; and you will see what is the word for it nowadays. A few words which cannot be translated within the metre you will find at the bottom of the page; but think for yourself before you look. There is nothing like thinking for one's self. Many of the words are like French or German words: so if you have learnt these languages you will be able often to guess what the word means.

For instance, you know how, in French, when you wish to say, I will not go or I am not sure, two no's are used, ne and pas: Je n'irai pas, or je ne suis pas sûr. Well, in Chaucer's time two no's were used in English. He would have said, "I n'ill nat go," and "I n'am nat sure."

There are many lines where you will see two no's. "I n'am nat precious." "I ne told no deintee." "I wol not leve no tales." "I ne owe hem not a word." "There n'is no more to tell," &c. Sometimes, however, ne is used by itself, without not or nat to follow. As "it n'is good," "I n'ill say—or sain," instead of "it is not good—I will not say."

And, as in this last word sain (which only means say), you will find often an n at the end of words, which makes it difficult to understand them; but you will soon cease to think that a very alarming difficulty if you keep looking at the modern version. As, "I shall nat lien" (this means lie). "I wol nat gon" (go): "withouten doubt" (without). "Ther wold I don hem no pleasance" (do); "thou shalt ben quit" (be). "I shall you tellen" (tell).

And I think you will also be able to see how much better some old words are for expressing the meaning, than our words. For instance, how much nicer 'flittermouse' is than 'bat.' That is an old North-country word, and very German (Fledermaus). When you see a little bat flying about, you know it is a bat because you have been told: but 'flitter-mouse' is better than bat, because it means 'floating mouse.' Now, a bat is like a mouse floating in the air. The word expresses the movement and the form of the creature.

Again—the old word 'herteles' (heartless), instead of without courage, how well it expresses the want of courage or spirit: we often say people have no heart for work, or no heart for singing, when they are sad, or ill, or weak. Heartless does not always mean cowardly; it means that the person is dejected, or tired, or out of spirits. We have left off using the word heartless

19

in that sense, however, and we have no word to express it. When we say heartless, we mean cruel or unkind, which is a perfectly different meaning.

Again, we have no word now for a meeting-time or appointment, as good as the old word 'steven:' we use the French word 'rendezvous' as a noun, which is not very wise. 'Steven' is a nice, short, and really English word which I should like to hear in use again.

One more instance. The word 'fret' was used for devouring. This just describes what we call 'nibbling' now. The moth fretting a garment—means the moth devouring or nibbling a garment.

This is a word we have lost sight of now in the sense of eating; we only use it for 'complaining' or 'pining.' But a fretted sky—and the frets on a guitar—are from the old Saxon verb frete, to eat or devour, and describe a wrinkly uneven surface, like the part of a garment fretted by the moth. So you must not be impatient with the old words, which are sometimes much better for their purpose than the words we use nowadays.

CANTERBURY TALES.

CHAUCER'S PILGRIMS.

SOME of Chaucer's best tales are not told by himself. They are put into the mouths of other people. In those days there were no newspapers—indeed there was not much news—so that when strangers who had little in common were thrown together, as they often were in inns, or in long journeys, they had few topics of conversation: and so they used to entertain each other by singing songs, or quite as often by telling their own adventures, or long stories such as Chaucer has written down and called the 'Canterbury Tales.'

The reason he called them the 'Canterbury Tales' was because they were supposed to be told by a number of travellers who met at an inn, and went together on a pilgrimage to a saint's shrine at Canterbury.

But I shall now let Chaucer tell you about his interesting company in his own way.

He begins with a beautiful description of the spring—the time usually chosen for long journeys, or for any new undertaking, in those days.

When you go out into the gardens or the fields, and see the fresh green of the hedges and the white May blossoms and the blue sky, think of Chaucer and his Canterbury Pilgrims!

Chaucer's Prologue.

Whan that Aprille with his schowres swoote	When, sweet
The drought of Marche hath perced to the roote,	root
And bathud every veyne in swich licour,	such liquor
Of which vertue engendred is the flour;	flower
Whan Zephirus[27] eek with his swete breeth	also, breath

21

Enspirud hath in every holte and heeth — grove
The tendre croppes, and the yonge sonne — young
Hath in the Ram his halfe cours i-ronne, — run
And smale fowles maken melodie, — small birds make
That slepen al the night with open yhe, — sleep, eye
So priketh hem nature in here corages:— — pricketh them, their impulses
Thanne longen folk to gon on pilgrimages, — long, go
And palmers[28] for to seeken straunge strondes, — seek, shores
To ferne halwes, kouthe[29] in sondry londes; — distant saints
And specially from every schires ende
Of Engelond, to Canturbury they wende, — go
The holy blisful martir[30] for to seeke, — blessed, seek
That hem hath holpen whan that they were seeke. — them, sick

When April hath his sweetest showers brought
To pierce the heart of March and banish drought,
Then every vein is bathéd by his power,
With fruitful juice engendering the flower;
When the light zephyr, with its scented breath,
Stirs to new life in every holt and heath
The tender crops, what time the youthful sun
Hath in the Ram his course but half-way run;
And when the little birds make melody,
That sleep the whole night long with open eye,
So Nature rouses instinct into song,—
Then folk to go as pilgrims greatly long,
And palmers hasten forth to foreign strands
To worship far-off saints in sundry lands;
And specially from every shire's end
Of England, unto Canterbury they wend,
Before the blessed martyr there to kneel,
Who oft hath help'd them by his power to heal.

It happened that one day in the spring, as I was resting at the Tabard[31] Inn, in Southwark, ready to go on my devout pilgrimage to Canterbury, there arrived towards night at the inn a large company of all sorts of people—nine-and-twenty of them: they had met by chance, all being pilgrims to Canterbury.[32] The chambers and the stables were roomy, and so every one found a place. And shortly, after sunset, I had made friends with them all, and soon became one of their party. We all agreed to rise up early, to pursue our journey together.[33]

But still, while I have time and space, I think I had better tell you who these people were, their condition and rank, which was which, and what they looked like. I will begin, then, with

The Knight.

A Knight[34] ther was and that a worthy man,	there, valuable
That from the tyme that he ferst bigan	
To ryden out, he lovede chyvalrye,	ride
Trouthe and honour, fredom and curtesie.	frankness
Ful worthi was he in his lordes werre,	war
And therto hadde he riden, noman ferre,	further
As wel in Cristendom as in hethenesse,	
And evere honoured for his worthinesse.	

A knight there was, and that a worthy man,
Who from the time in which he first began
To ride afield, loved well all chivalry,
Honour and frankness, truth and courtesy.
Most worthy was he in his master's war,
And thereto had he ridden, none more far,
As well in Christian as in heathen lands,
And borne with honour many high commands.

He had been at Alexandria when it was won: in Prussia he had gained great honours, and in many other lands. He had been in fifteen mortal battles, and had fought in the lists for our faith three times, and always slain his foe. He had served in Turkey and in the Great Sea. And he was always very well paid too. Yet, though so great a soldier, he was wise in council; and in manner he was gentle as a woman. Never did he use bad words in all his life, to any class of men: in fact

He was a verray perfight, gentil knight.

He was a very perfect, noble knight.

As for his appearance, his horse was good, but not gay. He wore a gipon of fustian, all stained by his habergeon;[35] for he had only just arrived home from a long voyage.

The Squire.

With him ther was his sone, a yong Squyer,	there, son
A lovyer, and a lusty bacheler,[36]merry	
With lokkes crulle as they were layde in presse.	locks curled
Of twenty yeer he was of age I gesse.guess	
Of his stature he was of evene lengthe,	
And wondurly delyver, and gret of strengthe.	wonderfully nimble, great
And he hadde ben somtyme in chivachie,[37]	had been
In Flaundres, in Artoys, and in Picardie,	
And born him wel, as in so litel space,	little
In hope to stonden in his lady grace.[38]	stand
Embrowdid[39] was he, as it were a mede	
Al ful of fresshe floures, white and reede.	
Syngynge he was, or flowtynge al the day;	playing on the flute
He was as fressh as is the moneth of May.	
Schort was his goune, with sleeves long and wyde.	
Wel cowde he sitte on hors, and faire ryde.	could, horse
He cowde songes wel make and endite,relate	
Justne and eek daunce, and wel purtray and write	.also, draw pictures

With him there was his son, a gay young squire,
A bachelor and full of boyish fire,
With locks all curl'd as though laid in a press,
And about twenty years of age, I guess.

In stature he was of an even length,
And wonderfully nimble, and great of strength.
And he had followed knightly deeds of war
In Picardy, in Flanders, and Artois,
And nobly borne himself in that brief space,
In ardent hope to win his lady's grace.
Embroidered was he, as a meadow bright,
All full of freshest flowers, red and white;
Singing he was, or flute-playing all day,
He was as fresh as is the month of May.
Short was his gown, his sleeves were long and wide,
Well he became his horse, and well could ride;
He could make songs, and ballads, and recite,
Joust and make pretty pictures, dance, and write.

As for the young squire's manners—

Curteys he was, lowly, and servysable,
And carf[40] byforn his fadur at the table.carved

Courteous he was, lowly, and serviceable,
And carved before his father at the table.

The Yeoman.

A Yeman had he, and servantes nomoo	no more
At that tyme, for him luste ryde soo;	it pleased him
And he was clad in coote and hood of grene.	
A shef of pocok arwes[41] bright and kene,	arrows
Under his belte he bar ful thriftily,	bore
Wel cowde he dresse his takel yomanly;	arrow

His arwes drowpud nought with fetheres lowe,[42]   arrows
And in his hond he bar a mighty bowe.bore
A not-heed hadde he, with a broun visage.   v. notes, p. 111.
Of woode-craft cowde he wel al the usage;   knew
Upon his arme he bar a gay bracer,[43]   bore
And by his side a swerd, and a bokeler,[44]   buckler
And on that other side a gay daggere,
Harneysed wel, and scharp at poynt of spere;   dressed well
A Cristofre on his brest of silver schene.   ornament representing St.
Christopher
An horn he bar, the bawdrik[45] was of grene:
A forster was he sothely, as I gesse.   forester, truly

A yeoman had he (but no suite beside:
Without attendants thus he chose to ride,)
And he was clad in coat and hood of green.
A sheaf of peacock-arrows bright and keen,
Under his belt he carried thriftily;
Well could he dress an arrow yeomanly!
None of his arrows drooped with feathers low
And in his hand he held a mighty bow.
A knot-head had he, and a sunburnt hue,
In woodcraft all the usages he knew;
Upon his arm a bracer gay he wore,
And by his side buckler and sword he bore,
While opposite a dagger dangled free;
Polished and smart, no spear could sharpe be.
A silver 'Christopher' on his breast was seen,
A horn he carried by a baldrick green:
He was a thorough forester, I guess.

The Prioress.

Ther was also a Nonne, a Prioresse,
That of hire smylyng was ful symple and coy; her
Hire grettest ooth[46] ne was but by seynt Loy, oath
And sche was cleped madame Eglentyne. called
Ful wel sche sang the servíse devyne,
Entuned in hire nose[47] ful semyly, seemly
And Frensch sche spak ful faire and fetysly, elegantly
Aftur the scole of Stratford atte Bowe, school
For Frensch of Parys was to hire unknowe. her unknown
At mete wel i-taught was sche withalle; meat, taught
Sche leet no morsel from hire lippes falle, let
Ne wette hire fyngres in hire sauce deepe.[48] wetted
Wel cowde sche carie a morsel, and wel keepe, carry
That no drope ne fil uppon hire breste. fell
In curtesie was sett al hire leste. courtesy, pleasure
Hire overlippe wypude sche so clene,[49]
That in hire cuppe ther was no ferthing sene scrap
Of grees, whan sche dronken hadde hire draught. had drunk
Ful semely aftur hire mete sche raught. seemly
And sikurly sche was of gret disport, assuredly
And ful plesant, and amyable of port,
And peyned hire to counterfete cheereways
Of court, and ben estatlich of manere, stately, manner
And to ben holden digne of reverence. worthy
But for to speken of hire conscience, speak
Sche was so charitable and so pitous[50]
Sche wolde weepe if that sche sawe a mous
Caught in a trappe, if it were deed or bledde.
Of smale houndes hadde sche, that sche fedde small hounds

With rostud fleissh, and mylk, and wastel breed.[51]
But sore wepte sche if oon of hem were deed,   them
Or if men smot it with a yerde smerte: rod
And al was conscience and tendre herte.
Ful semely hire wymple[52] i-pynched was:
Hire nose tretys: hire eyen grey as glas: well-proportioned, eyes, glass
Hire mouth ful smal, and therto softe and reed;
But sikurly sche hadde a faire forheed.   surely
It was almost a spanne brood, I trowe: broad, think
For hardily sche was not undurgrowe.   certainly, undergrown
Ful fetys was hire cloke, as I was waar.   neat
Of smal coral aboute hire arme sche baar   small
A peire of bedes[53] gaudid al with grene;   set of beads
And theron heng a broch of gold ful schene,   jewel, bright
On which was first i-writen a crowned A,   written
And after that, Amor vincit omnia.[54]

There also was a Nun, a Prioress,
Who of her smiling was most simple and coy;
Her greatest oath was only 'by St. Loy,'
And she was calléd Madame Eglantine.
Full well she sang the services divine,
Entunéd through her nose melodiously,
And French she spoke fairly and fluently,
After the school of Stratford atte Bow,
For French of Paris—that she did not know.
At meal-times she was very apt withal;
No morsel from her lips did she let fall,
Nor in her sauce did wet her fingers deep;
Well could she lift a titbit, and well keep,
That not a drop should fall upon her breast;
To cultivate refinement was her taste.
Her upper lip she ever wiped so clean
That in her drinking-cup no scrap was seen
Of grease, when she had drank as she thought good.
And gracefully she reach'd forth for her food.
And she was very playful, certainly,
And pleasant, and most amiable to see.
And mighty pains she took to counterfeit
Court manners, and be stately and discreet,
And to be held as worthy reverence.
But then to tell you of her conscience!
She was so charitable and piteous
That she would weep did she but see a mouse
Caught in a trap, if it were dead or bled;
And little dogs she had, which oft she fed
With roasted meat, and milk, and finest bread;
But sore she wept if one of them were dead,
Or, haply, with a rod were smitten smart.
And all was conscience and tender heart!
Most daintily her wimple plaited was:
Her nose was straight; her eyes were grey as glass;

Her mouth was little, and so soft and red!
Besides, she had a very fine forehead,
That measured nigh a span across, I trow!
For certainly her stature was not low.
And very dainty was the cloak she wore;
Around her arm a rosary she bore,
Of coral small, with little gauds of green,
And thereon hung a golden locket sheen,
On which was graven first a crownéd A,
And after, Amor vincit omnia.

The Prioress was attended by another nun, who acted as her chaplain, and three priests.

The Monk.

A Monk ther was, a fair for the maistrie,[55]mastery
An out-rydere, that lovede venerye;hunting
A manly man, to ben an abbot able.be
Ful many a deynte hors hadde he in stable:dainty horse
And whan he rood, men might his bridel heere[56]when, hear
Gyngle in a whistlyng wynd as cleere,jingling, clear
And eek as lowde as doth the chapel belle,
Ther as this lord was keper of the selle.where, religious house

A monk there was—one sure to rise no doubt,
A hunter, and devoted rider out;
Manly—to be an abbot fit and able,
For many a dainty horse had he in stable;
And when he rode, his bridle you could hear
Jingle along a whistling wind as clear
And quite as loud, as doth the chapel bell,

29

Where this good monk is keeper of the cell.

This jolly monk cared for little else but hunting, though this has never been considered a proper pursuit for the clergy. He was indifferent to what was said of him, and spared no cost to keep the most splendid greyhounds and horses for hard riding and hare-hunting. I saw his sleeves edged with the rare fur gris at the wrist, and that the finest in the land; his hood was fastened under his chin with a curious gold pin, which had a love-knot in the largest end. His pate was bald and shiny, his eyes rolled in his head; his favourite roast dish was a fat swan.[57]

The Friar.

A Frere ther was, a wantoun and a merye,	friar
A lymytour,[58] a ful solempne man.	solemn
In alle the ordres foure[59] is noon that can	Is able to do
So moche of daliaunce and fair langage.	dalliance
....	
Ful wel biloved and famulier was he	familiar
With frankeleyns[60] overal in his cuntre,	country
And eek with worthi wommen of the toun:	also, rich
....	
Ful sweetly herde he confessioun,	
And plesaunt was his absolucioun;[61]	
He was an esy man to yeve penance	eeasy
Ther as he wiste to han a good pitance;	when, knew
For unto a poure ordre for to geve	poor
Is signe that a man is wel i-schreve.	shriven
For if he yaf, he dorste make avaunt,	boast
He wiste that a man was repentaunt.	knew
For many a man so hard is of his herte,	heart
He may not wepe though him sore smerte;	he may smart
Therfore in-stede of wepyng and prayeres,	

Men moot yive silver to the poure freres.

A friar there was, so frisky and so merry—
A limitour, a most important man,
In the four orders there is none that can
Outdo him in sweet talk and playfulness.
....

He was most intimate and popular
With all the franklins dwelling near and far,
And with the wealthy women of the town.
....

So sweetly did he hear confession ay;
In absolution pleasant was his way.
In giving penance, very kind was he
When people made it worth his while to be;
For giving largely to some order poor
Shows that a man is free from sin, be sure,
And if a man begrudged him not his dole,
He knew he was repentant in his soul.
For many a man so hard of heart we see,
He cannot weep, however sad he be;
Therefore, instead of weeping and long prayers,
Men can give money unto the poor friars.

He carried a number of pretty pins and knives about him that he made presents of to people; and he could sing well, and play on the rotta.[62] He never mingled with poor, ragged, sick people—it is not respectable to have anything to do with such, but only with rich people who could give good dinners.

Somwhat he lipsede for his wantownesse,
To make his Englissch swete upon his tunge;   tongue

Somewhat he lispéd for his wantonness,
To make his English sweet upon his tongue;
and when he played and sang, his eyes twinkled like the stars on a frosty night.

The Merchant.

A Marchaunt was ther with a forked berd,   beard
In motteleye, and highe on hors he sat,motley,   horse
Uppon his heed a Flaundrisch bevere hat.   Flemish beaver

A merchant was there with a forkéd beard,
In motley dress'd—high on his horse he sat,
And on his head a Flemish beaver hat.

The Clerk.

A Clerk[63] ther was of Oxenford also, *Oxford*
That unto logik hadde longe ygo. *logic, gone*
As lene was his hors as is a rake, *lean, horse*
And he was not right fat, I undertake;
But lokede holwe, and therto soburly. *looked hollow*
Ful thredbare was his overest courtepy. *uppermost short cloak*
For he hadde geten him yit no benefice, *got*
Ne was so worldly for to have office,
For him was lever have at his beddes heede *he would*
Twenty bookes, clothed in blak or reede,
Of Aristotil, and his philosophie,
Than robus riche, or fithul, or sawtrie. *robes*

A clerk of Oxford was amid the throng,
Who had applied his heart to learning long.
His horse, it was as skinny as a rake,
And he was not too fat, I'll undertake!
But had a sober, rather hollow look;
And very threadbare was his outer cloak.
For he as yet no benefice had got:
Worldly enough for office he was not!
For liefer would he have at his bed's head
A score of books, all bound in black or red,
Of Aristotle, and his philosophy,
Than rich attire, fiddle, or psaltery.

Yet although the poor scholar was so wise and diligent, he had hardly any money, but all he could get from his friends he spent on books and on learning; and often he prayed for those who gave him the means to study. He spoke little—never more than he was obliged—but what he did speak was always sensible and wise.

Sownynge in moral vertu was his speche, *tending to*
And gladly wolde he lerne, and gladly teche. *would, learn*

Full of true worth and goodness was his speech,
And gladly would he learn, and gladly teach.
Then there was a

Serjeant-of-Law.

Nowher so besy a man as he ther nas,was not
And yit he seemede besier than he was.
....

He roode but hoomly in a medlé cootemixed fabric
Gird with a seynt of silk, with barres smale.belt

Never has been a busier man than he,
Yet busier than he was, he seemed to be.
....

He rode but homely-clad, in medley coat,
Girt with a belt of silk, with little bars.

The Franklin.

The Franklin.

Table Dormant.

A Frankelein was in his compainye;	
Whit was his berde, as is the dayesye.	daisy
Of his complexioun he was sangwyn,	
Wel loved he in the morwe a sop of wyn.	morning
…….	
Withoute bake mete was nevere his hous,	baked meats (pies)
Of flessch and fissch, and that so plentevous	
Hit snewed[64] in his hous of mete and drynke,	snowed
Of alle deyntees that men cowde thynke.	could think of
After the sondry sesouns of the yeersundry	sundry

35

So chaungede he his mete and his soper.   supper
....

His table dormant[65] in his halle alway
Stood redy covered al the longe day.

There was a Franklin in his company,
And white his beard was, as the daisies be.
With ruddy tints did his complexion shine;
Well loved he in the morn a sop of wine.
....

Without good meat, well cooked, was ne'er his house,
Both fish and flesh, and that so plenteous,
It seemed as though it snowed with meat and drink,
And every dainty that a man could think.
According to the seasons of the year
He changed his meats and varied his good cheer.
....

His table-dormant in his hall alway
Stood ready furnished forth throughout the day.

He was the most hospitable of men, and very well-to-do. He kept open house, for everybody
to come and eat when they liked. He had often been sheriff and knight of the shire; for he
was very highly thought of.

An anlas and gipser al of silk   all
Heng at his gerdul, whit as morne mylk.

A dagger and a hawking-pouch of silk
Hung at his girdle, white as morning milk.

A Haberdasher, a Carpenter, a Webber (weaver), a Dyer, and a Tapiser (tapestry-maker) came
next, with the Cook they brought with them, a Shipman, a Doctor of Physic, and a
'worthy[66] woman,' called the Wife of Bath, because she lived near that city.

The Doctor of Physic.

The Wife of Bath.

The Wife of Bath.

She was so expert in weaving cloth, that there was no one who could come up to her; and she thought so much of herself, that if another woman even went up to the church altar before her, she considered it a slight upon her. The Wife of Bath was middle-aged, and somewhat deaf: she had had five husbands, but they had all died—she was such a shrew: and she had taken pilgrimages to Cologne and Rome, and many other places; for she had plenty of money, as one might see by her showy dress.

Hire hosen weren of fyn scarlet reed,   hose
Ful streyte yteyd, and schoos ful moyst and newe.
Bold was hire face, and fair and rede of hew.

Her stockings were of finest scarlet red,
All straitly tied, and shoes all moist and new.
Bold was her face, and fair and red of hue.
She was well wimpled with fine kerchiefs, and her hat was as broad as a buckler or a target.

The Parson.

Then came the poor Parson—poor in condition, but 'rich in holy thought and work'—who was so good, and staunch, and true, so tender to sinners and severe to sin, regarding no ranks or state, but always at his post, an example to men.

Wyd was his parisch, and houses fer asondur,   wide
But he ne lafte not for reyne ne thondur,   ceased
In siknesse nor in meschief to visite
The ferrest in his parissche, moche and lite,   furthest
Uppon his feet, and in his hond a staf.
....
But Cristes lore and his apostles twelve
He taught, and ferst he folwed it himselve.[67]   followed

Wide was his parish, the houses far asunder,
But never did he fail, for rain or thunder,

In sickness and in woe to visit all
Who needed—far or near, and great and small—
On foot, and having in his hand a staff.
....

Christ's and the twelve apostles' law he taught,
But first himself obey'd it, as he ought.

The Ploughman.

Then the parson's brother, who was only a Ploughman, and worked hard in the fields, kind to his neighbours, ever honest, loving God above all things. He wore a tabard, and rode on a mare.[68]

There was also a Miller, a Manciple, a Reve, a Summoner, a Pardoner, and myself [Chaucer].

The Ploughman.

The Summoner.

The Pardoner.

The Summoner.

The Summoner[69] was a terrible-looking person, and rode with the Pardoner, who was his friend: the Pardoner singing a lively song, and the Summoner growling out a bass to it, with a loud, harsh voice. As for his looks, he had

A fyr-reed cherubynes face,[70]
For sawceflem he was with eyghen narwe.   pimply

40

A 'fiery-cherubin' red face,
For pimply he was, with narrow eyes.

Children were sore afraid of him when they saw him, he was so repulsive, and so cruel in extorting his gains. He was a very bad man: for though it was his duty to call up before the Archdeacon's court anybody whom he found doing wrong, yet he would let the wickedest people off, if they bribed him with money; and many poor people who did nothing wrong he forced to give him their hard earnings, threatening else to report them falsely to the Archdeacon. He carried a large cake with him for a buckler, and wore a garland big enough for the sign-post of an inn.[71]

The Pardoner.

The Pardoner[72] was a great cheat too, and so the friends were well matched; he had long thin hair, as yellow as wax, that hung in shreds on his shoulders. He wore no hood, but kept it in his wallet: he thought himself quite in the tip-top of fashion.

Dischevele, sauf his cappe, he rood al bare.	except
Suche glaryng eyghen hadde he, as an hare.	such, eyes
A vernicle[73] hadde he sowed on his cappe;	
His walet lay byforn him in his lappe.	before
....	
But trewely to tellen atte laste,	truly
He was in churche a noble ecclesiaste.	
Wel cowde he rede a lessoun or a storye,[74]	
But altherbest he sang an offertorie:	best of all
For wel he wyste, whan that song was songe	knew, when
He moste preche, and wel affyle his tonge,	preach, whet
To wynne silver, as he right wel cowde:	win
Therfore he sang ful meriely and lowde.	

Dishevell'd, save his cap, he rode barehead:
Such glaring eyes, like to a hare, he had!
A vernicle was sewed upon his cap;
His wallet lay before him, in his lap.
....
But honestly to tell the truth at last,
He was in church a noble ecclesiast.
Well could he read a lesson or a story,
But ever best he sang the offertory:
For well he knew that after he had sung,
For preaching he must polish up his tongue,
And thus make money, as he right well could:
Therefore he sang full merrily and loud.

Now I have told you as much as I can what people came into the Tabard Inn that night, and why they were all travelling together, and where they were going.

Mine Host.

Our host made us very welcome, and gave us a capital supper. He was a thoroughly good fellow, our host—a large, stout man, with bright, prominent eyes, sensible and well behaved, and very merry.

After supper, he made us all laugh a good deal with his witty jests; and when we had all paid our reckonings, he addressed us all:—

And sayde thus: Lo, lordynges, trewely   truly
Ye ben to me right welcome hertily:
For by my trouthe, if that I schal not lye,   shall, lie
I ne saugh this yeer so mery a companye   saw
At oones in this herbergh, as is now.   inn (auberge)
Fayn wolde I do yow merthe, wiste I how.
And of a merthe I am right now bythought,
To doon you eese, and it schal coste nought.   do, ease

And said to us: "My masters, certainly
Ye be to me right welcome, heartily:
For by my truth, and flattering none, say I,
I have not seen so large a company
At once inside my inn this year, as now!
I'd gladly make you mirth if I knew how.
And of a pleasant game I'm just bethought
To cheer the journey—it shall cost you nought!

"Whoever wants to know how, hold up your hands." We all held up our hands, and begged him to say on.

"Well, my masters," said he, "I say that each of you shall tell the rest four stories—two on the way to Canterbury, and two on the way home. For you know it is small fun riding along as dumb as a stone. And whichever in the party tells the best story, shall have a supper at this inn at the cost of the rest when you come back. To amuse you better, I will myself gladly join your party, and ride to Canterbury at my own expense, and be at once guide and judge; and whoever gainsays my judgment shall pay for all we spend by the way. Now, tell me if you all agree, and I will get me ready in time to start."

We were all well pleased; and the next morning, at daybreak, our clever host called us all together, and we rode off to a place called the Watering of St. Thomas.[75] There we halted, and drew lots who should tell the story first, knight, clerk, lady prioress, and everybody.

The lot fell to the knight, which every one was glad of; and as soon as we set forward, he began at once.

Notes by the Way.

One of the things most deserving of notice in reading Chaucer is his singularly strong grasp of character. In the 'Canterbury Tales' this is self-evident, and the succinct catalogue of the thirty-one pilgrims, which in feebler hands would have been dry enough, is a masterpiece of good-humoured satire, moral teaching, and, above all, photographic portraits from life. You will notice that Chaucer meant to make his 'Canterbury Tales' much longer than he lived to do. His innkeeper proposes that each of the pilgrims shall tell four stories. Only twenty-four of these exist.

You will never find any character drawn by Chaucer acting, speaking, or looking inconsistently. He has always well hold of his man, and he turns him inside out relentlessly. He very seldom analyzes thought or motives, but he shows you what is so clearly, that you know what must be without his telling you.

The good-humoured naïveté of mine host, like all his class, never forgetful of business in the midst of play, is wonderfully well hit off; for the innkeeper clearly would be the gainer by this pleasant stratagem: and he prevents any one's giving him the slip by going with them to Canterbury and back. The guests are glad enough of his company, for he could be especially useful to them on the way.

The stories, also, will be found perfectly characteristic of the tellers—there is no story given to a narrator whose rank, education, or disposition make it inconsistent. Each tells a tale whose incidents savour of his natural occupation and sympathies, and the view each takes of right or wrong modes of conduct is well seen in the manner as well as the matter.

Chaucer's personal distrust of and contempt for the contemporary Church and its creatures was the natural and healthy aversion of a pure mind and a sincerely religious heart to a form of godliness denying the power thereof—a Church which had become really corrupt. It is significant of his perfect artistic thoroughness that, with this aversion, he never puts an immoral or unfitting tale into the mouth of nun or friar; for it would be most unlikely that these persons, whatever their private character might be, would criminate themselves in public.

43

The Knight's Tale.

ONCE upon a time, as old stories tell us, there was a duke named Theseus, lord and governor of Athens, in Greece, and in his time such a conqueror that there was none greater under the sun. Full many a rich country owned his sway.

That with his wisdam and his chivalrie,	
He conquered al the regne of Femynye,	kingdom, Amazons
That whilom was i-cleped Cithea;	once, called
And wedded the fresshe quene Ipolita,[76]	fresh
And brought her hoom with him to his contre,	country
With mochel glorie and gret solempnite;	much, solemnity
And eek hire yonge suster Emelye.	also, sister
And thus with victorie and with melodye	music
Lete I this noble duk to Athenes ryde,	duke
And al his ost, in armes him biside.	arms

What with his wisdom and his chivalry
The kingdom of the Amazons won he,
That was of old time naméd Scythia,
And wedded the fresh Queen Ipolita,
And brought her to his own land sumptuously,
With pomp and glory, and great festivity;
And also her young sister Emelye.
And thus with victory and with melodie
Let I this noble duke to Athens ride,
And all his glittering hosts on either side.

And, certainly, if it were not too long to listen to, I would have told you fully how the kingdom of the Amazons was won by Theseus and his host. And of the great battle there was for the time between Athens and the Amazons; and how Ipolita—the fair, hardy queen of Scythia— was besieged; and about the feast that was held at the wedding of Theseus and Ipolita, and about the tempest at their home-coming. But all this I must cut short.

I have, God wot, a large feeld to ere;	plough
And wayke ben the oxen in my plough.	weak

I have, God knows, a full wide field to sow,
And feeble be the oxen in my plough.

I will not hinder anybody in the company. Let every one tell his story in turn, and let us see now who shall win the supper!

I will describe to you what happened as Theseus was bringing home his bride to Athens

This duk, of whom I make mencioun,	
Whan he was comen almost unto the toun,	come
In al his wele and in his moste pryde,	prosperity
He was war, as he cast his eyghe aside,	aware
Wher that ther knelede in the hye weye	kneeled
A compagnye of ladies, tweye and tweye,	two
Ech after other, clad in clothes blake;	each, black

But such a cry and such a woo they make,   woe
That in this world nys creature lyvynge,
That herde such another weymentynge,
And of that cry ne wolde they never stenten,   cease
Til they the reynes of his bridel henten.   caught
What folk be ye that at myn hom comynge
Pertourben so my feste[77] with cryinge?   perturb
Quod Theseus; Have ye so gret envye
Of myn honour, that thus compleyne and crie?
Or who hath yow misboden or offendid?   injured
And telleth me, if it may ben amendid;
And why that ye ben clad thus al in blak?   black
The oldest lady of hem alle spak....   them

This duke aforesaid, of deserved renown,
When he had almost come into the town
In all his splendour and in all his pride,
Perceivéd, as he cast his eyes aside,
A company of ladies, in a row,
Were kneeling in the highway—two by two,
Each behind each, clad all in black array;
But such an outcry of lament made they,
That in this world there is no living thing
That e'er heard such another outcrying;
Nor would they cease to wail and to complain
Till they had caught him by his bridle-rein.
"What folk are ye who at my home-coming
Perturb my festival with murmuring,"
Quoth Theseus. "Or do you envy me
Mine honour that ye wail so woefully?
Or who hath injured you, or who offended?
Tell me, if haply it may be amended,
And why are all of you in black arrayed?"
The oldest lady of them all then said—

"Lord, to whom fortune has given victory, and to live ever as a conqueror, we do not grudge your glory[78] and honour, but we have come to implore your pity and help. Have mercy on us in our grief. There is not one of us that has not been a queen or duchess; now we are beggars, and you can help us if you will.

"I was wife to King Capaneus, who died at Thebes[79]: and all of us who kneel and weep have lost our husbands there during a siege; and now Creon, who is king of Thebes, has piled together these dead bodies, and will not suffer them to be either burned or buried."

And with these words all the ladies wept more piteously than ever, and prayed Theseus to have compassion on their great sorrow.

The kind duke descended from his horse, full of commiseration for the poor ladies. He thought his heart would break with pity when he saw them so sorrowful and dejected, who had been lately of so noble a rank.

45

He raised them all, and comforted them, and swore an oath that as he was a true knight, he would avenge them on the tyrant king of Thebes in such a fashion that all the people of Greece should be able to tell how Theseus served Creon!

The duke sent his royal bride and her young sister Emelye on to the town of Athens, whilst he displayed his banner, marshalled his men, and rode forth towards Thebes. For himself, till he had accomplished this duty, he would not enter Athens, nor take his ease for one half-day therein.

The duke's white banner bore the red statue of Mars upon it; and by his banner waved his pennon, which had the monster Minotaur (slain by Theseus in Greece) beaten into it in gold. Thus rode this duke—thus rode this conqueror and all his host—the flower of chivalry—till he came to Thebes.

To make matters short, Theseus fought with the King of Thebes, and slew him manly as a knight in fair battle, and routed his whole army. Then he destroyed the city, and gave up to the sorrowful ladies the bones of their husbands, to burn honourably after their fashion.

When the worthy duke had slain Creon and taken the city, he remained all night in the field. During the pillage which followed, it happened that two young knights were found still alive, lying in their rich armour, though grievously wounded. By their coat-armour[80] the heralds knew they were of the blood-royal of Thebes; two cousins, the sons of two sisters. Their names were Palamon and Arcite.

These two knights were carried as captives to Theseus' tent, and he sent them off to Athens, where they were to be imprisoned for life; no ransom would he take.

Then the duke went back to Athens crowned with laurel, where he lived in joy and in honour all his days, while Palamon and Arcite were shut up in a strong tower full of anguish and misery, beyond all reach of help.

Thus several years passed.

This passeth yeer by yeer, and day by day,	
Till it fel oones in a morwe of May	morning
That Emelye, that fairer was to seene	see
Than is the lilie on hire stalkes grene,	
And fresscher than the May with floures newe—	flowers
For with the rose colour strof hire hewe,	strove, hue
I n'ot which was the fayrere of hem two—	
Er it were day as sche was wont to do,	
Sche was arisen, and al redy dight;	dressed
For May wole han no sloggardye a nyght.	sloth
The sesoun priketh every gentil herte,	
And maketh him out of his sleepe sterte,	
And seith, Arys, and do thin observaunce.[81]	arise, thine
This maked Emelye han remembraunce	
To don honour to May, and for to ryse.do	
I-clothed was sche fressh for to devyse.[82]	clothed
Hire yolwe heer was browdid in a tresse,	yellow
Byhynde hire bak, a yerde long I gesse.	
And in the gardyn at the sonne upriste	

Sche walketh up and doun wher as hire liste.   pleased
Sche gadereth floures, party whyte and reede,
To make a sotil gerland[83] for hire heede,
And as an aungel hevenly sche song.

Thus passeth year by year, and day by day,
Till it fell once upon a morn of May
That Emelye—more beauteous to be seen
Than is the lily on his stalk of green,
And fresher than the May with flowers new
(For with the rose's colour strove her hue
I know not which was fairer of the two)
Early she rose as she was wont to do,
All ready robed before the day was bright;
For May time will not suffer sloth at night;
The season pricketh every gentle heart,
And maketh him out of his sleep to start,
And saith, Rise up, salute the birth of spring!
And therefore Emelye, remembering
To pay respect to May, rose speedily:
Attired she was all fresh and carefully,
Her yellow hair was braided in a tress
Behind her back, a full yard long, I guess,
And in the garden as the sun uprose
She wandered up and down where as she chose.
She gathereth flowers, partly white and red,
To make a cunning garland for her head,
And as an angel heavenly she sang.

FAIR EMELYE GATHERING FLOWERS.

'The fairnesse of the lady that I see
Yonde in the gardyn romynge to and fro.'

The great tower, so thick and strong, in which these two knights were imprisoned, was close-joined to the wall of the garden.

Bright was the sun, and clear, that morning, as Palamon, by leave of his jailor, had risen, and was roaming about in an upper chamber, from which he could see the whole noble city of Athens, and also the garden, full of green boughs, just where fresh Emelye was walking.

48

This sorrowful prisoner, this Palamon, kept pacing to and fro in this chamber, wishing he had never been born; and it happened by chance that through the window, square and barred with iron, he cast his eyes on Emelye.

He started and cried out aloud, "Ah!" as though he were stricken to the heart.

And with that cry Arcite sprang up, saying, "Dear cousin, what ails you? You are quite pale and deathly. Why did you cry out? For God's love be patient with this prison life since it cannot be altered. What is Heaven's will we must endure."

Palamon answered, "Cousin, it is not that—not this dungeon made me cry out—but I was smitten right now through the eye into my heart. The fairness of a lady that I see yonder in the garden, roaming to and fro, made me cry out. I know not whether she be woman or goddess: but I think it is Venus herself!"

And he fell down on his knees and cried, "Venus, if it be thy will thus to transfigure thyself in the garden, help us to escape out of the tower."

Then Arcite looked forth and saw this lady roaming to and fro, and her beauty touched him so deeply that he said, sighing, "The fresh beauty of her will slay me. And if I cannot gain her mercy, I am but dead, and there is an end."

But Palamon turned furiously on him, and said, "Do you say that in earnest or in play?"

"Nay," cried Arcite, "in earnest by my faith—God help me, I am in no mood for play."

"It were no great honour to thee," cried Palamon, "to be false and a traitor to me, who am thy cousin and thy brother, sworn as we are both, to help and not hinder one another, in all things till death part us. And now you would falsely try to take my lady from me, whom I love and serve, and ever shall till my heart break. Now, certainly, false Arcite, you shall not do it. I loved her first, and told thee, and thou art bound as a knight to help me, or thou art false!"

But Arcite answered proudly, "Thou shalt be rather false than I—and thou art false, I tell thee, utterly! For I loved her with real love before you did. You did not know whether she were woman or goddess. Yours is a religious feeling, and mine is love as to a mortal; which I told you as my cousin, and my sworn brother. And even if you had loved her first, what matters it? A man loves because he can't help it, not because he wishes. Besides, you will never gain her grace more than I, for both of us are life-long captives. It is like the dogs who fought all day over a bone; and while they were fighting over it, a kite came and carried it off."

Long the two knights quarrelled and disputed about the lady who was out of their reach. But you shall see what came to pass.

There was a duke called Perithous, who had been fellow and brother in arms[84] of Duke Theseus since both were children, and he came to Athens to visit Theseus. These two dukes were very great friends: so much so that they loved no one so much as each other.

Now, Duke Perithous had known Arcite at Thebes, years before, and liked him, and he begged Theseus to let Arcite out of prison.

Theseus consented, but only on the condition that Arcite should quit Athens; and that he should lose his head, were he ever found there again.

So Arcite became a free man, but he was banished the kingdom.

How unhappy then Arcite was! He felt that he was worse off than ever. "Oh, how I wish I had never known Perithous!" cried he. "Far rather would I be back in Theseus' prison, for then I could see the beautiful lady I love."

O dere cosyn Palamon, quod he,
Thyn is the victorie of this aventure,   thine, chance
Ful blisfully in prisoun maistow dure;   may'st thou endure
In prisoun? certes nay, but in paradys!
Wel hath fortune y-torned the the dys.   thee

"O my dear cousin, Palamon," cried he,
"In this ill hap the gain is on thy side.
Thou blissful in thy prison may'st abide!
In prison? truly nay—but in paradise!
Kindly toward thee hath fortune turn'd the dice."

So Arcite mourned ever, because he was far away from Athens where the beautiful lady dwelt, and was always thinking that perhaps Palamon would get pardoned, and marry the lady, while he would never see her any more.

But Palamon, on the other hand, was so unhappy when his companion was taken away, that he wept till the great tower resounded, and his very fetters were wet with his tears.

"Alas, my dear cousin," he sighed, "the fruit of all our strife is thine!—You walk free in Thebes, and think little enough of my woe, I daresay. You will perhaps gather a great army and make war on this country, and get the beautiful lady to wife whom I love so much! while I die by inches in my cage."

And with that his jealousy started up like a fire within him, so that he was nigh mad, and pale as ashes. "O cruel gods!" he cried, "that govern the world with your eternal laws, how is man better than a sheep lying in the fold? For, like any other beast, man dies, or lives in prison, or is sick, or unfortunate, and often is quite guiltless all the while. And when a beast is dead, it has no pain further; but man may suffer after death, as well as in this world."

Now I will leave Palamon, and tell you more of Arcite.

Arcite, in Thebes, fell into such excessive sorrow for the loss of the beautiful lady that there never was a creature so sad before or since. He ceased to eat and drink, and sleep, and grew as thin and dry as an arrow. His eyes were hollow and dreadful to behold, and he lived always alone, mourning and lamenting night and day. He was so changed that no one could recognize his voice nor his look. Altogether he was the saddest picture of a man that ever was seen— except Palamon.

One night he had a dream. He dreamed that the winged god Mercury stood before him, bidding him be merry; and commanded him to go to Athens, where all his misery should end.

Arcite sprang up, and said, "I will go straight to Athens. Nor will I spare to see my lady through fear of death—in her presence I am ready even to die!"

He caught up a looking-glass, and saw how altered his face was, so that no one would know him. And he suddenly bethought him that now he was so disfigured with his grief, he might go and dwell in Athens without being recognized, and see his lady nearly every day.

He dressed himself as a poor labourer, and accompanied only by a humble squire, who knew all he had suffered, he hastened to Athens.

He went to the court of Theseus, and offered his services at the gate to drudge and draw, or do any menial work that could be given him. Well could he hew wood and carry water, for he was young and very strong. Now, it happened that the chamberlain of fair Emelye's house took Arcite into his service.

Thus Arcite became page of the chamber of Emelye the bright, and he called himself Philostrate.

Never was man so well thought of!—he was so gentle of condition that he became known throughout the court. People said it would be but right if Theseus promoted this Philostrate, and placed him in a rank which would better display his talents and virtues.

At last Theseus raised him to be squire of his chamber, and gave him plenty of gold to keep up his degree. Moreover, his own private rent was secretly brought to him from Thebes year by year. But he spent it so cunningly that no one suspected him. In this crafty way Arcite lived a long time very happily, and bore himself so nobly both in peace and war that there was no man in the land dearer to Theseus.

Now we will go back to Palamon.

Poor Palamon had been for seven years in his terrible prison, and was quite wasted away with misery. There was not the slightest chance of getting out; and his great love made him frantic. At last, however, one May night some pitying friend helped him to give his jailor a drink which sent him into a deep sleep: so that Palamon made his escape from the tower. He fled from the city as fast as ever he could go, and hid himself in a grove; meaning afterwards to go by night secretly to Thebes, and beg all his friends to aid him to make war on Theseus. And then he would soon either die or get Emelye to wife.

Now wol I torn unto Arcite agayn,	turn
That litel wiste how nyh that was his care,	know, near
Til that fortune hadde brought him in the snare.	
The busy larke, messager of day,	
Salueth in hire song the morwe gray;	saluteth
And fyry Phebus ryseth up so brighte,	
That al the orient laugheth of the lighte,	
And with his stremes dryeth in the greves	rays, groves
The silver dropes, hongyng on the leeves.	leaves
And Arcite, that is in the court ryal	royal[85]
With Theseus, his squyer principal,	squire
Is risen, and loketh on the merye day.	
And for to doon his observaunce to May,	do, ceremony
Remembryng on the poynt of his desir,	

He on his courser, stertyng as the fir,   *starting, fire*
Is riden into the feeldes him to pleye   *fields, play*
Out of the court, were it a myle or tweye.
And to the grove of which that I yow tolde,   *you*
By aventure his wey he gan to holde,   *chance, began*
To maken him a garland of the greves,   *make*
Were it of woodebynde or hawethorn leves,   *leaves*
And lowde he song ayens the sonne scheene: *sang, against*
O May,[86] with al thy floures and thy greene,
Welcome be thou, wel faire freissche May!
I hope that I som grene gete may.   *some, may get*
And fro his courser, with a lusty herte,   *heart*
Into the grove ful hastily he sterte,   *started*
And in a pathe he romed up and doun,   *roamed*
Ther as by aventure this Palamoun   *where, chance*
Was in a busche, that no man might him see,
For sore afered of his deth was he.   *afraid, death*
Nothing ne knew he that it was Arcite:
God wot he wolde han trowed it ful lite.   *knows, guessed, little*
For soth is seyd, goon sithen many yeres,   *truly, gone, since*
That feld hath eyen, and the woode hath eeres. *eyes, ears*

Now will I tell you of Arcite again,
Who little guess'd how nigh him was his care
Until his fortune brought him in the snare.
The busy lark, the messenger of day,
Saluteth in her song the morning grey;
And fiery Phœbus riseth up so bright,
That all the orient laugheth for the light;
And in the woods he drieth with his rays
The silvery drops that hang along the sprays.
Arcite—unknown, yet ever waxing higher
In Theseus' royal court, now chiefest squire—
Is risen, and looketh on the merry day:
And, fain to offer homage unto May,
He, mindful of the point of his desire,
Upon his courser leapeth, swift as fire,
And rideth to keep joyous holiday
Out in the fields, a mile or two away.
And, as it chanced, he made towards the grove,
All thick with leaves, whereof I spake above,
Eager to weave a garland with a spray
Of woodbine, or the blossoms of the may.
And loud against the sunshine sweet he sings,
"O May, with all thy flowers and thy green things,
Right welcome be thou, fairest, freshest May!
Yield me of all thy tender green to-day!"
Then from his courser merrily he sprang,
And plunged into the thicket as he sang;
Till in a path he chanced to make his way
Nigh to where Palamon in secret lay.
Sore frighted for his life was Palamon:

But Arcite pass'd, unknowing and unknown;
And neither guess'd his brother was hard by;
But Arcite knew not any man was nigh.
So was it said of old, how faithfully,
'The woods have ears, the empty field can see.'

A man should be prudent, even when he fancies himself safest: for oftentimes come unlooked-for meetings. And little enough thought Arcite that his sworn brother from the tower was at hand, sitting as still as a mouse while he sang.

Whan that Arcite hadde romed al his fill,	
And songen al the roundel lustily,	
Into a studie he fel sodeynly,	reverie
As don thes loveres in here queynte geeres,	curious fashions
Now in the croppe,[87] now doun in the breres,	briars
Now up, now doun, as boket in a welle.	

Now when Arcite long time had roam'd his fill,
And sung all through the rondel lustily,
He fell into dejection suddenly,
As lovers in their strange way often do,
Now in the clouds and now in abject wo,
Now up, now down, as bucket in a well.

He sat down and began to make a kind of song of lamentation. "Alas," he cried, "the day that I was born! How long, O Juno, wilt thou oppress Thebes? All her royal blood is brought to confusion. I myself am of royal lineage, and yet now I am so wretched and brought so low, that I have become slave and squire to my mortal foe. Even my own proud name of Arcite I dare not bear, but pass by the worthless one of Philostrate! Ah, Mars and Juno, save me, and wretched Palamon, martyred by Theseus in prison! For all my pains are for my love's sake, and Emelye, whom I will serve all my days."

Ye slen me with youre eyen, Emelye;	
Ye ben the cause wherfore that I dye:	be
Of al the remenant of myn other care	remnant
Ne sette I nought the mountaunce of a tare,	amount
So that I couthe don aught to youre pleasaunce!	were able to

"You slay me with your eyes, O Emelye!
You are the cause wherefore I daily die.
For, ah, the worth of all my other woes
Is not as e'en the poorest weed that grows,
So that I might do aught to pleasure you!"

Palamon, hearing this, felt as though a cold sword glided through his heart. He was so angry that he flung himself forth like a madman upon Arcite:—

And seyde: False[88] Arcyte—false traitour wikke,	wicked
Now art thou hent, that lovest my lady so,	
For whom that I have al this peyne and wo,	
And art my blood, and to my counseil sworn,	counsel

As I ful ofte have told the heere byforn,   *before now*
And hast byjaped here duke Theseus,   *tricked*
And falsly chaunged hast thy name thus;
I wol be deed, or elles thou schalt dye.   *dead, else*
Thou schalt not love my lady Emelye,
But I wil love hire oonly and no mo;   *more*
For I am Palamon, thy mortal fo.foe
And though that I no wepne have in this place,   *weapon*
But out of prisoun am astert by grace,   *escaped*
I drede not, that outher thou schalt dye,   *fear*
Or thou ne schalt not loven Emelye.
Ches which thou wilt, for thou schalt not asterte.   *escape*
This Arcite, with ful dispitous herte,   *there*
Whan he him knew, and hadde his tale herde,
As fers as a lyoun, pulleth out a swerde,   *fierce*
And seide thus: By God that sitteth above,
Nere it that thou art sike and wood for love,   *were it not*
And eek that thou no wepne hast in this place,   *also*
Thou schuldest nevere out of this grove pace,   *step*
That thou ne schuldest deyen of myn hond.   *die*
For I defye the seurté and the bonddefy
Which that thou seyst that I have maad to the;   *sayest*
What, verray fool, thenk wel that love is fre!
And I wol love hire mawgré al thy might.   *In spite of*
But, for thou art a gentil perfight knight,   *because*
And wilnest to dereyne hire by batayle,   *art willing*
Have heere my trouthe, to morwe I nyl not fayle,   *pledge*
Withouten wityng of eny other wight,   *without knowledge*
That heer I wol be founden as a knight,   *will, found*
And bryngen harneys[89] right inough for the;
And ches the best, and lef the worst for me.
And mete and drynke this night wil I brynge
Inough for the, and clothes for thy beddynge.
And if so be that thou my lady wynne,   *win*
And sle me in this wode, ther I am inne,   *wood*
Thou maist wel have thy lady as for me.
This Palamon answerde, I graunt it the.

Crying, "False, wicked traitor! false Arcite!
Now art thou caught, that lov'st my lady so,
For whom I suffer all this pain and wo!
Yet art my blood—bound to me by thy vow,
As I have told thee oftentimes ere now—
And hast so long befool'd Duke Theseus
And falsely hid thy name and nurture thus!
For all this falseness thou or I must die.
Thou shalt not love my lady Emelye—
But I will love her and no man but I,
For I am Palamon, thine enemy!
And tho' I am unarmed, being but now
Escap'd from out my dungeon, care not thou,
For nought I dread—for either thou shalt die

Now—or thou shalt not love my Emelye.
Choose as thou wilt—thou shalt not else depart."
But Arcite, with all fury in his heart,
Now that he knew him and his story heard,
Fierce as a lion, snatch'd he forth his sword,
Saying these words: "By Him who rules above,
Were't not that thou art sick and mad for love,
And hast no weapon—never should'st thou move,
Living or like to live, from out this grove,
But thou shouldest perish by my hand! on oath
I cast thee back the bond and surety, both,
Which thou pretendest I have made to thee.
What? very fool! remember love is free,
And I will love her maugré all thy might!
But since thou art a worthy, noble knight,
And willing to contest her in fair fight,
Have here my troth, to-morrow, at daylight,
Unknown to all, I will not fail nor fear
To meet thee as a knight in combat here,
And I will bring full arms for me and thee;
And choose the best, and leave the worst for me!
And I will bring thee meat and drink to-night,
Enough for thee, and bedding as is right:
And if the victory fall unto thine hand,
To slay me in this forest where I stand,
Thou may'st attain thy lady-love, for me!"
Then Palamon replied—"I grant it thee."

Then these, who had once been friends, parted till the morrow.

O Cupide, out of alle charite!	all
O regne that wolt no felaw have with the!	kingdom
Ful soth is seyd, that love ne lordschipe	truly, nor
Wol not, thonkes, have no felaschipe.	willingly, fellowship
Wel fynden that Arcite and Palamoun.	find
Arcite is riden anon unto the toun	
And on the morwe, or it were dayes light,	before
Ful prively two harneys hath he dight,	prepared
Bothe suffisaunt and mete to darreyne	sufficient
The batayl in the feeld betwix hem tweyne.	field, them, two
And on his hors alone as he was born,	carried
He caryed al this harneys him byforn;	before
And in the grove, at tyme and place i-sette,	
This Arcite and this Palamon ben mette.	be
Tho chaungen gan here colour in here face,	then, their
Right as the honter in the regne of Trace	kingdom
That stondeth in the gappe with a spere,	
Whan honted is the lyoun or the bere,	
And hereth him come ruschyng in the greves,	groves
And breketh bothe the bowes and the leves,	breaking
And thenketh, Here cometh my mortel enemy,	
Withoute faile, he mot be deed or I;	without

For eyther I mot slen him at the gappe,
Or he moot slee me, if it me myshappe:
So ferden they, in chaungyng of here hew,   *their hue*
As fer as eyther of hem other knewe. *far, them*
Ther nas no good day, ne no saluyng;   *was not, saluting*
But streyt withouten wordes rehersyng,
Everich of hem helpeth to armen other,   *each, helped*
As frendly, as he were his owen brother;   *own*
And thanne with here scharpe speres stronge
They foyneden ech at other wonder longe,   *foined*
Tho it semede that this Palamon *then, seemed*
In his fightyng were as a wood lyoun,   *mad*
And as a cruel tygre was Arcite:[90]
As wilde boores gonne they to smyte,   *began*
That frothen white as fome, for ire wood,   *their madness*
Up to the ancle faught they in here blood.[91]   *their*
And in this wise I lete hem fightyng dwelle;
And forth I wol of Theseus yow telle.   *you*

O god of love, that hast no charity!
O realm, that wilt not bear a rival nigh!
Truly 'tis said, that love and lordship ne'er
Will be contented only with a share.
Arcite and Palamon have found it so.
Arcite is ridden soon the town unto:
And, on the morrow, ere the sun was high,
Two harness hath he brought forth privily,
Meet and sufficing for the lonely fight
Out in the battle-field mid daisies white.
And riding onward solitarily
All this good armour on his horse bore he:
And at the time and place which they had set
Ere long Arcite and Palamon are met.
To change began the colour of each face—
Ev'n as the hunter's, in the land of Thrace,
When at a gap he standeth with a spear,
In the wild hunt of lion or of bear,
And heareth him come rushing through the wood,
Crashing the branches in his madden'd mood,
And think'th, "Here com'th my mortal enemy,
Now without fail or he or I must die;
For either I must slay him at the gap,
Or he must slay me if there be mishap."
So fared the knights so far as either knew,
When, seeing each, each deepen'd in his hue.
There was no greeting—there was no 'Good day,'
But mute, without a single word, straightway
Each one in arming turn'd to help the other,
As like a friend as though he were his brother.
And after that, with lances sharp and strong,
They dash'd upon each other—lief and long.
You might have fancied that this Palamon,

Fighting so blindly, were a mad lìòn,
And like a cruel tiger was Arcite.
As two wild boars did they together smite,
That froth as white as foam for rage—they stood
And fought until their feet were red with blood.
Thus far awhile I leave them to their fight.
And now what Theseus did I will recite.

Then something happened that neither of them expected.

It was a bright clear day, and Theseus, hunting with his fair queen Ipolita, and Emelye, clothed all in green, came riding by after the hart, with all the dogs around them; and as they followed the hart, suddenly Theseus looked out of the dazzle of the sun, and saw Arcite and Palamon in sharp fight, like two bulls for fury. The bright swords flashed to and fro so hideously that it seemed as though their smallest blows would fell an oak. But the duke knew not who they were that fought.[92]

Theseus smote his spurs into his horse, and galloped in between the knights, and, drawing his sword, cried, "Ho![93] No more, on pain of death! By mighty Mars, he dies who strikes a blow in my presence!" Then Theseus asked them what manner of men they were, who dared to fight there, without judge or witness, as though it were in royal lists?[94]

You may imagine the two men turning on Theseus, breathless and bloody with fight, weary with anger, and their vengeance still unslaked.

This Palamon answerde hastily,	
And seyde: Sire, what nedeth wordes mo?	need
We han the deth deserved bothe tuo.	two
Tuo woful wrecches ben we, tuo kaytyves	wretches, captives
That ben encombred of oure owne lyves,	encumbered by
And as thou art a rightful lord and juge	
Ne yeve us neyther mercy ne refuge.	give us not
And sle me first, for seynte charite;	holy
But sle my felaw eek as wel as me.	also
Or sle him first; for, though thou know him lyte,	little
This is thy mortal fo, this is Arcite,	
That fro thy lond is banyscht on his heed	
For which he hath i-served to be deed.	deserved
For this is he that come to thi gate	
And seyde, that he highte Philostrate.	was named
Thus hath he japed the ful many a yer,	befooled
And thou hast maad of him thy cheef squyer.	made
And this is he that loveth Emelye.	
For sith the day is come that I schal dye,	
I make pleynly my confessioun,	
That I am thilke woful Palamoun,	that
That hath thy prisoun broke wikkedly.	wickedly
I am thy mortal foo, and it am I	
That loveth so hoote Emelye the brighte,	
That I wol dye present in hire sighte.	
Therfore I aske deeth and my juwyse;	sentence
But slee my felaw in the same wyse,	slay

For bothe we have served to be slayn.
This worthy duk answerde anon agayn,
And seyde: This is a schort conclusioun:
Your owne mouth, by your confessioun,   own
Hath dampned you bothe, and I wil it recorde.   condemned
It needeth nought to pyne yow with the corde.[95]
Ye schul be deed by mighty Mars the reede!   dead

And Palamon made answer hastily,
And said—"O Sire, why should we waste more breath?
For both of us deserve to die the death.
Two wretched creatures are we, glad to die
Tired of our lives, tired of our misery—
And as thou art a rightful lord and judge
So give us neither mercy nor refùge!
And slay me first, for holy charity—
But slay my fellow too as well as me!
—Or slay him first, for though thou little know,
This is Arcite—this is thy mortal foe,
Who from thy land was banished on his head,
For which he richly merits to be dead!
Yea, this is he who came unto thy gate,
And told thee that his name was Philostrate—
Thus year by year hath he defied thine ire—
And thou appointest him thy chiefest squire
—And this is he who loveth Emelye!
"For since the day is come when I shall die,
Thus plain I make confession, and I own
I am that miserable Palamon
Who have thy prison broken wilfully!
I am thy mortal foe,—and it is I
Who love so madly Emelye the bright,
That I would die this moment in her sight!
Therefore I ask death and my doom to-day—
But slay my fellow in the selfsame way:—
For we have both deservëd to be slain."
And angrily the duke replied again,
"There is no need to judge you any more,
Your own mouth, by confession, o'er and o'er
Condemns you, and I will the words record.
There is no need to pain you with the cord.
Ye both shall die, by mighty Mars the red!"

Then the queen, 'for verray wommanhede,' began to weep, and so did Emelye, and all the
ladies present. It seemed pitiful that two brave men, both of high lineage, should come to
such an end, and only for loving a lady so faithfully. All the ladies prayed Theseus to have
mercy on them, and pardon the knights for their sakes. They knelt at his feet, weeping and
entreating him—

And wold have kist his feet ther as he stood,
Till atte laste aslaked was his mood;
For pite renneth sone in gentil herte,   runneth

And though he first for ire quok and sterte,   shook
He hath considerd shortly in a clause
The trespas of hem bothe, and eek the cause:
And although that his ire hire gylt accusede,   their
Yet in his resoun he hem bothe excusede.   them

And would have kissed his feet there as he stood,
Until at last appeasëd was his mood,
For pity springeth soon in gentle heart.
And though he first for rage did quake and start,
He hath considered briefly in the pause
The greatness of their crime, and, too, its cause;
And while his passion had their guilt accused,
Yet now his calmer reason both excused.

Everybody had sympathy for those who were in love;[96] and Theseus' heart 'had compassion of women, for they wept ever in on' (continually).

So the kindly duke softened, and said to all the crowd good-humouredly, "What a mighty and great lord is the god of love!"

Lo, her this Arcite and this Palamoun,   here
That quytely weren out of my prisoun,   freely (quit)
And might have lyved in Thebes ryally,   royally
And witen I am here mortal enemy,   know, their
And that here deth lith in my might also,   their, lieth
And yet hath love, maugré here eyghen tuo,
I-brought hem hider bothe for to dye.
Now loketh, is nat that an heih folye?   look, high
Who may not ben a fole, if that he love?   be
Byholde for Goddes sake that sitteth above,
Se how they blede! be they nought wel arrayed!
Thus hath here lord, the god of love, hem payed   them
Here wages and here fees for here servise.   their
And yet they wenen for to ben ful wise,   think
That serven love, for ought that may bifalle.   serve
But this is yette the beste game of alle,
That sche, for whom they have this jolitee,   fun
Can hem therfore as moche thank as me.   can them, much
Sche woot no more of al this hoote fare,   knows
By God, than wot a cuckow or an hare.   knows
But al moot ben assayed, hoot or colde;   must be tried
A man moot ben a fool other yong or olde;   must be, either
I woot it by myself ful yore agon:
For in my tyme a servant was I on.   one

"Here are this Arcite and this Palamon,
Safe out of prison both, who might have gone
And dwelt in Thebes city royally,
Knowing I am their mortal enemy,
And that their death within my power lies:

59

Yet hath blind Love, in spite of both their eyes,
Led them both hither only to be slain!
Behold the height of foolishness most plain!
Who is so great a fool as one in love?
For mercy's sake—by all the gods above,
See how they bleed! a pretty pair are they!
Thus their liege lord, the god of love, doth pay
Their wages, and their fees for service done;
And yet each thinks himself a wise man's son
Who serveth Love, whatever may befall.
But this is still the greatest joke of all,
That she, the cause of this rare jollity,
Owes them about as many thanks as I!
She knew no more of all this hot to-do,
By Mars! than doth a hare or a cuckoo!
But one must have one's fling, be't hot or cold;
A man will play the fool either young or old.
I know it by myself—for long ago
In my young days I bowed to Cupid's bow."

This is as if he should say, "These two foolish boys have got nothing from their liege lord,
the god of love, but a very narrow escape with their heads. And Emelye herself knew no more
of all this hot business than a cuckoo! But I, too, was young once, and in love, and so I won't
be hard upon them!" "I will pardon you," he added, "for the queen's sake and Emelye's, but
you must swear to me never to come and make war on me at any time, but be ever my friends
in all that you may for the future."

And they were very thankful and promised as he commanded.

Then Theseus spoke again, in a kind, half laughing way:—

To speke of real lynage and riches,	speak, royal
Though that sche were a quene or a prynces,	princess
Ilk of yow bothe is worthy douteles	each
To wedden, when time is, but natheles	marry, nevertheless
I speke as for my suster Emelye,	
For whom ye have this stryf and jelousye,	
Ye woot youreself, sche may not wedde two	know
At oones, though ye faughten ever mo;	once, fought
That oon of yow, or be him loth or leef,	unwilling or willing
He mot go pypen in an ivy leef;[97]	must
This is to say, sche may nought now have bothe,	
Al be ye never so jelous, ne so wrothe.	angry

"And as for wealth and rank, and royal birth,
Although she were the noblest upon earth,
Each of you both deserves to wed your flame
Being of equal worth; but all the same
It must be said, my sister Emelye
(For whom ye have this strife and jealousy),
You see yourselves full well that she can never
Wed two at once although ye fought for ever!

60

But one of you, whether he likes or no,
Must then go whistle, and endure his wo.
That is to say, she cannot have you both,
Though you be never so jealous or so wroth."

With that he made them this offer—that Palamon and Arcite should each bring in a year's time (50 weeks) a hundred knights, armed for the lists,[98] and ready to do battle for Emelye; and whichever knight won, Palamon and his host or Arcite and his host, should have her for his wife.

Who looks happy now but Palamon? and who springs up with joy but Arcite! Every one was so delighted with the kindness of Theseus that they all went down on their knees to thank him—but of course Palamon and Arcite went on their knees most.

Now, would you like to know all the preparations Theseus made for this great tournament?

First, the theatre for the lists had to be built, where the tournament was to take place. This was built round in the form of a compass, with hundreds of seats rising up on all sides one behind another, so that everybody could see the fight, and no one was in anybody's way. The walls were a mile round, and all of stone, with a ditch running along the outside. At the east and at the west stood two gates of white marble, and there was not a carver, or painter, or craftsman of any kind that Theseus did not employ to decorate the theatre. So that there never was such a splendid place built in all the earth before or since.

Then he made three temples: one over the east gate for Venus, goddess of love; one over the west gate for Mars, who is god of war; and towards the north, he built a temple all of alabaster and red coral; and that was for Diana. All these beautiful things cost more money than would fill a big carriage.

Now I will tell you what the temples were like inside.

First, in the Temple of Venus were wonderful paintings of feasts, dancing, and playing of music, and beautiful gardens, and mountains, and people walking about with the ladies they liked. All these were painted on the walls in rich colour.

There was a statue of Venus besides, floating on a sea of glass, and the glass was made like waves that came over her. She had a citole in her hand, which is an instrument for playing music on; and over her head doves were flying. Little Cupid was also there, with his wings, and his bow and arrows, and his eyes blinded, as he is generally made.

Then, in the Temple of Mars, who is the god of war, there were all sorts of dangers and misfortunes painted. Battles, and smoke, and forests all burning with flames, and men run over by carts, and sinking ships, and many other awful sights. Then a smith forging iron—swords and knives for war.

The statue of Mars was standing on a car, armed and looking as grim as possible: there was a hungry wolf beside him.

As for the Temple of Diana, that was very different from Venus's. Venus wishes everybody to marry the one they love. Diana does not want any one to marry at all, but to hunt all day in the fields. So the pictures in Diana's Temple were all about hunting, and the merry life in the forest.

61

Her statue showed her riding on a stag, with dogs running round about, and underneath her feet was the moon. She was dressed in the brightest green, and she had a bow and arrows in her hand.

Now you know all about the splendid theatre and the three temples.

At last the day of the great tournament approached!

Palamon and Arcite came to Athens as they had promised, each bringing with him a hundred knights, well armed; and never before, since the world began, was seen a sight so magnificent. Everybody who could bear arms was only too anxious to be among the two hundred knights—and proud indeed were those who were chosen! for you know, that if to-morrow there should be a like famous occasion, every man in England or anywhere else, who had a fair lady-love, would try to be there.

All the knights that flocked to the tournament wore shining armour according to their fancy. Some wore a coat of mail, which is chain-armour, and a breast-plate, and a gipon: others wore plate-armour, made of broad sheets of steel; some carried shields, some round targets. Again, some took most care of their legs, and carried an axe; others bore maces of steel.

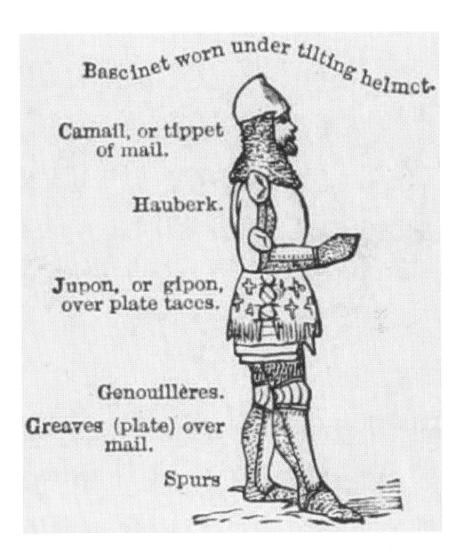

Bascinet worn under tilting helmet.

Camail, or tippet of mail.

Hauberk.

Jupon, or gipon, over plate taces.

Genouillères.

Greaves (plate) over mail.

Spurs

Mail habergeon seen at neck.
Tabard (coat armour)
over a plate hauberk.

Gauntlets.

Genouillères.

Jambes of plate.

It was on a Sunday, about nine o'clock in the morning, when all the lords and knights came into Athens.

With Palamon came the great Licurgus, King of Thrace; with Arcite came the mighty King of India, Emetrius: and I must give you the exact account of how these two kings looked, which is most minute. I should not wonder if these were the likenesses of Palamon and Arcite themselves.[99]

First, then, comes—

Ligurge himself, the grete kyng of Trace;	
Blak was his berd, and manly was his face.	
The cercles of his eyen in his heed	eyes
They gloweden bytwixe yolw and reed,	between
And lik a griffoun loked he aboute,	
With kempe heres[100] on his browes stowte;	stout
His lymes grete, his brawnes hard and stronge,	limbs, muscles
His schuldres brood, his armes rounde and longe.	shoulders
And as the gyse was in his contre,	guise
Ful heye upon a chare of gold stood he,	high, car

With foure white boles in a trays.   *bulls, the traces*
In stede of cote armour on his harnays,[101]
With nales yolwe, and bright as eny gold,
He had a bere skyn, cole-blak for-old.   *very old*
His lange heer y-kempt byhynd his bak,   *long hair combed*
As eny raven fether it schon for blak.   *shone*
A wrethe of gold arm-gret, and huge of wighte,
Upon his heed, set ful of stoones brighte,
Of fyne rubies and of fyn dyamauntz.   *diamonds*
Aboute his chare ther wenten white alauntz,[102]
Twenty and mo, as grete as eny stere,   *steer (bullock)*
To hunt at the lyoun or at the bere,
And folwed him, with mosel fast i-bounde,   *muzzle*
Colerd with golde, and torettz[103] fyled rounde.   *spikes, filled*

Licurge himself, the mighty king of Thrace;
Black was his beard, and manly was his face,
The circles of his eyes within his head
Glow'd of a hue part yellow and part red,
And like a griffon lookëd he about,
With hair down-combed upon his brows so stout;
His limbs were great, his muscles hard and strong,
His shoulders broad, his arms were round and long.
According to the fashion of his land,
Full high upon a car of gold stood he,
And to the car four bulls were link'd, milk-white.
'Stead of coat-armour on his harness bright,
With yellow nails and bright as any gold,
A bear's skin hung, coal-black, and very old.
His flowing hair was comb'd behind his back,
As any raven's wing it shone for black.
A wreath of gold, arm-thick, of monstrous weight,
Crusted with gems, upon his head was set,
Full of fine rubies and clear diamonds.
About his car there leapëd huge white hounds,
Twenty and more, as big as any steer,
To chase the lion or to hunt the bear,
And follow'd him, with muzzles firmly bound,
Collar'd in gold, with golden spikes around.

The other portrait has a less barbaric splendour about it.

The gret Emetreus, the kyng of Ynde,   *India*
Uppon a steede bay, trapped in steel,
Covered with cloth of gold dyapred wel,   *diapered like*
Cam rydyng lyk the god of armes, Mars.
His coote armour was of a cloth of Tars,[104]
Cowched of perlys whyte, round and grete.   *overlaid*
His sadil was of brend gold new i-bete;   *burnished*
A mantelet[105] upon his schuldre hangyng   *mantle*
Bret-ful of rubies reed, as fir sparclyng.   *cram-full, fire*
His crispe her lik rynges was i-ronne,   *run*

65

And that was yalwe, and gliteryng as the sonne.   *yellow-brown*
His nose was heigh, his eyen bright cytryn,
His lippes rounde, his colour was sangwyn,
A fewe freknes in his face y-spreynd,   *sprinkled*
Betwixe yolwe and somdel blak y-meynd,   *somewhat, mixed*
And as a lyoun he his lokyng caste.   *looking*
Of fyve and twenty yeer his age I caste.   *suppose*
His berd was wel bygonne for to sprynge;
His voys was as a trumpe thunderynge.
Upon his heed he wered of laurer grene   *laurel*
A garlond freische and lusty for to sene.
Upon his hond he bar for his deduyt[106]   *hand, delight*
An egle tame, as eny lylie whyt.   *eagle, any*

The great Emetrius, the Indian King,
Upon a bay steed trapp'd in shining steel,
Covered with cloth of gold from head to heel,
Came riding like the god of armies, Mars;
His coat-armour was made of cloth of Tars,
O'erlaid with pearls all white and round and great:
His saddle was of smooth gold, newly beat.
A mantlet on his shoulder as he came,
Shone, cramm'd with rubies sparkling like red flame,
And his crisp hair in shining rings did run,
Yellow it was, and glittering as the sun.
His nose was high, his eyes were bright citrine,
His lips were round, his colour was sanguine,
With a few freckles scattered here and there,
'Twixt black and yellow mingling they were,
And lion-like his glance went to and fro.
His age was five and twenty years, I trow.
A downy beard had just begun to spring,
His voice was like a trumpet thundering.
Upon his head he wore a garland green,
Of laurel, fresh, and pleasant to be seen.
Upon his wrist he bore for his delight
An eagle, tame, and as a lily white.

There was a great festival, and the dancing, and minstrelsy, and feasting, and rich array of Theseus' palace were most wondrous to behold. I should never have time to tell you

What ladies fayrest ben, or best daunsynge,   *be*
Or which of hem can carole[107] best and singe,   *sing*
Ne who most felyngly speketh of love;
What haukes sitten on the perche above,   *sit*
What houndes liggen on the floor adoun.   *lie*

What ladies danced the best, or fairest were,
Or which of them best sung or carol'd there;
Nor who did speak most feelingly of love,
What hawks were sitting on the perch above,
What hounds lay crouching on the floor adoun.

Then there were the temples to visit, to ask grace and favour from the gods. Palamon went to the Temple of Venus, the goddess of love, and prayed her to help him to gain his lady. Venus promised him success.

Arcite thought it more prudent to go to the god of war, Mars; so he sacrificed in his temple, and prayed for victory in the lists. Mars promised him the victory.

But Emelye did not wish to marry either of her lovers. She went to the temple of Diana early in the morning, and asked the goddess to help her not to get married! She preferred her free life, walking in the woods and hunting. She made two fires on Diana's altar: but Diana would not listen to her, and both the fires went out suddenly, with a whistling noise, and Emelye was so frightened that she began to cry. Then Diana told her she was destined to marry one of these poor knights who had suffered so much for her, and so she must make up her mind to it.

Emelye then departed: but Mars and Venus had a great dispute, because, as you know, they had promised success to each of the two knights, and Emelye could not marry both. Now, you shall see how each of them managed to gain a victory.

All Monday was spent in jousting and dancing, and early on Tuesday began the great tourney.

Such a stamping of horses and chinking of harness![108] Such lines and crowds of horsemen! There you might see armour so rare and so rich, wrought with goldsmith's work, and embroidery, and steel! Helmets and hauberks and trappings—squires nailing on the spearheads, and buckling helmets—rubbing up the shields, and lacing the plates with thongs of leather. Nobody was idle.

The fomy stedes on the golden bridel
Gnawyng, and faste the armurers also
With fyle and hamer prikyng to and fro;
Yemen on foote, and communes many oon   commons many a one
With schorte staves, thikke as they may goon.   go

The foamy steeds upon the golden bridle
Gnawing, and fast the armourers also
With file and hammer pricking to and fro;
Yeomen on foot, and flocking thro' the land
Commons with short staves, thick as they can stand.

Pipes, trumpets, drums, and clarions were heard, that serve to drown the noise of battle with music—little groups of people gathered about the palace, here three—there ten—arguing the merits of the two Theban knights. Some said one thing, some another. Some backed the knight with the black beard, others the bald one, others the knight with close hair. Some said, "He looks grim, and will fight!" and "He hath an axe that weighs twenty pound!"

Duke Theseus sits at a window, like a god on his throne. The masses of people are pressing towards him to see him, and to salute him humbly, and to hear his commands, and his decree!

A herald on a tall scaffold shouts out "Ho!" till all the noise of the people is hushed, and when all is quiet, he tells them the duke's will:—

"My lord hath of his wisdom considered that it were destruction to gentle blood to fight in this tourney, as in mortal battle. Therefore, to save life, he now changes his first purpose.

"No arrows, pole-axe, or short knife shall be brought into the lists, no short sword, either in the hand or worn at the side. No man shall ride more than one course with a sharp spear. Whoso comes to harm shall be taken, and not slain, but brought to the stake, there to abide according to order. And should a chieftain on either side be taken, or slay his fellow, no longer shall the tourney last. God speed you, go forth, and lay on fast! Fight your fill with mace and longsword!"[109]

The shouts of all the people rang right up to the sky, "God save such a good lord, who will have no bloodshed!"

Up go the trumpets and the music, and through the broad city, all hung with cloth of gold, the crowds ride to the lists. The noble duke rode first, and the Theban knights on either side, afterwards came the queen and fair Emelye, and then all the company followed according to their rank.

When they came to the lists, everybody pressed forward to the seats. Arcite goes in at the west gate by Mars' temple, with a red banner, and all his hundred knights. At the same moment Palamon enters the east gate by Venus' temple, with his white banner and brave host. Never was there such a sight. The two companies were so evenly matched there was no choosing between them. Then they ranged themselves in two ranks; the names were read out, that there might be no cheating in the numbers; the gates were shut, and loud was the cry, "Do now your devoir, young knights proud!"

The heralds have ceased to ride up and down. The trumpets ring out—in go the spears steadily to the rests—the sharp spur is in the horse's side. There you may see who can joust and who can ride—there the shafts of the spears shiver on the thick shields—he feels the thrust right through the body. Up spring the lances twenty foot high, out fly the swords like silver—helmets are crushed and shivered—out bursts the blood in stern, red streams! See, the strong horses stumble—down go all—a man rolls under foot like a ball. See, he fences at his foe with a truncheon, and hustles him while his horse is down. He is hurt through the body, and is dragged off to the stake—and there he must stay. Another is led off to that other side. All the humane orders of Theseus are forgotten.

From time to time Theseus stops the fray to give time for refreshment and drink, should the combatants need it.

Often have these two Thebans fought before now; each has often unhorsed the other. But in spite of Theseus' commands, never was tiger bereft of its young so cruel in the hunt, as Arcite in his jealousy was on Palamon. Never was hunted lion, mad with hunger, so eager for blood as Palamon for Arcite's life. See, they are both bleeding.

As the day went by, many in the field were carried away by excitement. The strong King Emetrius flew at Palamon as he fought with Arcite, and ran his sword into him. Then there was a frightful uproar. Emetrius could not govern himself, and was dragged off to the stake by the force of twenty men, and while trying to rescue Palamon, the great King Licurge was borne down; and King Emetrius, despite his strength, was flung out of his saddle a sword's length, so violently Palamon hit at him; but he was carried to the stake for all that, and this tumult put an end to the tourney, according to the rule Theseus had made.

How bitterly wretched was Palamon, now that he could not ride any more at his foe! Only by an unfair attack had he lost ground. Theseus, seeing them all fighting together wildly, cried out "Ho!" and stopped the tourney. Then he said, "I will be a true judge, and impartial. Arcite of Thebes shall have Emelye, who, by good luck, has fairly won her!"

Shouts of delight answered Theseus, till it seemed as if the theatre would fall with the noise.

It is said that Venus was so disappointed at Palamon, her knight, losing, that she wept, and went for help to her father, the god Saturn. Saturn said to her, "Daughter, hold thy peace; Mars has had his way, but you shall yet have yours!"

Now you shall see what happened.

This fierce Arcite, hearing the duke's decision, and the cries and yells of the heralds and all the people, raised his visor and spurred his horse along the great place and looked up at Emelye. And Emelye looked down at him kindly (for women always follow the favour of fortune), and smiled.

It was in this sweet moment, when he was off his guard, that something startled his tired and excited horse, and it leapt aside and foundered as it leapt, and before Arcite could save himself, he was flung down, and his breast-bone smashed against the saddle-bow—so that he lay as dead, his face black with the sudden rush of blood.

Poor Arcite! to lose all, just in the moment of supreme joy and victory!

He was carried out of the lists, broken-hearted, to Theseus' palace, where his harness was cut off him, and he was laid in a beautiful bed. He was still conscious, and always asking piteously for Emelye.

As for Duke Theseus, he came back to the town of Athens in great state and cheer. Were it not for this unlucky accident at the end, there had not been a single mishap, and as the leeches said Arcite would soon be well again, that was no such great disaster. None had been actually killed, though many had been grievously wounded: which was very gratifying. For all the broken arms could be mended, and the bruises and cuts healed with salves and herbs and charms.

There had even been no discomfiture, for falls did not count as shame, nor was it any disgrace to be dragged to a stake with kicks and hootings, and held there hand and foot all alone, whilst one's horse was driven out by the sticks of the grooms. That was no disgrace, for it was not cowardice; and such things must happen at a tourney. And so all the people made mirth.

The duke gave beautiful gifts to all the foreign knights, and there were ever so many more shows and feasts for the next three days, and the two mighty kings had the greatest honour paid them, till all men had gone home to their houses.

So there was an end of the great battle.

But Arcite did not get well so soon as they thought he would. His wound swelled up, and the sore increased at his heart more and more. He was so injured that the balms and the salves gave him no ease, and nature could not do her part. And when nature cannot work, farewell physic! there is no more to be done but carry the man to the churchyard.

In short, Arcite was evidently dying, and he sent for Emelye, who held herself his wife, and for Palamon, his cousin, and they both came to his bedside.

Then he told Emelye all the sorrow that was in his heart, at losing her whom he had loved so dearly; and how he still loved her, and wanted her to pray for him when he was dead.

Allas, the woo! allas, the peynes stronge	pains
That I for you have suffred, and so longe!	suffered
Allas, the deth! allas, myn Emelye!	death
Allas, departyng of our compainye!	separating
Allas, myn hertes queen! allas, my wyf!	
Myn hertes lady, endere of my lyf!	
What is this world? what asken men to have?	ask
Now with his love, now in his colde grave	
Allone, withouten eny compainye!	any
Farwel, my swete foo! myn Emelye![110]	foe
And softe tak me in youre armes tweye,	two
For love of God, and herkneth what I seye.	hearken

"Alas, the woe! alas, the trials strong
That I for you have borne—and, ah, so long!
Alas, to die! alas, mine Emelye!
Alas, that we so soon part company!
Alas, my heart's one queen! alas, my wife!
Ah, my heart's lady, ender of my life!
What is life worth? what do men yearn to have?
Now with his darling—now in his cold grave,
Alone, alone, and with no company!
Farewell, my sweet foe—farewell, Emelye,
And softly take me in your arms to-day
For love of God, and listen what I say."

Then Arcite pointed to Palamon, and said—

I have heer with my cosyn Palamon
Had stryf and rancour many a day agon
For love of yow, and for my jelousie.
. . . .
So Jupiter have of my soule part,
As in this world right now ne knowe I non
So worthy to be loved as Palamon,
That serveth you, and wol don al his lyf.

And if that evere ye schul ben a wyf,	shall
Foryet not Palamon, the gentil man.	forget

And with that word his speche faille gan,	began to fail
For fro his feete up to his brest was come	
The cold of deth, that hadde him overnome.[111]	
And yet moreover in his armes twoalready	
The vital strengthe is lost, and al ago.	gone
Only the intellect, withouten more,	without

That dwellede in his herte sik and sore,
Gan fayllen, when the herte felte deth;   began to fail
Dusked his eyen two, and failled his breth.   darkened, failed
But on his lady yit caste he his eye;
His laste word was—Mercy, Emelye.

"I have here with my cousin Palamon
Had strife and hatred days and years agone
For love of you, and for my jealousy.
....
So Jupiter have of my soul a part,
As in the whole wide world now know I none
So worthy to be loved as Palamon,
Who served you well, and will do all his life.
Therefore, if ever you shall be a wife,
Forget not Palamon, that noble man."

And with that word his speech to fail began,
For from his feet up to his breast was come
The cold of death, that hath him overcome.
And now moreover, in his arms at last
The vital strength is lost, and all is past.
Only the intellect, all clear before,
That lingered in his heart so sick and sore,
Began to falter when the heart felt death,
Then his two eyes grew dark, and faint his breath,
But on his lady yet cast he his eye;
And his last word was—"Mercy, Emelye."

He was dead.

Emelye was carried away from Arcite, fainting; and the sorrow she felt is more than I can tell.
Day and night she wept, for she had learned to love Arcite as much as if he had been already
her husband, so that she was nigh to dying.

All the city mourned for him, young and old. Theseus, and Palamon, and everybody was filled
with grief. Never had there been such sorrow.

Theseus had a splendid bier made, for Arcite to be burned according to the custom, with the
greatest honours. Huge oak trees were cut down on purpose to burn on his pile. Arcite's body
was covered with cloth of gold, with white gloves on his hands, his sword by his side, and a
wreath of laurel on his head. His face was uncovered, so that all the people might see him,
when he was carried forth from the great hall of the palace.

Theseus ordered that Arcite should be burned in that very grove where Palamon and Arcite
had first fought for love of Emelye, on that sweet May morning a year ago. So the funeral
pile was raised in that grove.

Three beautiful white horses, covered with glittering steel harness and the arms of Arcite,
bore all his armour and weapons before him to the spot.

The whole city was hung with black, and the noblest Greeks in the land carried the bier. Duke Theseus, and his old father Egeus, and Palamon, walked beside it, carrying in their hands golden cups, full of milk and wine and blood, to throw upon the pile. Then came Emelye, weeping, with fire in her hand, as the custom was, wherewith to set light to the pile.

With great care and ceremony the wood and straw were built up around the body, so high that they seemed to reach to the sky, and cloth of gold and garlands of flowers were hung all round it.

Poor Emelye fainted when she set fire to the pile, in the course of the funeral service, for her grief was more than she could bear. As soon as the fire burned fast, perfumes and jewels were flung in, and Arcite's shield, spear, and vestments, and the golden cups. Then all the Greeks rode round the fire to the left, three times shouting, and three times rattling their spears; and three times the women cried aloud.

And when all was over, Emelye was led home; and there were curious ceremonies performed, called the lykewake, at nightfall.

Long afterwards, Theseus sent for Palamon. The mourning for Arcite was over in the city, but Palamon came, still wearing his black clothes, quite sorrowful.

Then Theseus brought Emelye to Palamon, and reminded them both of Arcite's dying words. He took Emelye's hand and placed it in the hand of Palamon. Then Palamon and Emelye were married, and they lived happy ever after.

For now is Palamon in alle wele,   welfare
Lyvynge in blisse, in richesse, and in hele; health
And Emelye him loveth so tendrely,
And he hire serveth al so gentilly,   nobly
That nevere was ther no word hem bitweene there, between
Of jelousye, or any other teene.   affliction

Thus endeth Palamon and Emelye,
And God save al this fayre compainye.fair

For now this Palamon hath all the wealth,
Living in bliss, in riches, and in health;
And Emelye loveth him so tenderly,
And he doth cherish her so faithfully,
That all their days no thought they had again
Of jealousy, nor any other pain.

Thus endeth Palamon and Emelye,
And God save all this kindly company!

Notes by the Way.

The outline of the foregoing Tale was borrowed by Chaucer from Boccaccio's 'Theseida:' but the treatment and conception of character are wholly his own.

It is a common thing to say of the Knight's Tale that with all its merits the two principal actors, Arcite and Palamon, are very much alike, and constantly may be mistaken for each other. It seems to me that to say such a thing is a proof of not having read the tale, for the characters of the two men are almost diametrically opposed, and never does one act or speak as the other would do.

Notice, therefore, the striking contrast all through the story between the characters. From the first, Arcite in the prison is seen to be cooler and more matter-of-fact than Palamon, whose violent nature suffers earliest from imprisonment, mentally, perhaps morally; and whom we find pacing restlessly about, and ceaselessly bemoaning his fate, while Arcite is probably sitting still in philosophic resignation.

Palamon is clearly a man of violent, uncontrolled passions—reckless, even rash, and frantically jealous. Arcite's is by far the stronger mind—wise, clever, cool, but quite as brave and fervent as his friend. Every incident brings out their character in strong relief. To Palamon it is given to see Emelye first. He mistakes her for Venus, and prays to her as such—his mind being probably slightly disordered by the privations of mediæval prison life, as a mind so excitable would soon become. Arcite recognizes her instantly as a woman, and claims her calmly. Palamon 'flies out,' reproaches him bitterly, violently, with the term most abhorrent to the chivalrous spirit of the time—'false.' Arcite answers with passion, but he is matter-of-fact in the midst of it, reminding his friend how little consequence it is to either of them, for both are perpetual prisoners; and he can even wind up with a touch of humour, quoting the two fighting dogs and the kite.

On his release from prison, Arcite follows out successfully a most difficult rôle, concealing his identity in the midst of Theseus' court, and in the agitating presence of his lady, at the risk of his life—for years: a stratagem requiring constant sang-froid and self-control, which would have been as impossible to Palamon, as mistaking a beautiful woman for a divine vision would have been to Arcite. He does not forget Palamon during this time, though powerless to help him. He is unselfish enough to pray Juno for him, in his soliloquy in the wood.

At the meeting of the rivals in the wood, Palamon, mastered at once by rage, bids Arcite fight with him, that instant, regardless of his (Palamon's) being unarmed: he fears nothing, he only wants to fight. Arcite, also furious, can nevertheless see the common-sense side of the affair, and the need for fair play and proper accoutrements; and enumerates very sensibly the arms and other necessaries he will bring Palamon, including (so matter-of-fact is he) food and bedding for the night.

When the combatants are discovered in their illegal and unwitnessed fight, Palamon does not fear death. He is only anxious that, whether he be dead or alive, Arcite shall not have Emelye; and reiterates his entreaty that Arcite may be slain too—before or after, he doesn't care which, as long as he is slain.

Palamon's intense jealousy, which could face death cheerfully, but not the yielding up of his beloved to another man, and his anxiety that Arcite should not survive him, are of course less ignoble than they seem if viewed in the light of the times. It was this same jealousy which prompted him to betray Arcite as soon as he got the chance—forgetting that Arcite had not betrayed him, the day before, when he was in his power. But Chaucer himself once or twice refers to his mind being unhinged—'wood for love'—which claims our forbearance.

Again, the appearance of Licurge (taken as Palamon's portrait) is very characteristic. His eye is fierce, his get-up is mighty, barbaric, bizarre; but Emetrius (Arcite) appears in a much more usual way. Licurge mounts a chariot drawn by bulls—Emetrius rides on horseback, like an ordinary knight. Licurge is enveloped in a bear's hide—Emetrius is properly caparisoned.

It is also noteworthy that Palamon entreats Venus for success, for he can think of nothing but his love: Arcite thinks it more prudent to address Mars, since he has got to win Emelye by fight—he has considered the question, you see; and it is therefore (I think) that the preference is given to Palamon in marrying Emelye, because society so exalted the passion of love in those days, while Arcite is made to suffer for his very prudence, which might argue a less absorbing passion.

It was a master-thought to make Arcite die by an accident, so that neither of the rivals vanquished the other, and Palamon escapes the possible reproach of winning his happiness by slaying his friend.

The sympathy, however, remains with Arcite. His character is beautifully developed. It is not inconsistent with his power of self-control and brave heart, noble throughout, that he is able to make such a sacrifice on his death-bed as to give Emelye to Palamon. It is a sign of forgiveness of Palamon, who, at the point of death, showed no such generosity; and the greatness of the sacrifice must be estimated by remembering the mediæval view of love and love-matters.

I do not think that Palamon could have done that, any more than he could have concealed his identity in Theseus' court.[112]

The Friar's Tale.

THIS worthy Friar (Chaucer says), as he rode along with the rest of the company, kept looking askance at the Summoner, whom he evidently regarded as an enemy,[113] and though, as yet, for common civility's sake, he had not said anything to him which could cause a regular quarrel, it was quite plain there was little love lost between them.

When his turn came to tell his story, he saw a chance of annoying the Summoner, which he didn't mean to lose; and, disagreeable as the Summoner was, it is not very surprising.

But if it like to this companye,	
I wil yow of a Sompnour telle a game;	joke
Pardé, ye may wel knowe by the name,	
That of a Sompnour may no good be sayd;	
I pray that noon of yow be evel apayd.	disappointed

"But if agreeable to the company,
I'll tell you of a Summoner such a game
Belike you may imagine from the name,
That of a Summoner can no good be said.
I pray that none of you be ill repaid!"

The Summoner, who was inoffensive enough just then, whatever he might have been at other times, was not very well pleased at having his trade spoken of in such terms, and felt that it was all a hit at himself; and mine host, to prevent further squabbling, breaks in with—"Now, Friar, it is not very courteous to speak at a companion in that style; a man of your calling ought to know better:—

In companye we wol have no debaat:

74

Telleth your tale, and let the Sompnour be.   tell
Nay, quoth the Sompnour, let him saye to me
What so him list; whan it cometh to my lot
By God I schal him quyten every grot.   requite, groat
I schal him telle which a gret honour   great
Is to ben a fals flateryng lymytour!   be, false

"In company we will have no debate,
Tell on your tale, and let the Summoner be."
"Nay," cried the Summoner, "let him say of me
What he may choose. When my turn comes, good lack!
All he has said I'll pay him fairly back!
I'll tell him what a pretty trade is his,
Beggar and flattering limitor that he is!"

Mine host cries out, "Peace, no more of this!" and begs the Friar to go on.

ONCE upon a time there was an archdeacon in my country who punished with great severity all kinds of misdoings.

He had a Summoner ready to his hand, who worked under this strict archdeacon with equal severity. A slyer fellow was there none in England; and most cunningly he watched the people in secret, so as to find out how best to catch them tripping.

I shall not spare this Summoner here, though he be mad as a hare with it all; for Summoners have no jurisdiction over us Friars, you know, and never will have, all the days of their lives. We are out of their power!

["So are other refuse of the people[114] besides Friars!" interrupted the angry Summoner, when he heard that.

"Peace, with bad luck to you!" cries mine host, also getting angry; "and let the Friar tell his story. Now tell on, master, and let the Summoner gale!"[115]]

This false thief—this Summoner—used to find out, in all sorts of underhand ways, what people did, right or wrong, by spying in secret, and by keeping people to spy for him. And when he found out anybody doing wrong, he would threaten to summon them before the court, and they used to bribe him with money to let them off. If they were too poor to bribe him, he would make the archdeacon punish them; but if they had enough money to give him, he did not care how many bad things they did, and never told the archdeacon. This was very unjust and wicked, as it encouraged people to do wrong; and the Summoner grew quite rich in this evil way, for he kept all the money himself, and did not give it to the archdeacon. He was, you see, a thief as well as a spy;

For in this world nys dogge for the bowe[116]
That can an hurt dere from an hol y-knowe   ,whole

No dog on earth that's trainëd to the bow
Can a hurt deer from an unhurt one know,
better than this cunning man knew what everybody was about,—

And for that was the fruyt of al his rent,   because

Therfore theron he set all his entent.   thereon, purpose
And so bifel, that oones on a daybefell, once
This Sompnour, ever wayting on his pray,
Rod forth to sompne a widew, an old ribibe,[117]
Feynyng a cause, for he wolde han a bribe.
And happede that he say bifore him ryde   saw
A gay yeman under a forest syde.
A bowe he bar, and arwes bright and kene;
He had upon a courtepy of grene;   short cloak
An hat upon his heed with frenges blake.   head
Sir, quoth this Sompnour, heyl and wel overtake.   overtaken
Welcome, quod he, and every good felawe.   fellow
Whider ridestow under this grene schawe?   ridest thou, wood
(Sayde this yiman) wiltow fer to-day?
This Sompnour him[118] answerd and sayde, Nay:
Here faste by, quod he, is myn entent   purpose
To ryden, for to reysen up a rent   raise
That longith to my lordes dueté.   duty

And, since that was the source of all his pelf,
To winning gain he did devote himself.
And so it chanc'd that, once upon a day,
This Summoner, ever waiting for his prey,
Rode forth to summon a widow, a poor soul,
And feign'd a cause, that he might get a dole.
It happen'd that he saw before him ride
A yeoman gay, along the forest side.
A bow he bore, and arrows, bright and keen;
He had on a short upper cloak of green;
A black-fringed hat upon his head was set.
The Summoner cried out, "Hail, sir, and well met!"
"Welcome," quoth he, "and every one as good!
And whither ridest thou in this green wood?
(The yeoman said) and is it far you go?"
The Summoner made answer, and said, "No:
Close handy here my errand lies," quoth he,
"I ride to raise a rent that's owing me,
Belonging to my master's property."

"Art thou a bailiff, then?" asks the yeoman. The Summoner was ashamed to say what he really was, so he said, "Yes."

"Good," said the stranger. "Thou art a bailiff and I am another. Let us be friends. I am unknown in this country; but if you will come and see me in my country, I have plenty of gold and silver in my chest, and I will share it all with you."

"Thank you," said the greedy Summoner; and they shook hands, and promised to be staunch friends and sworn brothers till they died! And thus they rode on together.

The Summoner, who was always inquisitive and asking questions, was very anxious to know where he could find this amiable new friend, who was so free with his money.

Brother, quoth he, wher now is your dwellyng,
Another day if that I schulde yow seeche?   seek

"Brother," quoth he, "your dwelling now, where is't,
If I some future day the place could reach?"
Notice the cunning yeoman's answer:—

This yiman him answered in softe speche:
Brother, quod he, fer in the north[119] contre,
Wheras I hope somtyme I schal the se;   where
Er we depart I schal the so wel wisse,   separate, teach
That of myn hous ne schaltow never misse.   shalt thou, miss

The yeoman answered him in softest speech:
"Brother," quoth he, "far in the north countree,
Whereat I hope sometime I shall thee see.
Before we part I shall direct thee so,
Thou canst not fail my dwelling-place to know."

You will see later why he was so anxious to bring the Summoner to his own dwelling.

Now, brother, quod this Sompnour, I yow pray   you
Teche me, whil that we ryden by the way,   ride
Syn that ye ben a baily as am I,   since, be
Som subtilte, as tel me faithfully   subtilty
In myn office how I may moste[120] wynne.   my
And spare not for consciens or for synne,   refrain
But, as my brother, tel me how do ye?

"Now, brother," said the Summoner, "I pray,
Teach me while we are riding on our way,
Since you a bailiff are, as well as I,
Some subtle craft, and tell me faithfully
How in my office I most gold may win,
And hide not aught for conscience or for sin,
But as my brother, tell me how do ye?"

The strange yeoman is delighted at these questions, and you will see that in his answer he pretends to describe himself, but he is really describing all the Summoner does!

Now, by my trouthe, brothir myn, sayde he,
As I schal telle the a faithful tale.
My wages ben ful streyt and eek ful smale;   narrow, small
My lord to me is hard and daungerous,   severe
And myn office is ful laborous,   laborious
And therfor by extorciouns[121] I lyve.
Forsoth I take al that men wil me yive,   give
Algate by sleighte or by violence,   always, cunning
Fro yer to yer I wynne my despence,
I can no better telle faithfully.

Now, certes, quod this Sompnour, so fare I.

I spare not to take, God it woot,   knows
But-if it be to hevy or to hoot.[122]   unless
What I may gete in counseil prively,   get
No more consciens of that have I;   conscience
Nere myn extorcions I mighte not lyven,   were it not for
Ne of such japes I wil not be schriven.   games, shriven
Stomak ne conscience know I noon.
I schrew thes schrifte-fadres, everichoon.   curse
Wel be we met, by God and by seint Jame!
But, leve brother, telle me thy name?
Quod this Sompnour. Right[123] in this menewhile
This yeman gan a litel for to smyle.   began
Brothir, quod he, woltow that I the telle?   wilt thou
I am a feend, my dwellyng is in helle,
And her I ryde about my purchasyng,   here
To wite wher men wol yive me eny thing.   know
My purchas is theffect of all my rent. the effect
Loke how thou ridest for the same entent
To wynne good, thou rekkist never how,
Right so fare I, for ryde I wolde now
Unto the worldes ende for a praye.   prey
A, quod the Sompnour, benedicite, what say ye?[124]   ah

"Now, by my troth, my brother dear," quoth he,
"I will be frank with you, and tell you all:
The wages that I get are very small,
My master's harsh to me, and stingy too,
And hard is all the work I have to do;
And therefore by extortion do I live.
Forsooth, I take what any one will give;
Either by cunning or by violence
From year to year I snatch my year's expense.
No better can I tell you honestly."

"Now, truly," cried the Summoner, "so do I!
I never spare to take a thing, God wot,
Unless it be too heavy or too hot.
What I can grasp by counsel privily,
No scruples in that matter trouble me.
Without extortion I could ne'er subsist,
So in my pranks I ever will persist;
Stomach nor conscience truly I have none.
I hate all these shrift-fathers, every one!
Well met are we, our ways are just the same.
But, my dear fellow, tell me now your name?"
The Summoner entreated him. Meanwhile
That yeoman broke into a little smile.
"Brother," he answered, "wilt thou have me tell?
—I am a fiend, my dwelling is in hell,
And here I ride about my purchasing
To know what men will give me anything.
Such gains make up the whole of all my rent.

Look how thou journeyest for the same intent
To reap thy gains, thou carest never how!
Just so I do—for I will journey now
Unto the wide world's end to get my prey."
"Mercy!" the Summoner cried, "what is't ye say?"

He is rather aghast at this awful confession, bad as he admits himself to be. He had sincerely thought it was a real yeoman; and when he says to him, with a strange and evil smile, "Shall I tell you?—I am a fiend, my dwelling is in hell," the horrible candour strikes him dumb for a minute. He rather wishes he wasn't his sworn brother. But he very soon gets over this, thinking of the gold and silver, and begins to talk quite friendly.

I wende ye were a yemen trewely:	truly
Ye have a mannes schap as wel as I.	shape

"I thought you were a yeoman, verily:
Ye have a human shape as well as I."
"Have you then a distinct form in hell like what I see?"

"No, certainly," says the fiend, "there we have none, but we take a form when we will."

Or ellis make yow seme that we ben schape	It seem to you
Somtyme like a man, or like an ape;	
Or lik an aungel can I ryde or go;	
It is no wonder thing though it be so.	

"Or else we make you think we have a shape,
Sometimes like to a man, or like an ape;
Or like an angel I can ride or go;
It is not wondrous that it should be so."

"Why, a common conjurer can deceive you any day, and I have tenfold more cunning than a conjurer!"

"Why," said the Summoner, quite interested, "do you have several shapes, and not only one?"

"We borrow whatever shape is best to catch our prey," said the evil one.

"What makes you take all that trouble?" says the Summoner.

Ful many a cause, lieve sir Sompnour,	dear
Sayde this feend. But al thing hath a tyme;	
The day is schort, and it is passed prime,[125]	
And yit ne wan I nothing in this day;	won
I wol entent to winning, if I may,	attend
And not entende our thinges to declare.	

"Full many a cause, my good sir Summoner,"
Replied the fiend. "But all things have a time;
The day is short, and it is now past prime,
Yet have I not won anything to-day;
I'll give my mind to winning, if I may,

And not our privy doings to declare."

For you see the fiend was more intent upon his business than even the Summoner. However, he goes on to say, that sometimes he is obliged to work under the great God, without whose sufferance he could never have any power at all.

For somtyme we ben Goddis instruments	God's
And menes to don his comaundementes,	means
When that Him list, upon His creatures,	He chooses
In divers acts and in divers figures.	various

"Sometimes God uses us as instruments
And means, to work out His all-wise intents:
When on us this divine command He lays,
We serve in divers forms and divers ways."

"But you needn't be in such a hurry," he says to the Summoner. "You'll know more than you like perhaps before long."

But oon thing warne I the, I wol not jape,	one, jest
Thou wilt algates wite how we ben schape.	always know
Thou schalt herafterward, my brother deere,	
Com wher the nedith not of me to leere,[126]	come, learn
For thou schalt by thin oughn experienceown	
Conne,[127] in a chayer, reden of this sentence	be able, to counsel, meaning
Bet than Virgile[128] when he was on lyve,	better, alive
Or Daunt also. Now let us ryde blyve,	quickly
For I wol holde companye with the	
Til it be so that thou forsake me.	

"But of one thing I warn thee, not in play,
That thou shalt know what we are like, some day.
Thou shalt hereafter come, my brother dear,
Whither thou wilt not need of me to hear;
For thou shalt learned be—nay, specially wise
By self-experience—in these mysteries:
Wiser than Virgil ere from earth he past,
Or Dante either. Let us now ride fast,
For I will keep companionship with thee
Till thou desirest to depart from me."

A pleasant prospect! However, the Summoner was quite content, so long as the silver and gold were shared with him. He declares he will never forsake his sworn brother, though he be a fiend, and promises to share all his own goods with the evil one! adding—

Tak thou thi part, and that men wil the yyven,	thee, give
And I schal myn, thus may we bothe lyven;	mine, live
And if that eny of us have more than other,	either
Let him be trewe, and part it with his brother.	
I graunte, quod the devel, by my fay.	
And with that word thay riden forth hir way.	ride

"Take thou thy part, whatever men will give,
And I will do the same, so both shall live;
And if the one get more than doth the other,
Let him be true and share it with his brother."
"I grant it," said the devil, "by my fay."
With that, they rode together on their way.

As they proceeded they saw right at the town's end a cart laden with hay. The road was heavy with mud, so that the cart stuck. The carter smote his horses, and cried like mad, "Hait! go on![129] The fiend take you—what a labour I have with you. The fiend have it all, cart, horse, and hay!"

The Summoner, hearing this, remembered he was to have half of all the evil one's goods, and whispered to him, "Don't you hear what the carter says? Take it all quick—he has given it you—hay, and cart, and the three horses!"

"Nay," said the evil one, "he does not mean what he says. He is only in a passion. Ask him yourself, or else wait and see what comes next."

The carter whacked his horses, and they began to stoop and pull the cart out, and then he said, "Hait! bless you—good Dobbins—well pulled, my own grey boy! Now is my cart out of the mud."

"There, brother, what did I tell you?" says the fiend. "Now, you see the churl said one thing, but he thought another. Let us go on; I shall get nothing here."

With that they went a little way outside the town. The Summoner began to whisper to his companion, "Here there lives an old beldame who would almost as soon lose her head as give up a penny of her goods. But I mean to have twelve pence[130] out of her, though she should go mad; or else I'll haul her up before the court. And yet, all the same, I know no harm of her. But if you want a lesson how to extort your gains in your country, you may take example of me!"

The Summoner goes and raps at the old widow's gate. "Come out, you old crone. I dare say you are in mischief there!" he cried.

"Who knocks?" said the old woman. "God save you, sir. What is your will?"

"I've a bill of summons against you. On pain of cursing, see that you are to-morrow before the archdeacon, to answer to the court."

"God help me," says the poor old woman, in great distress. "I have been ill a long time, and cannot walk so far, and to ride[131] would kill me, my side pricks so. May I not ask for a libel,[132] and answer there by my procurator whatever there is against me?"

"Yes," says the Summoner, "pay me—let's see—twelve pence, and I will let you off. I shall not get much profit out of that. My master gets it, and not I. Make haste and give me twelve pence—I can't wait."

"Twelve pence!" said the poor widow. "Now, heaven help me out of this. I have not so much as twelve pence in the whole wide world. You know that I am old and poor. Rather give me alms."

"Nay, then," cries the hard-hearted Summoner, "I will not let you off, even if you die of it."

"Alas!" says she, "I am not guilty."

"Pay me!" cried he, "or I will carry off your new pan besides, which you owe me, for when you were summoned to the court before, I paid for your punishment!"

"You lie," cried the poor old woman. "I was never summoned before to that court in all my life; and I have done no wrong. May the evil one catch you for your wickedness, and carry you away, and my pan too!"

And when the fiend heard her curse the Summoner on her knees, he came forward and said, "Now, good mother, are you in earnest when you say that?"

"May the devil fetch him, pan and all, before he dies, if he doesn't repent!"

"Repent!" cries the wicked Summoner, "I don't mean to repent anything I do, I can tell you. I wish I had everything you possess besides—even every rag you have on!"

"Now, brother," says the evil one, "don't be angry; for you and this pan are mine by right. This very night you shall go with me to hell, and you will soon know more about our mysteries than a master of divinity!"

And with that word the foule fend him hente;	caught
Body and soule, he with the devyl wente,	
Wher as the Sompnours han her heritage;	their
And God, that maked after His ymage	made
Mankynde, save and gyde us alle and some,	
And leene this Sompnour good man to bycome.	grant

With that the foul fiend took him for his own,
Body and soul he's with the devil gone,
Whither these Summoners have their heritage
And God, who did create in His image
Mankind, protect and guide us all our days,
And lead this Summoner here to mend his ways.

Lordings, I could have told you, if I had time, all the pains and punishments which came to this wicked Summoner in hell. But let us all pray to be kept from the tempter's power. The lion lies in wait always to slay the innocent, if he can. Dispose your hearts ever to withstand the evil fiend who longs to make you his slaves! He will not tempt you above what you can bear, for Christ will be your champion and your knight.[133] And pray that this Summoner with us, may repent of his misdeeds before the devil carries him away.

Legends of the kind told by the Friar were very popular in the mediæval times, believed in by some as they were laughed at by others. Mr. Wright conjectures that this tale was translated from some old fabliau. The Friar evidently counted on the unpopularity of this class of men, the Summoners, when he held his fellow-traveller up to general ignominy in this way. It seems a breach of civility and fair-play to modern minds, but the Summoners were in reality hated universally for their extortion or for their secret power among the people. As you have seen, the host begins by calling for justice, but the popular feeling was but too clearly on the Friar's side from the first, and mine host shares it. (Vide notes, pp. 31, 57.)

This Tale would appear by no means to discourage swearing; but mark the distinction drawn between a hearty, deliberate malediction, and the rapid unmeaning oath which sowed the common talk. The lesson was probably the more forcible through the absence of any hypercritical censure of 'strong language'—censure which would have been vain indeed, in an age when common oaths were thought as much less of, as positive cursing was more of, than in the present day.

The rough moral deduced was admirably suited to the coarse and ignorant minds of the lower orders.

The Clerk's Tale.

This Sompnour in his styrop up he stood,	
Upon the Frere his herte was so wood	mad
That lyk an aspen leef he quok for ire.	quaked
Lordyngs, quod he, but oon thing I desire;	
I yow biseke that of your curtesye,	
Syn ye han herd this false Frere lye,	
As suffrith me, I may my tale telle.	pray suffer
This Frere bosteth that he knowith helle,	
And God it wot, that is but litel wonder,[134]	
Freres and feendes been but litel asonder.[135]	

Sir Clerk of Oxenford, our hoste sayde,	Oxford
Ye ryde as stille and coy as doth a mayde[136]	
Were newe spoused, syttyng at the bord;[137]	
This day ne herde I of your mouth a word.	
I trow ye study aboute som sophyme.	sophism
But Salomon saith, everythyng hath tyme.	
For Goddis sake as beth of better cheere,	be
It is no tyme for to stodye hiere.	study

Up in his stirrups did the Summoner start,
For with this Friar such rage was in his heart,
That like an aspen-leaf he shook for ire.
"Lordings," cried he, "but one thing I desire,
And I beseech you of your courtesy,
Since you have heard this falsest Friar lie,
Suffer me, pray, my story now to tell.
This Friar boasts of how he knoweth hell;
Heav'n knows, that if he does it is no wonder,

For fiends and Friars are not far asunder."

"Sir Clerk of Oxford," then our landlord said
"You ride as shy and quiet as a maid
Newly espous'd, who sits beside the board;
All day we have not had from you a word.
I guess, some subtle lore you're studying.
But Solomon says there's time for everything.
Prithee, rouse up, and be of better cheer,
It is no time for your deep studies here.

"Do not give us a sermon, or something so learned that we cannot understand it.

Spekith so playn at this tyme, we yow praye,
That we may understonde that ye saye.

"Speak to us very plainly, now, we pray,
That we may understand the whole you say."
This worthy Clerk answered pleasantly, "Host, I am under your orders, so I will obey you,
and tell you a tale which I learned at Padua, of a worthy clerk, who has been proved by his
words and work.

He is now deed and nayled in his chest,	coffin
Now God yive his soule wel good rest!	give
Fraunces Petrark,[138] the laureat poete,	
Highte this clerk, whos rethorique swete	was named
Enlumynd al Ytail of poetrie,	Italy
As Linian[139] did of philosophie,	
Or lawue, or other art particulere;	law
But deth, that wol not suffre us duellen here,	
But as it were a twyncling of an ye,	eye
Hem bothe hath slayn, and alle schul we dye.	

"Now he is dead, and nailéd in his chest,
I pray to God to give his spirit rest!
Francis Petrarch, the poet laureate,
This clerk was call'd, whose rhetoric sweet did late
Illume all Italy with poetry,
As Linian did with his philosophy,
And law, and other noble arts as well;
But death, that will not suffer us here to dwell,
But, as it were, a twinkling of an eye,
Hath slain them both, and we, too, all shall die."

Part I.

TO the west of Italy there is a territory called Saluces,[140] which once belonged to a marquis
very much beloved by all his people. They all obeyed and respected him, both lords and
commoners, and he was very happy.

84

Besides, he was the noblest born of any one in Lombardy—handsome, and strong, and young—courteous to all, and discreet enough, except in some things where he was not quite perfect! and his name was Walter.

The worst fault of him was the careless sort of life he led. He did nothing but hunt, and hawk, and amuse himself, instead of attending to more serious duties. This made his people very sorry, and they thought if Walter had a wife he would get more steady, and not waste his time so sadly.

One day all his people went in a great crowd to see him; and the wisest one among them said—"O noble marquis, your goodness gives us courage to come to you and tell you what we want. Do not be angry, but deign to listen to us, for we all love you. The only thing needed to make us quite happy is for you to marry. We pray you, then, to let us find you a nice wife, and we will choose the noblest and best in the land."

Walter listened, and then answered—"My dear people, you know I am very comfortable as I am, and enjoy my liberty: I don't want a wife. But if it makes you any happier, I will try and get one as soon as I can. As for choosing me one, pray don't take so much trouble. I would much rather do that for myself. Only remember that when I am married, you must always show the greatest honour and respect to whoever she may be. For since I consent to give up my freedom to please you, you must not find fault with any one whom I choose."

All the people promised they would be quite content with any wife he liked, for they were so much afraid he would not marry at all if they didn't.

Then, to make quite sure, they begged him to fix exactly the day when the wedding should take place, and he did so, promising to get everything ready, according to their request. And the people thanked him on their knees and went away.

Part II.

NOW, near the marquis's palace, there was a village in which dwelt a poor man—poorer than the poorest of his neighbours. His name was Janicula, and he had a young daughter who was fair enough to see, called Griselda.

But, in beauty of mind, Griselda was the fairest maiden under the sun. She had been brought up very humbly, and more often drank water than wine, and she worked so hard that she was never idle.

But though this mayden tender were of age,	
Yet in the brest of her virginité	breast, girlhood
Ther was enclosed rype and sad corrage;[141]	mature, serious
And in gret reverence and charité	love
Hir olde pore fader fostered sche;	
A fewe scheep spynnyng on the feld sche kepte,	field
Sche nolde not ben ydel til sche slepte.	would not be

And when sche hom-ward com, sche wolde brynge	came, bring
Wortis or other herbis tymes ofte,	worts
The which sche schred and seth for her lyvynge,	chop, boil, living
And made hir bed ful hard, and nothing softe.	
And ay sche kept hir fadres lif on lofte	ever, supported

85

With every obeissance and diligence,
That child may do to fadres reverence.   father's

But though this maiden was as yet so young,
Under her girlish innocence there lay
A brave and serious spirit, ever strong;
And with good heart she laboured day by day
To tend and help her father, poor and grey.
Some sheep while spinning in the fields she kept,
For never was she idle till she slept.

And she would often, as she homeward sped,
Bring with her herbs and cresses gathered there,
Which for a meal she fain would seethe and shred.
Hard was her bed and frugal was her fare,
Keeping her father with untiring care,
And all obedience, and all diligence
That child can give to filial reverence.

On this poor hard-working Griselda, the marquis Walter had often cast his eyes when he happened to pass her while hunting. And when he looked at her it was with no foolish thoughts, but with serious admiration for her virtue. He had never seen any one so young who was so good, and he made up his mind if ever he married anybody he would marry her.

So, after the people's visit, according to his promise to them, Walter began to prepare beautiful dresses and jewels, brooches and rings of gold, and everything proper for a great lady. And the wedding-day arrived, but no one had seen any bride, or could think where she was to come from!

At last all the feast was ready, all the palace beautifully adorned, upstairs and downstairs— hall and chambers. The noble guests arrived who were bidden to the wedding—lords and ladies richly arrayed—and still there was no bride!

The marquis made them all follow him into the village, to the sound of music.

Now, Griselda, who knew nothing of all this, went that morning to fetch water from the well; and she heard say that this was to be the marquis's wedding-day.

So she hastened home, and thought to herself she would get through her work as fast as she could, and try to see something of the sight.

"I will stand with the other girls at the door," she said to herself innocently, "and I shall see the new marchioness, if she passes by this way to the castle."

Just as she crossed the door, the marquis came up, and called her.

Griselda set down her water-cans beside the door in an ox's stall,[142] and, dropping on her knees,[143] waited for the great lord to speak.

The marquis said gravely, "Where is thy father, Griselda?" and Griselda answered humbly, "He is all ready here," and hurried in to fetch him.

Then the marquis took the poor man by the hand, saying, "Janicula, I shall no longer hide the wish of my heart. If you will consent, I will take your daughter for my wife before I leave this house. I know you love me, and are my faithful liegeman. Tell me, then, whether you will have me for your son-in-law."

This sudden offer so astonished the poor man that he grew all red, and abashed, and trembling. He could say nothing but—"My lord, it is not for me to gainsay your lordship. Whatever my lord wishes."

Yit wol I, quod this markys softly,	yet
That in thy chambre, I and thou and sche	
Have a collacioun, and wostow why?	meeting, knowest thou
For I wol aske if that it hir wille be	
To be my wyf, and reule hir after me;	according to
And al this schal be doon in thy presence,	done
I wol nought speke out of thyn audience.	hearing

"Yet," said the marquis, softly, "fain would I
That in thy chamber I and thou and she
Confer together—dost thou wonder why?
For I would ask her whether she will be
My wife—and rule herself to pleasure me;
And in thy presence all things shall be said:
Behind thy back no contract shall be made."

And while the three were talking in the chamber all the people came into the house without,[144] and wondered among themselves how carefully and kindly she kept her father. But poor Griselda, who had never seen such a sight before, looked quite pale. She was not used to such grand visitors.

GRISELDA'S MARRIAGE

'This is ynough, Grisilde myn, quod he.'

This is what the marquis said to her.

"Griselda, it pleases your father and me that I should marry you, and I suppose you will not be unwilling.[145] But first I must ask you, since it is to be done in such a hurry, will you say yes now, or will you think it over? Are you ready to obey me in all things when you are my wife, whether I am kind to you or not? and never to say no when I say yes—either by word or by frowns? Swear that, and I will swear to marry you."

Wondering at all this, and trembling with fear, Griselda answered—

"My lord, I am quite unworthy of the great honour you offer me; but whatever my lord wishes I will consent to. And I will swear never, so far as I know, to disobey you—not even if you wish to kill me, though I don't want to die."

"That is enough, my Griselda," said Walter, and he went gravely out at the door, and showed her to the people. "This is my wife, who stands here," he said: "honour and love her, whoever loves me."

Then, so that she might not enter his castle in her poor gown, he bade all the gentlewomen robe her at once in beautiful clothes; and though these smart ladies did not much like touching the old clothes she had on, still they stript them all off her, and clad her all new and splendidly, from head to foot.

Then they combed and dressed her hair, which was quite loose and disarranged, and with their delicate fingers they placed a crown on her head, and covered her with jewels, great and small. They hardly knew her, so beautiful she looked when she was thus richly attired.

The marquis put a ring on her finger, which he had brought on purpose, and set her on a snow-white horse; and she was conducted, with great rejoicings, to the palace, where the day was spent in feasting and merriment till the sun set.[146]

In short, heaven so favoured the new marchioness, that in a little time you would never have guessed she was of so humble birth; she might have been brought up in an emperor's hall, and not in a hut with oxen. The people who had known her from her childhood could hardly believe she was Janicle's daughter, she was so changed for the better.

Moreover, her virtue and gentle dignity made her beloved by everybody, so that her fame was spread throughout all the country, and people even took long journeys to come and look upon her.

Walter had not a fault to find with her. She made him happy by her excellence and her wifely homeliness, just as she made the people happy by her kindness and cleverness in redressing their wrongs.

Part III.

GRISELDA had a little girl at last, which was a great joy to them both, and to all the people. But Walter had a great longing to put his wife to the test—to see whether she was really as meek and patient and submissive as she seemed.

I know not why he wanted to do this, for he had often tried her in little ways before, and had found her perfect; and for my part I think it is a cruel deed to grieve and torment a wife who does not deserve it, for the sake of needless proof.

However, Walter did as follows. One night, while the baby was still very young, he came to her, looking stern and troubled; she was all alone, and he said, "Griselda, you have not forgotten the day when I took you out of your poor home. Well, although you are very dear to me, to my people you are not dear; they feel it a great shame to be the subjects of one who came of such mean rank. And since thy daughter was born they have murmured so greatly that I cannot disregard them, so I must do with the baby as the people choose, if I want to live in peace with them all. Yet what I must do is much against my will, and I will not do it without your consent; but I pray you to show me now how patient you can be, even as you swore to be, on our marriage day."

When Griselda heard this she did not know that it was all untrue, and she said calmly, "My lord, all shall be as you will. My child and I, we are both yours, living or dying. Do as you choose. For my part, there is nothing I fear to lose, but you."

The marquis was overjoyed to hear that, but he concealed his pleasure, and kept a very stern and sad face, and presently departed.

He went to a man, to whom he gave certain directions how to act; then he sent the man to Griselda.

This man was a sergeant,[147] the trusted servant of the marquis, and he stalked into Griselda's chamber. "Madam," he said, "you must forgive me if I do what I am compelled to by my lord. This child I am ordered to take away," and the man made as though he would kill it at once.

Suspecious was the defame of this man,	ill-fame
Suspect his face, suspect his word also,	
Suspect the tyme in which he this bigan.	
Allas! hir doughter, that she lovede so,	
Sche wende he wold han slayen it right tho;	believed, then
But natheles sche neyther weep ne sikede,	nevertheless, sighed
Conformyng hir to that the marquis likede.	

But atte laste speke sche bigan,	to speak
And mekely sche to the sergeant preyde,	
So as he was a worthy gentil man,	
That she moste kisse hir child er that it deyde.	might
And in hir barm[148] this litel child sche leyde,	lap
With ful sad face, and gan the child to blesse,	
And lullyd it, and after gan it kesse.	began, kiss

Suspicious of repute was this stern man,
Suspicious in his look, and speech also,
So was the time when he the deed began.
Alas! her baby, that she lovëd so,
Would he destroy it ere he turned to go?—
And yet she did not weep, she was resign'd
To all the wishes of her master's mind.

To say a few meek words she then began,
And for one boon she pitifully pray'd,
That as he was a kind and worthy man
She might but kiss her baby ere it died.
And in her lap the little child she laid,
With mournful face, and did the baby bless,
And lull'd it with how many a soft caress!

And then she said, in her gentle voice, "Farewell, my child; I shall never see thee again; but since I have marked thee with the cross, may He who died for us all bless thee! To him, little child, I give thy soul, for this night thou shalt die for my sake."

Truly, even to a nurse, this would have been hard to bear, but to a mother how far more grievous! Still she was so firm and brave that she soon gave up the baby to the sergeant, saying, "Take the little, tiny maid, and go, do my lord's command. But one thing I pray you, that when it is dead you will bury the little body in some place where birds and beasts will not mangle it."

The sergeant would not promise her even that, but carried the child off with him.[149]

He took the babe to the marquis, and told him exactly all that Griselda had said. The marquis certainly showed some little feeling and regret; yet he kept to his purpose, as men will when they are determined. He then bade the sergeant wrap up the child softly and tenderly, and carry it in secret, in a box or the skirt of a garment, to Bologna, where dwelt his sister, Countess of Panik.[150] She would foster it kindly; but whom the child belonged to was to be kept from all men's knowledge.

The sergeant did as he was commanded, and the marquis watched his wife to see if there should be any rebellion in her manner. But she did not change. She was always kind, and loving, and serious, and as busy and humble as ever. Not a word she spoke of the poor baby.

Part IV.

A FEW years afterwards, Griselda had another child—a little boy. This was still more joy to the people and to Walter than the other baby, because it was the heir.

When the babe was two years old, the marquis took it into his head to tempt again his poor wife. Ah! how needless to torture her! but married men care for no limits when they find a patient wife!

"Wife," said the marquis, "I have told you how discontented are the people with our marriage; and since the boy's birth their anger has been greater. Their murmuring destroys all my comfort and courage. They grumble, because when I am dead the blood of Janicle shall succeed to my heritage; and I cannot disregard the words they say! So I think I will serve him as I served his sister; but do not suddenly fly out with grief. Be patient, I beg of you, and command your feelings."

Griselda answered, sadly and calmly, when she heard this—

I have, quod sche, sayd thus, and ever schal,	
I wol no thing, ne nil no thing certayn,	will not
But as yow list: nought greveth me at al,	please
Though that my doughter and my sone be slayn	
At your comaundement: this is to sayn,	say
I have not had no part of children twayne,	
But first syknes, and after wo and payne.	sickness

Ye ben oure lord: doth with your owne thingbe, master	
Right as yow list: axith no red of me;	ask, advice
For as I left at hom al my clothing	

Whan I first com to yow, right so, quod sche,
Left I my wille and al my liberte,
And took your clothing; wherfor, I yow preye   you
Doth your plesaunce, I wil youre lust obeye.   desire

"I have," quoth she, "said this, and ever shall,
I wish not, nor will wish, it is certain,
But as you choose: I grieve me not at all,
Although my daughter and my son be slain
At your commandment: nor will I complain
That I have had no part in children twain,
But sickness first, and then a bitterer pain.

"Thou art our lord: do, then, with what is thine
E'en as thou wilt: ask not assent of me;—
For as I left at home all that was mine
When I came first to thee, right so," quoth she,
"Left I my will and all my liberty,
And took new habits: wherefore, now, I pray
Do but thy pleasure, and I will obey."

"If I knew beforehand what your wish was," said poor Griselda, "I would do it without delay; but now that I know your will, I am ready to die if you desire it; for death is nothing compared with your love!"

When the marquis heard that, he cast down his eyes, and wondered how she could endure it all; and he went forth looking very dreary, but in reality he felt extremely pleased.

The ugly sergeant came again, and took away the little boy: Griselda kissed it and blessed it, only asking that his little limbs might be kept from the wild beasts and birds; but the sergeant promised nothing, and secretly took him with great care to Bologna.

The marquis was amazed at her patience; for he knew that, next to himself, she loved her children best of anything in the world. What could he do more to prove her steadfastness, and faithfulness, and patience? But there are some people who, when they have once taken a thing into their head, will stick to it as if they were bound to a stake. So this marquis made up his mind to try his wife still further.

He watched her closely, but never could he find any change in her: the older she grew, the more faithful and industrious she was. Whatever he liked, she liked: there seemed but one will between them; and, God be thanked, all was for the best.

But all this time the slander against Walter spread far and near; and the people said he had wickedly murdered both his children, because his wife was a poor woman. For the people had no idea what had really become of them. And they began to hate Walter instead of loving him, as they had once done; for a murderer is a hateful name.

Still the marquis was so determined to test his wife, that he cared for nothing else.

When Griselda's daughter was twelve years old, Walter sent secretly to Rome, commanding that false letters, seeming to come from the Pope, should be made according to his will. These letters, or 'bulls,' were to give him leave to quit his first wife, for the sake of his people, and marry another woman; but they were none of them really from the Pope: they were all counterfeit and false, made by Walter's order, to deceive Griselda.

The common people did not know the difference between true letters and false; but when the tidings arrived, Griselda was very sorrowful; for she loved Walter best of all things, as he very well knew.

I deeme that hir herte was ful wo;[151]   judge, sad
But sche, ylike sad for evermo,   alike, firm
Disposid was, this humble creature,   disposed
Th'adversite of fortun al tendure.   fortune, to endure

Full sure am I her heart was full of wo;
But she, as though serene for evermo,
Was ready, in her humbleness of mind,
In all adversity to be resign'd.

GRISELDA'S SORROW.

'And as a lamb sche sitteth meeke and stille,
And let this cruel sergeant doon his wille.'

Then the marquis sent to the Earl of Panik, who had married his sister, begging him to bring both his children home, openly and in great honour; but no one was to know whose children they were. He was to answer no questions—

But saye the mayde schuld i-wedded be[152]	should
Unto the Markys of Saluce anoon.	immediately
And as this eorl was prayd, so dede he;	did
For at day set he on his way is goon	gone
Toward Saluce, and lordes many oon,	many a one
In riche array, this mayden for to guyde,	

94

Hir yonge brother rydyng by hir syde.

Arrayed was toward hir mariage
This freisshe may, al ful of gemmes clere; *maiden, gems*
Hir brother, which that seven yer was of age,
Arrayed eek ful freissh in his manere; *also, manner*
And thus in gret noblesse and with glad chere, *nobleness*
Toward Saluces shaping her journay, *their*
Fro day to day thay ryden in her way. *their*

But say the maiden should, ere long, be wed
Unto the Marquis of Saluce so high.
And as this earl was pray'd to do, he did,
And started on his journey speedily
Towards Saluces, with lordly company
In rich array, this maiden fair to guide,
Her little brother riding by her side.

And this fresh maid was robed for marriage
Full of clear gems, in goodly raiment rare;
Her brother, who was seven years of age,
Was in his fashion clad all fresh and fair;
And thus, in splendour, and with joyous air,
Towards Saluces following the way,
The cavalcade advances day by day.

Part V.

IN order to put the last trial upon Griselda, to the uttermost proof of her courage, the marquis one day, before all the household, said to her in a boisterous way—

Certes, Grisildes, I had y-nough plesaunce *certainly, pleasure*
To have yow to my wif, for your goodnesse
And for youre trouthe, and for your obeissaunce; *truth, obedience*
Nought for your lignage, ne for your richesse; *lineage, wealth*
But now know I in verray sothfastnesse *truth*
That in gret lordschip, if I wel avyse, *am not mistaken*
Ther is gret servitude in sondry wyse. *sundry wise*

I may not do, as every ploughman may;
My poeple me constreignith for to take *constrain*
Another wyf, and crien day by day;
And eek the Pope, rancour for to slake,
Consentith it, that dar I undertake; *dare*
And trewely, thus moche I wol yow saye, *much*
My newe wif is comyng by the waye.

Be strong of hert, and voyde anoon hir place, *heart*
And thilke dower that ye broughten me *that*
Tak it agayn, I graunt it of my grace.
Retourneth to your fadres hous, quod he, *return*
No man may alway have prosperité,

95

With even hert I rede yow endure *advise*
The strok of fortune or of adventure. *chance*

And sche agayn answerd in paciènce:
My lord, quod sche, I wot, and wist alway,
How that bitwixe your magnificence
And my poverté, no wight can ne may *nobody*
Make comparisoun, it is no nay;
I ne held me neuer digne in no manere *worthy, manner*
To ben your wif, ne yit your chamberere. *chambermaid*

And in this hous, ther ye me lady made,
(The highe God take I for my witnesse,
And al-so wisly he my soule glade) *cheer*
I never huld me lady ne maistresse,
But humble servaunt to your worthinesse,
And ever schal, whil that my lyf may dure, *life*
Aboven every worldly creature. *above*

That ye so longe of your benignité *benignity*
Han holden me in honour and nobleye, *nobleness*
Wher as I was not worthy for to be, *where*
That thonk I God and yow, to whom I preye *thank*
For-yeld it yow, ther is no more to seye. *repay*
Unto my fader gladly wil I wende, *go*
And with him duelle unto my lyves ende.

Ther I was fostred as a child ful smal,
Til I be deed my lyf ther wil I lede,
A widow clene in body, hert, and al: *clean*
For sith I yaf to yow my maydenhede, *since, maidenhood*
And am your trewe wyf, it is no drede,
God schilde such a lordes wyf to take *shield (forbid)*
Another man to housbond or to make. *for, for mate*

And of your newe wif, God of his grace
So graunte yow wele and prosperité,
For I wol gladly yelden hir my place, *yield*
In which that I was blisful wont to be.
For sith it liketh yow, my lord, quod sche,
That whilom were al myn hertes reste, *once*
That I schal gon, I wol go whan yow leste. *please*

But ther as ye profre me such dowayre *proffer*
As I ferst brought, it is wel in my mynde,
It were my wrecchid clothes, no thing faire, *wretched*
The whiche to me were hard now for to fynde.
O goode God! how gentil and how kynde
Ye semede by your speche and your visage, *speech*
That day that maked was our mariage! *made*

"'Tis true, Griselda, I was once content
To marry you—because you were so good,
And true, and faithful, and obedient—
Not for your wealth, nor for your noble blood;
Still one thing must be clearly understood,
That in this rank and riches men so praise
There is great servitude in many ways.

"I may not do as every ploughman may:
My people urge me evermore to take
Another wife, and clamour day by day.
And now the Pope, their rancour swift to slake,
Gives glad consent to any change I make;
And more than that—I need not fear to say—
My new wife is already on her way.

Make way for her, be brave, give up her place,
And, see, the dowry that you brought to me
I will restore—I grant it of my grace.
Go back unto your father's house," quoth he,
"No one can always have prosperity.
With equal spirit suffer weal or woe,
The gifts of chance or luck that come and go."

And she replied, with perfect patience:
"My lord, I know, and knew alway," quoth she,
"Too well, that 'tween your own magnificence
And my great poverty, there cannot be
Comparison at all, and verily
I held myself unworthy every way
To be your wife—or servant—for a day.

"And in this house wherein ye made me great
(High God my witness, who shall haply set
Some coming comfort in my altered state),
Lady nor mistress never was I yet;
But humble servant to the grace I get:
This I shall be, with spirit ever strong,
More than all others, yea, my whole life long.

"And for your charity in keeping me
In dignity and honour day by day
So many years, unworthy though I be,
Now thank I God and you, to whom I pray
That He will all your graciousness repay.
Unto my father cheerfully I wend
To dwell with him from now to my life's end.

"There I was fostered as an infant small,
There till I die my life I will lead through,
Dwell as an honest widow, heart and all.
For since I gave my girlhood unto you,

And am your wife, most loving and most true,
It were not fitting that a great lord's wife
Should wed another husband all her life.

"And with your wife to be, God of his grace
Grant you all welfare and prosperity;
For I will yield her cheerfully my place,
In which I once so happy used to be;
For since it pleaseth you, my lord," quoth she,
"Who ever were the dearest to my heart,
That I should go, content I will depart.

"But when you bid me take again that dower
That I first brought, it still is in my mind:
It was my wretched clothing, coarse and poor—
Rags that it were not easy now to find.
And, O good God! how gentle and how kind
You then seemed, by your words and by your look,
That day whereon the name of wife I took!"

Griselda said no word of reproach to her cruel husband, except one touching remark, which
he may have felt as one—

"Love is not old as when that it is new." (Love is not the same in after years as when it first
comes.)

Then she appeals to him in a way that must have touched a heart of stone, for she saw no
sign of relenting in his face: she does not know how far his brutality will go, and will not be
surprised at the last insult.

My lord, ye wot that in my fadres place	
Ye dede me strippe out of my pore wede,	strip, attire
And richely me cladden of your grace;	
To yow brought I nought elles, out of drede,	else
But faith, and nakednesse, and maydenhede;	maidenhood
And her agayn my clothyng I restore,	
And eek my weddyng ryng for evermore.	

The remenant of your jewels redy beremainder	
Within your chambur, dar I saufly sayn.	dare
Naked out of my fadres hous, quod sche,	
I com, and naked moot I torne agayn.	return
Al your pleisauns wold I folwen fayn;[153]	follow gladly
But yit I hope it be not youre entente,	intention
That I smocles out of youre paleys wente.	smockless, palace

"My lord, you know that in my father's place
You stript me of my poor attire, for ruth:
Anew you richly clad me, of your grace.
And I brought nothing unto you, in truth,
But honesty, and poverty, and youth.
And here again your clothing I restore,

And ev'n your wedding-ring for evermore.

"The remnant of your jewels ready be
Within your chamber, I can safely say.
With nothing from my father's house," quoth she,
"I came, with nothing I shall go away.
In all things as you bid I will obey;
But yet I hope you will not let me go
Quite as bereft as when I came to you."

A faint sparkle of human spirit comes into her entreaty—"Ye could not do so dishonest
(shameful) a thing:"—

Remembre yow, myn oughne lord so deere,   own
I was your wyf, though I unworthy were.

Wherfor, in guerdoun of my maydenhede,   girlhood
Which that I brought, and not agayn I bere,   carry away
As vouchethsauf as yeve me to my meedevouch   safe, reward
But such a smok as I was wont to were.   smock, wear

"Remember yet, my lord and husband dear,
I was your wife, though I unworthy were!

"Thus, in requital of the youth I brought,
But never can take back, nor have it more,
Give me, I pray, a garment of such sort
As in those days of poverty I wore."

Walter accepts this humble claim; mark the calm dignity with which she refrains from giving
way before her 'folk.'

The smok,[154] quod he, that thou hast on thy bak,   smock
Let it be stille, and ber it forth with the.
But wel unnethes thilke word he spak,   scarcely, this
But went his way for routhe and for pité.   compassion
Byforn the folk hirselven strippith sche,   herself
And in hir smok, with heed and foot al bare,   head and feet
Toward hir fader house forth is she fare.   went

The folk hir folwen wepyng in hir weye,   follow her
And fortune ay thay cursen as thay goon;   curse
But she fro wepyng kept hir eyen dreye,   dry
Ne in this tyme word ne spak sche noon.   none
Hir fader, that this tyding herd anoon,
Cursede the day and tyme that nature
Schoop him to ben a lyves creäture.   formed, living

For oute of doute this olde pore man
Was ever in suspect of hir mariage;   suspicion
For ever he deemede, sith that it bigan,   believed
That whan the lord fulfilled had his corrage,   impulse

Him wolde thinke that it were disparage disparagement
To his estate, so lowe for to lighte,
And voyden hire as sone as ever he mighte. put her away

Agayns his doughter hastily goth he goeth
(For he by noyse of folk knew hir comyng),
And with hir olde cote, as it might be,   coat
He covered hir, ful sorwfully wepynge,   sorrowfully
But on hir body might he it nought bringe,
For rude was the cloth, and mor of age,   coarse, more
By dayes fele than at hir mariage.   many (viel)

Thus with hir fader for a certeyn space
Dwellith this flour of wifly pacience,   flower
That neyther by hir wordes, ne by hir face,
Byforn the folk nor eek in her absence,   also, their
Ne schewed sche that hir was doon offence; showed, done
Ne of hir highe astaat no remembraunce   nor, estate
Ne hadde she, as by hir countenaunce.

"The shift," he said, "thou hast upon thy back,
Let it remain, and bear it forth with thee."
But scarcely that hard word for pain he spake,
And went his way for sorrow and pity.
Before the household all her robes stript she;
And in her shift, barefoot and bare of head,
Toward her father's house forth is she sped.

The household follow, tears in every eye,
Bewailing her ill-fortune as they go;
But she from weeping kept her own eyes dry,
Nor spake a word to those who murmur'd so.
Her father heard the news awhile ago,
And sore laments the day that he was born,
To be a thing so helpless and forlorn.

For ever without doubt the poor old man
Distrusted heartily her altered rank;
Believing inly since it first began,
That when my lord had wearied of his prank,
He would conceive it far beneath his rank
To have a low-born wife, however good,
And rid himself of her whene'er he could.

Unto his daughter hastily he goes,
(For by the noise of crowds he knew her nigh),
And her old garb about her form he throws,
And covers her, with tears and many a sigh,
But could not draw it round her properly,
For coarse and shrunk the cloth was—worse for age
By many days, than at her marriage.

Thus with her father for a certain space
Did dwell this flower of wifely patience;
And neither by her speech nor by her face,
Before the folk, nor e'en in their absènce,
Seem'd she to feel that she endured offence.
As far as any living soul could see
She had of her past state no memory.

And after all it was scarce any wonder. For in her days of wealth her spirit had always been humble and meek. No dainty fare, no foolish pomp or luxury, no semblance of splendid rank, had she allowed herself; but, ever wise and humble and firm, when reverses came she was ready to bear them.

Men speak of Job's patience; but, though some praise women little enough, no man can be as patient as a woman can—no man be faithful as a woman can.

Part VI.

AT last the Earl of Panik arrived, whose fame had been spreading among great and small. The people had all found out that he was bringing them a new marchioness, in such pomp and state, that never before had a like splendour been seen throughout West Lombardy.

The marquis, who had arranged all these things, sent for this poor innocent Griselda; and she came with humble mind and joyful face, and no proud notions in her heart, and knelt before him and asked his will.

"Griselda," he said, "my will is that the maiden whom I am to marry be received here as royally as it is possible in my house to be, and that everybody, according to his degree, shall be made thoroughly welcome and happy. I have no woman able to arrange my rooms fully to my liking, and therefore I want you to take everything in hand. You know of old my ways and my tastes; therefore, though your dress is ragged and you look very bad, you must do your duties to the very best of your power."

Griselda answered, "Not only, lord, am I glad to do anything for you, but I love you enough to work all my days to please you."

And with that worde sche gan the hous to dighte,
And tables for to sette, and beddes make:

And with that word she 'gan the house to deck,
To set the tables and to make the beds:
begging all the chambermaids to hasten and hurry and shake and sweep smartly; and she, most serviceable of them all, got every chamber and the great hall garnished and adorned.

Abouten undern gan this lord alighte,	forenoon
That with him broughte these noble children tweye;	two
For which the peple ran to se that sighte	
Of hir array, so richely biseye;	rich to be seen
And than at erst amonges hem thay seye	at first
That Walter was no fool, though that hem leste	he pleased
To chaunge his wyf; for it was for the beste.	

101

For sche is fairer, as thay demen alle,   deem
Than is Grisild, and more tendre of age.   younger

Somewhat ere noonday did this earl alight,
Who with him brought the unknown children fair,
And all the people ran to see the sight
Of their array, resplendent as they were;
And soon the common thought was whispered there,
That Walter was no fool for being glad
To change his wife—a good exchange he had!

For she is fairer, as they notice all,
Than is Griselda, tenderer of age.
And the throngs of admiring serfs stood making their light remarks, forgetful of the victim of it all, and her undeserved disgrace. They watch the fair bride and the handsome boy beside her, and every moment the marquis seems to get more popular.

O stormy poeple, unsad and ever untrewe,   unsteady
And undiscret and chaunging as a fane,   indiscreet
Delytyng ever in rombel that is newe,   noise
For lik the moone ay waxe ye and wane,
Ay ful of clappyng, dere ynough a jane,[155]   chattering
Youre doom is fals, your constaunce yvil previth, judgment, ill proveth
A ful gret fool is he that on yow leevith.   believeth

O stormy people, light, and ever untrue,
And undiscerning—changing as a fane,
Delighting in new noise, because 'tis new,
How like the moon do ye, too, wax and wane!
Your empty praise, like worthless coin, is vain:
False is your judgment, frail your constancy,
Who trusts to you—a full great fool is he.

That is what the graver people in the city said when the populace were gazing up and down, glad for the novelty, to have a new lady in the castle.

Meanwhile Griselda was working busily at everything that was needed for the feast. She was nothing abashed at her clothing, though it was rude and coarse, and somewhat torn besides. She went to the gate with the rest to salute the bride, and hurried back at once to her work.

She received every one cheerfully, and in such a manner that no one had a fault to find with her; but some of them wondered who this woman was, in such shabby clothes, but who behaved with so much grace and propriety; and many praised her diligence and wisdom.

When all the great lords were about to sit down to supper, Walter called to Griselda, who was working in the hall.

Grisyld, quod he, as it were in his play,
How likith the my wif and hir beauté?   do you like
Right wel, my lord, quod sche, for in good fay faith

A fairer saugh I never noon than sche.   *none*
I pray to God yive hir prosperité;
And so hope I that he wol to yow sende
Plesaunce ynough unto your lyves ende.   *pleasantness*

On thing biseke I yow, and warne also,[156]   *beseech*
That ye ne prike with no tormentynge   *prick*
This tendre mayden, as ye han doon mo: *more (others)*
For she is fostrid in hir norischinge   *fostered, nourishing*
More tendrely, and to my supposyng: *as I suppose*
Sche couthe not adversité endure,
As couthe a pore fostrid creature.   *could, poorly*

And whan this Walter saugh hir pacience,
Hir glade cheer, and no malice at al,
And he so oft hadde doon to hir offence,
And sche ay sad, and constant as a wal,   *steady*
Continuyng ever hir innocence overal:
This sturdy marquis gan his herte dresse   *direct*
To rewen upon hir wyfly stedefastnesse.   *to pity*

This is ynough, Grisilde myn, quod he,
Be now no more agast, ne yvel apayed,   *afraid, disappointed*
I have thy faith and thy benignité,   *goodness*
As wel as ever womman was, assayed   *essayed*
In gret estate, and pourliche[157] arrayed.   *poorly*
Now knowe I, dere wyf, thy stedefastnesse.
And hir in armes took and gan hir kesse.   *kiss*

And sche for wonder took of it no keepe,   *heed*
Sche herde not what thing he to hir sayde,
Sche ferd as sche hadde stert out of a sleepe,   *fared, started*
Til sche out of hir masidnesse abrayde.   *awoke*
Grisild, quod he, by God that for us deyde,   *died*
Thou art my wyf, non other I ne[158] have,
Ne never had, as God my soule save.

This is thy[159] doughter, which thou hast supposed
To be my wif: that other faithfully
Shal be myn heir, as I have ay purposed.
Thow bar hem of thy body trewely.
At Boloyne have I kept hem prively.
Tak hem agayn, for now maistow not seye   *mayest thou*
That thou hast lorn noon of thy children tweye.   *lost*

And folk, that other weyes han seyd of me,
I warn hem wel, that I have doon this deede   *done*
For no malice, ne for no cruelté,
But for tassaye in thee thy wommanhede;   *to assay, womanhood*
And not to slen my children (God forbede!)   *forbid*
But for to kepe hem prively and stille   *quietly*
Til I thy purpos knewe, and al thy wille!

"Grisild," he said to her, as if in play,
"How seems my wife and her fair looks to thee?"
"Right well, my lord," said she, "for in good fay
I never saw a fairer bride than she;
I pray God give you both prosperity;
And so I hope that He will ever send
You happiness enough to your lives' end.

"One thing I pray of you, and warn beside,
That you goad not with any torturing
This tender maid—like some you have sore tried
For she is nurtured in her upbringing
More tenderly—and such a gentle thing
Might haply not adversity endure
Like one whose nurture had been hard and poor."

And when this Walter saw her patientness,
Her cheerful mien, and malice none at all;
Though he so oft had tried her more or less,
And she still firm and constant as a wall,
Continuing ever her innocence over all:
This sturdy marquis 'gan his heart to chide,
Touch'd by her steadfast faith that never died.

"This is enough, Griselda mine," said he,
"Be no more ill at ease, and fear no more!
I have thy faith and strength and charity
Tempted, as woman never was before,
Both in thy wealth, and in thy rags so poor.
Now do I know, dear wife, thy steadfastness:"
And clasp'd her in his arms with many a kiss.

But she for wonder took no heed of him,
She heard not any of the words he spoke,
She seemed as one that starteth from a dream
Till she from her astonishment awoke.
"Griselde," cried he, "it was a cruel joke:
Thou art my wife, none other one I have,
Nor ever had—as God my soul shall save!

"This is thy daughter, whom thou hast supposed
To be my wife—that other faithfully
Shall be my heir, as I have long disposed;
For they are both thy children, verily.
I kept them at Bologna privily.
Take them again, thou canst not say, as once,
Thou hast lost either of thy little ones.

"And folk, who otherwise have said of me,
I warn them well that I have acted thus,
Neither in malice nor in cruelty,

Solely to prove thy patience marvellous,
And not to slay my babes (God hinder us!)
But to conceal them secretly apart
Until I learned thy purpose and thy heart!"
You may fancy you see Griselda at this moment, standing in her rags before the glittering company, and her brain dazed with wondering whether this were some new freak, or the truth that brought unheard-of joy. But nature had been taxed too far, and all her courage could not bear up against the shock.

Whan sche this herd, aswone doun she fallith,	in a swoon
For pitous joy, and after her swownyng	swooning
Sche bothe hir yonge children to hir callith,	
And in hir armes, pitously wepyng,	
Embraseth hem, and tendrely kissyng,	
Ful lik a moder, with hir salte terestears	
Sche bathide bothe hir visage and hir heres.[159]	their hair

When she heard this, all senseless down she falleth,
For piteous joy—and half unconsciously
Both her young children unto her calleth,
And in her arms, weeping so piteously,
Embraceth them, with kisses tenderly,
Full like a mother, and the tears she sheds
Bathe the fair faces and the dear loved heads.

Piteous it was to hear her humble voice, thanking Walter so fervently. "Graunt mercy, lord, God thank you," cried she, "for saving me my children. Now I care not how soon I die, since your love has come back to me.

O tendre, O dere, O yonge children myne,[160]	
Youre woful moder wende steadfastly	believed
That cruel houndes or som foul vermyne	wild dogs
Had eten yow: but God of his mercy,	
And your benigne fader tenderly	
Hath doon yow kepe. And in that same stounde	preserved you, moment
Al sodeinly sche swapped doun to grounde.	sank

And in hir swough so sadly holdith sche	swoon, firmly
Hir children tuo, whan sche gan hem tembrace,	to embrace them
That with gret sleight and gret difficulté	skill
The children from her arm they gonne arace.	tear away
O! many a teer on many a pitous face	
Doun ran of hem that stooden hir bisyde,	down, stood, beside
Unnethe aboute hir mighte thay abyde.	hardly

Waltier hir gladith, and hir sorwe slakith,	cheers, sorrow
Sche rysith up abaisshed from hir traunce,	abashed
And every wight hir joy and feste makith,	everybody
Til sche hath caught agayn hir continaunce;	countenance
Wauter hir doth so faithfully plesaunce,	comforts her
That it was daynté for to see the cheere	dainty
Bitwix hem tuo, now thay be met in feere.	company

These ladys, whan that thay hir tyme save,   their, saw
Han taken hir, and into chambre goon,   have
And strippen hir out of hir rude arraye,
And in a cloth of gold that brighte schon,   shone
With a coroun of many a riche stoon   crown, stone
Upon hir heed, they into hallo hir broughte,
And ther sche was honoured as hir oughte.   she ought to be

Thus hath this pitous day a blisful ende;
For every man and womman doth his might   best
This day in mirth and revel to despende,
Til on the welken schon the sterres brighte;   welkin
For more solempne in every mannes sighte   stately, man's
This feste was, and gretter of costage,   greater, cost
Than was the revel of hir mariage.

"O young, O dear, O tender children mine,
Your hapless mother thought in all her wo
That cruel beasts of prey and foul vermine
Had slain you both; but God had mercy—lo!
He and your loving father will'd it so
That you should be preserved:" and said no more,
But suddenly fell fainting on the floor.

And in her swoon so closely holdeth she
Her new-found children in a strong embrace.
That those around unclasp not easily
The fingers which so firmly interlace:
O! many a tear on many a pitying face
Ran down in token of deep sympathy—
Scarce could they bear to watch her agony.

Walter consoleth her as she awaketh:
She riseth up bewildered from her trance:
Each presseth round about and merry maketh
Until she hath recovered countenance.
With kisses and with loving word and glance
Walter doth cheer her—sweet it was to see
The joy they felt—united happily.

And when they saw their time, these ladies gay
Unto a chamber led her forth with them,
And stript her out of all her rude array,
And in apparel bright with many a gem
Clad her, and, crownëd with a diadem
Upon her head, they brought her to the hall,
Where she was meetly honoured of them all.

Thus hath this piteous day a blissful end,
Till every man and woman in the rout
Striveth the day in mirth and glee to spend,

106

Till in the darken'd sky the stars shone out;
For greater and more sumptuous, without doubt,
This revel was—and there was more to pay—
Than the rejoicings on her marriage-day.

Thus dwelt, for many years after, Walter and his wife in peace and joy; and I hope that the suffering of that day was the last Griselda had to bear at the hands of her capricious and wilful spouse. The pretty daughter Walter married to one of the greatest lords in Italy; and he then brought Griselda's old father to dwell in peace and comfort in his own court.

His son succeeded to his state and rank, and married happily, though he did not tempt and torment his wife as Walter did; for the world is not so strong as it once was, and people cannot bear such treatment now!

The story is told, not that wives should imitate Griselda in humility, for it would be unbearable, even if they did; but that every one in his degree should be constant in adversity as Griselda was. For if one woman could be so submissive to a mortal man, how much more ought we to take patiently all that God sends as our lot in life.

But one word before I stop! It would be hard to find in a whole city three, or even two, Griseldas nowadays. The gold in their nature is now so mixed with base metal that in any great trial the coin would sooner break than bend.

Grisild is deed, and eek hir pacience,	also
And bothe at oones buried in Itayle;	once
For whiche I crye in open audience	
No weddid man so hardy be to assayle	
His wyves pacience, in hope to fynde	
Grisildes, for in certeyn he schal fayle.	

Dead is Griselda, and her patience,
Both buried in one grave in Italy;
So I entreat in open audience
No wedded man be rash enough to try
His own wife's patience, in the hope to find
Griselda's, for he'll fail most certainly!

Notes by the Way

The tender pathos in Chaucer's telling of this story (which he borrowed from Petrarch, but which is really much older than his time), cannot be excelled in any story we know of. The definite human interest running all through it points to some living Griselda, but who she was, or where she came from, no one knows. Resignation, so steadfast and so willing, was the virtue of an early time, when the husband was really a 'lord and master'; and such submission in a woman of the present civilization would be rather mischievous than meritorious. If a modern wife cheerfully consented to the murder of her children by her spouse, she would probably be consigned to a maison de santé, while her husband expiated his sins on the scaffold; and if she endured other persecutions, such as Griselda did, it is to be hoped some benevolent outsider would step in, if only to prevent cruelty to animals.

But it must be remembered that in the old world wives held a very different position in society, and the obedience of all the household to the lord of the castle was the chief secret of peace, discipline, and unity, as obedience to the captain of a vessel is now. We may also infer, from many hints in this Tale, the admiration felt for that kind of self-command in which people of a ruder time were so deficient. When almost everybody gave way habitually to violent emotions of all sorts, those who could rein in feeling were held in high esteem. Perhaps Walter himself may not have been wantonly cruel, but only so bewildered by these unaccustomed virtues that he could not trust their sincerity without experiments.[161]

Chaucer seems to me to have devoted especial pains to the Clerk's Tale, relating it in the same careful versification as the history of the pious Constance (Man of Law's Tale), the holy St. Cecilia (second Nonne's Tale), and the Prioress's Tale—all religious, and undoubtedly written con amore.

The story of Griselda winds up with real artistic power, the Clerk concluding with an ironical little song addressed to ordinary wives, so as to leave his hearers laughing, instead of depressed by the inadequate reward of patient Grizel's virtues. This little song consists of six beautiful verses, of six lines only each, and in which every line rhymes with the corresponding line in the five other verses. Clearly great labour has been lavished on it—but I have not included it, as the ironical directions to wives to be bad wives would be probably not understood by a child, and superfluous if they were.

The Franklin's Tale.

MINE host would not suffer long delay between the stories; and as soon as the last story was at an end, he called upon the Franklin to begin.

IN Armorike,[162] that is called Brittany, there was a knight named Arviragus, who loved the lady Dorigene. Much he laboured, and many a brave deed he performed for her sake. He loved her so dearly that no trouble seemed to him too great to win her love, for she was the fairest lady under the sun, and, moreover, came of high lineage. But, at last, seeing his worthiness and meek obedience, she consented to take him for her husband and her lord (such lordship as men have over their wives); and, in order that they might live more happily together, Arviragus, of his own free will, swore, as a knight, that he would never tyrannize over her, but follow her wishes in all things, as he had done ever.[163]

This kindness touched the lady deeply, and she thanked Arviragus; and, with great humility, she said, "Since of your gentillesse you proffer me so much power, I will always be a humble and true wife to you. Have here my troth, until my life shall end."

Thus they lived happily and at peace; for those who would live long together must give in to each other.

Love wol nought ben constreigned by maystrie:	mastery
Whan maystrie cometh, the god of love anon	soon
Beteth his winges, and fare wel—he is gon!	

Love will not be constrained by tyranny;
When mastery cometh, the god of Love anon
Beateth his wings, and farewell!—he is gone!
For women wish for liberty, and not to be kept like slaves—and so do men also, if I tell truth. And whoever is patient in love, has all the advantage. Patience is a high virtue, for it overcomes things that rigour cannot do.

Arviragus went home with his wife to his own country, not far from Penmark,[164] where they dwelt 'in bliss and in solace.'

When a year had passed away, this knight Arviragus made ready to go to England[165] to seek fame and honour in the service of arms, and there he dwelt two years.

But Dorigene loved her husband so dearly that she wept and fell sick when she was left alone. She could not sleep or eat, and as time went on, all her friends thought she would die. They tried to amuse her all that they could. Night and day they strove to comfort her, she was so sad, and begged her to go and roam with them in the fields and on the sea-shore.

You know even a stone will show some pattern at last if you cut long enough at it: and after a while Dorigene began to try and cheer up a little. Meanwhile, Arviragus sent letters home to tell her he would speedily return, else grief had slain her heart!

Now, Dorigene's castle stood near the sea; and sometimes she used to walk with her friends and her people on the cliffs, from whence she could see ever so many great ships and barges sailing by. But even the sea began to make her sad, for she said to herself, "Of all these ships that I see, is there not one will bring me back my lord?"

At other times she would sit and look down from the brink of the cliff; but when she saw the grisly black rocks that wrecked so many ships, her heart quaked with fear, and she sank on the green grass, and cried, with deep sighs of grief, "Would to God that all these black rocks were sunk into the earth, for my lord's sake!" and the piteous tears fell from her eyes.

Her friends soon saw it did her no good looking at the sea, but only made her worse. So they led her by rivers, and in beautiful green places, where they danced, and played at chess and tables.[166]

So on a day, right in the morwe tyde,	morning
Unto a gardyne that was ther besyde,	
In which that thay hadde made here ordinaunce	
Of vitaile, and of other purvyaunce,	victual
They gon and pleyen hem al the longe day.	go, play
And this was on the sixte morwe of May,[167]	
Which May had peynted with his softe schoures	
This gardyn ful of leves and of floures.	

So on a day, before the sun was high,
Unto a garden fair that was hard by
(Wherein they had spread forth their meat and drink,
And every comfort that the heart could think),
They went—and sported all the whole long day,
And this was on the sixth sweet morn of May,
When May had painted, with his tender showers,
This garden full of fragrant leaves and flowers.

The odour of flowers and the fresh scene would have made any heart light that ever was born except one burdened by great sickness or great sorrow. After dinner they began to dance and sing—all save Dorigene, whose heart was sad. He whom she loved best was not among them.

There danced, among others, a squire before Dorigene, who was handsomer, and more radiant in array, and fresher than a May morning. He sang and danced better than anybody ever danced before, or will again! And, besides, he was young, strong, and virtuous, and rich and wise, and held in great esteem.

This squire, whose name was Aurelius, had long loved the Lady Dorigene, but she knew nothing of it. He did not dare to tell her his grief, and could only sing songs, in which he complained in a general way that he loved some one who regarded him not.

He made a great many songs in this strain.

But at last, on this day it happened, as Aurelius was her neighbour, and a man of worship and honour, Dorigene fell a-talking with him; and when he saw a chance, Aurelius said to her, "Madam, I wish when Arviragus went over the sea, I had gone whither I could never come back! For well I know you do not care for me. Madam, forget Arviragus: and love me a little, or I shall die!"

Dorigene looked at him, and said, "Is this your will? I never knew what you meant. But now, this is my answer: I cannot forget my Arviragus, and I do not care for any one but him!"

But afterwards she said in play, "Aurelius, I will love you when you have taken away all the rocks and stones that hinder the ships from sailing. And when you have made the coast so clear that there is not a single stone to be seen, then I will love you best of any man." For she well knew the rocks could never be moved.

But Aurelius was sorely grieved. "Is there no other grace in you?" said he. "No, by that Lord who made me," Dorigene answered. "Madam, it is an impossibility," he said; "I must die."

Then came Dorigene's other friends, who knew nothing of this. They roamed up and down the green alleys, and betook themselves to new sports and new revels; but Aurelius did not mingle with them. He went sorrowfully to his own home, for it seemed as though he felt his heart grow cold.

He was so sad that he fell sick, and so suffered a long, long time, telling his trouble to nobody in the world; except to his brother, who was a clerk,[168] and who was very sorry for him.

| His breast was hole withouten for to sene, | see |
| But in his herte ay was the arwe kene. | ever |

His breast was whole without, to every eye,
But in his heart the arrow keen did lie.
And well you know that it is a perilous cure when a wound is healed outwardly only!

Meanwhile, Arviragus came home from England to his faithful wife, and there were great rejoicings, and feasts, and jousting; and these two were so glad to see each other that they thought of nothing else. Dorigene cared nothing at all for Aurelius; and Arviragus had no suspicion that Aurelius had spoken to her of love.

DORIGEN AND AURELIUS IN THE GARDEN.

'Have mercy, swete, or ye wol do me deye.'

Now Aurelius' brother was a very learned man; and as he saw Aurelius got no better, he was very unhappy about him. At last he remembered that he had once seen at Orleans, in France, a book on conjuring,[169] which had been left in his way. This book was full of all sorts of curious tricks which were performed by the 'tregetoures' or jugglers of that day. He was glad when he thought of this book, feeling sure he saw a chance of curing Aurelius.

And whan this boke was in his remembraunce,
Anon for joye his herte gan for to daunce,   immediately
And to him selve he sayde pryvely,

111

My brother shal be warisshed hastely,   cured
For I am siker that ther ben sciencessure
By whiche men maken dyverse apparences, various
Swiche as thise subtile tregetoures pleyen,
For oft at festes have I wel herde seyen
That tregettoures withinne an halle large
Han made come in a water and a barge,
And in the halle rowen up and doun.
Sometyme hath semed come a grym leoun, seemed, grim
And sometyme floures spring as in a mede,[170]
Sometyme a vine, and grapes white and rede,
Sometyme a castel al of lym and ston,
And whan hem liked voyded it anon.   dispersed
Thus semeth it to every mannes sight.

And when this book came, by a lucky chance,
Into his mind, his heart began to dance,
And to himself he whispered privily,
"My brother shall be healed full speedily,
For I am sure that there be sciences
By which men raise divers appearances,
Such as the cunning jugglers do in play;
For oftentimes at feasts have I heard say
That jugglers playing in a hall so large,
Have seemed to bring in waters and a barge,
And in the hall they row it to and fro.
Sometimes a lion fierce will come and go,
Sometimes, as in a meadow, flowers upspring,
Sometimes a vine, with rich fruit clustering,
Sometimes a castle all of lime and stone,
And when they wish, at once the whole is gone!
Thus seemeth it to be, in all men's sight."

Therefore he thought that if he could find any old friend at Orleans, who knew anything of magic, he might help Aurelius to win the beautiful Dorigene.

He went to his brother's bed, and gave him so much hope that he sprang up at once and started off to Orleans.

When they were nearly arrived at the city, they met a young clerk, roaming by himself, who greeted them in Latin, saying, to their great wonder, "I know the cause that brings you here," and, ere they went a step farther, he told them all that was in their minds!

This clerk was, you see, a magician, and having saved them the trouble of explaining their business, he brought them to his house, where he feasted them in splendid style, and showed them many wonderful visions.

He schewed hem, er they went to soupere, supper
Forestes, parkes, full of wilde dere;
There[171] saw he hartes with hir hornes hie,
The gretest that were ever seen with eie!
He saw of hem an hundred slain with houndes,

And som with arwes blede of bitter woundes.
He saw, when voided were the wilde dere,   departed
Thise faukoneres upon a faire rivere,
That with hir haukes han the heron slein.   hawks
Tho saw he knyhtes justen in a pleyn;   joust
And after this he dide him such plesaunce,
That he him schewed his lady in a daunce,
On which himself he dauncéd, as him thouht.
And when this mayster that this magique wrouht,
Sawh it was tyme, he clapped his hondes tuo,   two
And, fare wel! al the revel is y-do!   done
And yet remued they never out of the hous
While they saw alle this sightes mervelous;
But in his studie, ther his bookes be,
They saten stille, and no wighte but they thre.

He made appear, before they went to meat,
Forests and parks, with wild deer fair and fleet;
There saw he harts that tossed their antlers high,
The greatest that were ever seen with eye!
He saw a hundred of them slain by hounds,
While some with arrows bled of bitter wounds,
And when the wild deer were no longer there,
Came falconers upon a river fair,
Who, with their falcons, have the heron slain;
Then saw he knights all jousting in a plain;
And after this he gave him such pleasance,
That he could see his lady in a dance,
In which himself was dancing, as he thought.
And when this master, who the magic wrought,
Saw it was time, he clapped his hands, and eh!
Farewell! for all the revel fades away!
And yet they never moved from out the house,
While they did see these visions marvellous;
But in his study, where his volumes lay,
They sat alone, and no man else but they.

Therefore, after all these wondrous sights, inside the magician's study, there was no doubt that he could make the rocks disappear on the coast of Brittany!

Aurelius asked him how much money he should give him to perform that feat, and the magician said he must have no less than a thousand pounds;[172] but Aurelius said he would give him the whole world if he could; and it was agreed that for this sum he should make the rocks vanish, and that without delay!

The next morning, at daybreak, Aurelius, his brother, and the magician, went to the sea-side of Brittany, where the feat was to be done: it was the cold frosty month of December.

Aurelius paid the magician every attention in his power, and entreated him to hasten to alleviate his misery; he rather ungraciously added, that he would slit his heart with his sword if he didn't.

The cunning sorcerer made as much haste as he could with his spells and trickeries to make all the rocks sink, or seem to sink, before the eyes of all that looked at them, right underground; at last he succeeded. By his magic arts it really did seem to everybody, for a week or two, that the rocks were all gone.

Aurelius thanked him with joy, and then hastened to the castle, where he knew he should see Dorigene, to remind her of what she had promised.

"My sovereign lady," he said, saluting her humbly—

Ye wot right wel what ye byhighte me,	promised
And in myn hond your trouthe plighte ye	my
To love me best; God woot ye sayde so,	
Al be that I unworthy am therto.	
Madame, I speke it for thonour of yow	you
More than to save myn hertes lif right now:	
I have do so as ye comaundede me,	
And if ye vouchesauf ye maye go se.	vouchsafe
In yow lith al to do me lyve or deye,	lieth
But wel I wote the rokkes ben aweye.	are

"You know right well what you have promised me,
And hand in mine your fair trouth plighted ye
To love me best; God knoweth you said so,
Although I be unworthy thereunto.
Madam, I speak for th' honour of the vow
More than to urge my heart's deep longing now:
For I have done as you commanded me,
And if you please it, you may go and see.
It rests with you, to let me live or die,
But that the rocks have vanish'd, well know I."

Poor Dorigene had little expected to fall into such a trap! She stood astonished, and her face grew white—all the colour left her cheeks. How bitterly she repented her rash promise! for she did not want to go away with Aurelius. "Alas!" she cried, "that such a thing should be! how could I guess so monstrous a marvel could come to pass?" and her terror made her like one desperate.

Her husband, Arviragus, too, was absent, and there was no one she could tell her trouble to. She cried and lamented for three days, vainly thinking how she could get out of the scrape; and at last she determined to die. So three days passed, and all the time she was weeping and resolving on her death.

However, on the third night, Arviragus came home again; and, when he knew what she was weeping so bitterly for, he said, cheerfully and kindly, "Is that all, Dorigene?"

Is ther aught elles, Dorigen, but this?	else
Nay, nay, quod sche, God me so rede and wis	reads, knows
This is to moche, and it were Goddes wille!	if
Ye, wyf, quod he, let slepe that may be stille,[173]	
It may be wel, paraunter, yet to-day.	peradventure
Ye schal your trouthe holden, by my fay,	faith

114

For God so wisly have mercy on me,   wisely
I hadde wel lever i-stekid for to be,   rather, slain
For verray love which that I to you have,
But if ye scholde your trouthe kepe and save,   unless
Trouthe is the hiest thing that man may kepe.
And with that word he brast anon to wepe.   burst

"Is there aught further, Dorigene, than this?"
"Nay, nay," cried she, "God help me, for it is
Too much already—were it but His will!"
"Yea, wife," he answered, "what has been is still,
But yet, perchance, it may be well to-day.
That promise you shall hold to, by my fay,
For as I hope for mercy from on high,
I would more willingly consent to die,
Yea for the love's sake that I bear to you,
Than you should break the honour of a vow
Faith is the highest thing that can be kept."
And with that word he broke away and wept.

Poor Arviragus, this brave and just knight, bade Dorigene keep her word at any cost to herself or him, but he could not keep up his cheerful tone. He was too deeply grieved and hurt, and even wept with her for sorrow.

Then he commanded a squire and a maid to attend Dorigene for a part of the way to the garden, where Aurelius would fetch her.

Now, Aurelius happened to meet her on her way to the garden, in one of the busiest streets of the town. He saluted her joyfully, and asked her whither she was going. But Dorigene was distracted with grief.

And sche answered, half as sche were mad,
Unto the gardyn, as myn housbond bad,
My trouthe for to holde, allas! allas!

And she made answer half as she were mad,
"Unto the garden, as my husband bade,
To keep my troth to you, alas! alas!"

When Aurelius heard that, he was deeply touched that Arviragus should have sent her, weeping as she was, rather than she should break her promise. See how proud and how strong the sense of honour was in those days! He felt that after such a sacrifice he would rather forego everything than insist upon his right to take away Dorigene, which, he felt, would be 'churlish wretchedness against fraunchise of all gentillesse'[174]—a deed against courtesy and honour. And he said, "Madam, say to your lord, Arviragus, that since I see he would rather suffer anything than that you should fail in truth, and since I see that you care far more for Arviragus than ever you will for me—even if you went away with me, you would never love me as much as Arviragus—I would rather be unhappy all my life than make you so. I release you from your promise for ever."

Thus can a squyer doon a gentil dede,   do
As wel as can a knyghte, withouten drede.

Thus can a squire do a noble deed
As nobly as a knight can, without dread.

Dorigene fell down on her knees and thanked him, and went back to her husband happy, and they lived in bliss ever after.

Aurelius, however, though his conscience was clear, bethought him of all his trouble and the money he had spent to no purpose. He had willingly promised all his fortune when he thought he could win beautiful Dorigene; but now he said, "I must sell my heritage, but I cannot live here a beggar to shame my kindred; unless the magician would be so kind as to let me pay the thousand pounds little by little. I will not break my promise to him. He shall have the money though I have got nothing by it."

With herte soor he goth unto his cofre,	sore
And broughte gold unto this philosophre,	philosopher
The value of fyf hundred pound, I gesse,	
And him bysecheth of his gentillesce,	beseecheth
To graunte him dayes of the remenaunt;	remnant
And sayde, Maister, I dar wel make avaunt	boast
I fayled never of my trouthe as yit,	
For sikerly my dettes schall be quyt	surely
Towardes yow, how so that ever I fare	
To goon and begge in my kurtil bare,	beg, tunic
But wolde ye vouchesauf upon seurté,	vouchsafe, surety
Tuo yere or thre for to respite me,	
Than were I wel, for elles most I selle	
Myn heritage, ther is nomore to telle.	

With mournful heart he went unto his coffer
And took such gold as he was free to offer,
The value of five hundred pounds, I guess;
Beseeching him, of his kindheartedness,
To grant him for the rest some time to pay,
And said, "Master, I do not fear to say
I never failed to keep my word as yet;
Truly my debt to you I shall acquit,
Whatever comes—though I must needs at best
Go begging in my shirt to find the rest.
But would ye grant, on good security,
To give me credit for two years, or three,
Then all were well, for else I must needs sell
My heritage—there is no more to tell."

The magician soberly answered, "Did I not keep my covenant with you?"

"Yes, well and truly," said Aurelius.

"And did you not take the lady away with you?"

"No, no," said Aurelius, sadly; and he told him all that had happened.

The magician answered, "Dear friend, every one of you has behaved honourably. Thou art a squire, and he is a knight, but a simple clerk can do a gentle deed, as well as any of you! Sir, I release you from your thousand pounds: I will not take a penny from you." And he took his horse and rode away.

Chaucer winds up by saying—

Lordynges, this questioun wold I axe now—	ask
Which was the moste free, as thinketh yow?	liberal

Masters, a little question answer me—
Which one was the most generous of the three?

And you, tell me which you think was the most honourable in keeping faith, and most generous in giving up his rights.

But beware of the folly that Dorigene committed, in making rash promises; for when you make a promise you must be prepared to keep it, and cannot always expect to be let off as she was.

Notes by the Way.

One of the most interesting illustrations of the singular morality which was the outcome of woman's transition state from a position of slavery to one of equality with man, is to be found in this curious but beautiful tale: a tale which in any other age could scarcely have been popular. The Franklin tells us it was an old Breton lay; which, however, is now not known to exist.

It is seen that woman, from being regarded as a mere chattel, like horse or dog, came to be unnaturally exalted; and, as new movements often outshoot their mark and go too far, she came to be held as something god-like and ideal, the moving spring of all heroic virtues. Valour, courtesy, self-control, obedience, were taught by her, and she could give no higher guerdon than herself. (See note to 'Knight's Tale,' p. 45.)

It is the young and inexperienced hound which outruns the scent, not the fully trained dog, and we must remember that society had then the virtues and vices of immaturity. The Franklin's Tale, with its pathos and earnestness, passing at times into burlesque, is as quaint and instructive as an early effigy on some cathedral door.

A certain soft and refined luxuriousness seems to hang like a gossamer veil over a sentiment of genuine and vigorous chivalry, carried too far for our 19th century notions, but, like the generous mistakes of youth, none the less touching.

The moral of this striking tale points out the danger of giving even the smallest inlet to wrong dealing; since a condition apparently impossible to realize may after all work our ruin.

THEN mine host turned to the Pardoner: "Thou, pardoner, thou, my good friend," he said—

Tel us a tale, for thou canst many oon.
It schal be doon, quod he, and that anoon.
But first, quod he, her at this ale-stake[175]
I wil bothe drynke and byten on a cake.

"Tell us a tale; thou knowest many an one."
"I will!" he said; "it shall at once be done.
But first," he added, "here at this ale-stake
I'll take a drink, and have a bite of cake."

When he had done so (for they were passing a roadside inn), he began, as you shall hear:—

THERE was in Flanders a company of young folk, who gave themselves up to folly and wrong-doing. They did nothing but gamble and riot, and drink wine, and dance, and swear; and their gluttony and idleness made them wicked, so that when they heard of other people committing sin they laughed and did as much wrong as ever they could.

This kind of life degrades every one. Gluttony was the first cause of our confusion: Adam and Eve were driven from Paradise for that vice. And drunkenness leads to many other sins, as is shown in Holy Writ.

Three of these bad young men were sitting in a tavern one morning very early, drinking, when they heard the clinking of a bell[176] before a corpse that was being carried to the grave. One of them called to his boy, "Go out, and ask who that dead man is who passes by; and mind you bring his name back right!"

"Master," said the boy, "there is no need to go and ask, for I heard who the dead man was two hours before you came into this tavern. He was one of your own companions, and he was slain last night as he sat in his chair drinking, by a privy thief named Death, who kills everybody in this country. With his spear he smote his heart in two, and went away without speaking. About a thousand has he killed this pestilence.[177] And, master, it seems to me, that before he comes to you too, it were as well to be prepared. Beware of him, be ready for him! my dame ever taught me that."

By seinte Mary, sayde this taverner,	innkeeper
The child saith soth, for he hath slayn this yeer,	true
Hens over a myle, withinne a gret village,	
Bothe man and womman, child, and hyne, and page.	labourer

"By holy Mary," said the innkeeper,
"The child says true, for he hath slain this year,
Within a mile hence, in a large village,
Both man and woman, servant, child, and page.

"I should think he lived there, this Death, so many have died. It were wise to be warned before he came suddenly on a man!"

"Good lack," cried one of the rioters with an oath, "is it then such danger to meet him? I'll seek him out by street and stile.

Herkneth, felaws, we thre ben all oones,	hearken, be
Let ech of us hold up his hond[178] to other,	hand
And ech of us bycome otheres brother;	
And we wil slee this false traitour Deth;	
He shall be slayne, that so many sleeth.	slain, slayeth

"Now listen, mates, for all we three are one,
Let each hold up his hand unto the other,
And each of us become the others' brother.
And we will slay this sneaking traitor Death,
He shall be slain, he that so many slay'th."

So these three men, half drunk as they were, plighted faith to live and die for each other, as though they were brothers born. And up they started, and went forth to this village, of which the innkeeper had spoken, where they thought Death lived. And much bad language they used, and many wicked things they said, resolving to catch Death before night fell.

Right as thay wolde han torned over a style,	turned
Whan thai han goon nought fully half a myle,	
An old man and a pore with hem mette.	
This olde man ful mekely hem grette,[179]	meekly, greeted
And saide thus, Lordynges, God yow se!	God see you
The proudest of these ryotoures threrioters	
Answerd ayein, What, carle, with sory grace,	churl
Why artow al for-wrapped save thi face?[180]—	wrapped up
Why lyvest thou longe in so great an age?	

This olde man gan loke on his visage,	began, look
And saide thus: For that I can not fynde	because
A man—though that I walke into Inde—	
Neither in cité noon, ne in village,	
That wol chaunge his youthe for myn age;	
And therfore moot I have myn age stille	
As longe tyme as it is Goddes wille,	
Ne Deth, allas! ne wil not have my lif,	
Thus walk I lik a resteles caytif,[181]	
And on the ground, which is my modres gate,	
I knokke with my staf, erly and late,	
And saye, Leeve moder, let me in.	dear
Lo, how I wane, fleisch, and blood, and skyn—	
Allas, whan schuln my boones ben at rest?	shall, bones
Moder, with yow wil I chaunge my chest,	
That in my chamber longe tyme hath be,	
Ye, for an haire clout[182] to wrap-in me.enwrap	
But, yet to me sche wol not do that grace,	favour
For which ful pale and welkid is my face.	withered

But sires, to yow it is no curtesye
To speke unto an old man vilonye,

But he trespas in word or elles in dede. *unless, else*
In holy writ ye may yourself wel rede, *read*
Ayens an old man, hoor upon his hede, *in presence of*
Ye schold arise: wherefor I you redeexhort
Ne doth unto an old man more harm now, *do not*
Namore than ye wolde men dede to yow
In age, if that ye may so long abyde. *live so long*
And God be with you, wherso ye go or ryde! *walk*
I moot go thider as I have to goo. *thither*

Nay, olde cherl, by God thou shalt not so,
Sayde that other hasardour anoon,
Thou partist nought so lightly, by seint Johan! *departest, easily*
Thou spak right now of thilke traitour Deth,
That in this contré alle our frendes sleth;
Have her my trouth, as thou art his aspye; *here*
Tel wher he is, or elles thou schalt dye.[183]

Just as they were about to cross a stile,
When they had gone not fully half a mile,
A poor and aged man did meet them there.
This old man greeted them with civil air,
And said, "Good day, my lords, God look on ye."
Then the most arrogant of the noisy three
Answered him thus—"What, churl, with sorry grace,
Why art thou all wrapped up except thy face?
Why livest thou so long, and art so grey?"

The old man looked him in the face straightway,
And answer'd thus: "Because I cannot find
A man—e'en though I walk'd as far as Inde—
Neither in any city, nor villàge,
Willing to change his youth for mine old age;
And therefore must I have my old age still
As long a time as it is heaven's will.
Nor will e'en Death receive my life, alas!
Thus like a restless wayfarer I pass,
And on the ground, which is my mother's gate,
Keep knocking with my staff early and late,
And say to her—'Dear mother, let me in.
Lo, how I vanish, flesh and blood and skin—
Alas, when shall my bones remain at rest?
Mother, I want to change with you my chest,
Which in my room so long a time hath been,
Yea, for a cloth of hair to wrap me in!'
But yet to me she will not do that grace,
Wherefore so pale and wrinkled is my face.

"But, sirs, in you it is no courtesy
To speak to an old man disdainfully,
Unless he shall offend in word or deed.
In Holy Writ ye may your own selves read,

120

Before an aged man whose hair is grey
Ye should rise up—and therefore I you pray
Offer to an old man no mischief now
More than you would that men did unto you
In your old age, if you so long abide,
And God be with you, whither you walk or ride!
I must go on, whither I have to go."

"Nay, thou old churl, thou shalt not quit us so."
Cried out the other rioter anon,
"Thou partest not so lightly, by St. John!
Thou hast just spoken of that traitor Death
Who all our friends through all the country slay'th,
So now I warrant thee, thou art his spy;
Tell where he is, this Death, or thou shall die.

"You needn't deny that you know of his whereabouts—for you are in his plot to get rid of
us young folks, you wretched old thief!"

Now, sires, than if that yow be so leef
To fynde Deth, torn up this croked way,
For in that grove I laft him,[184] by my fay,
Under a tree, and ther he wil abyde.   remain
Ne for your bost he nyl him no thing hyde.   boast
Se ye that ook? right ther ye schuln him fynde.
God save yow, that bought agein mankynde,   again
And yow amend. Thus sayth this olde man,

And everich of these riotoures ran,   every one
Til thay come to the tre, and ther thay founde
Of florins fyn of gold ycoyned rounde,   coined
Wel neygh a seven busshels, as hem thoughte.
No lenger thanne after Deth thay soughte,
But ech of hem so glad was of that sighte,
For that the florens so faire were and brighte,
That doun thai sette hem by the precious hord.
The werste[185] of hem he spake the firste word.
Bretheren, quod he, take kepe what I schal saye,
My witte is gret, though that I bourde and playe,   wisdom, jest
This tresour hath fortune to us yiven,   given
In mirth and jollyté our lif to lyven,   jollity, live
And lightly as it comth, so wil we spende.   cometh
Ey, Goddis precious dignite, who wendesupposed
Today, that we schuld have so fair a grace?
But mighte this gold be caried fro this place
Hom to myn hous, or ellis unto youres,
(For wel I wot that this gold is nought oures),   know
Than were we in heyh felicité.   high
But trewely by day it may not be,
Men wolde saye that we were theves stronge,
And for our tresour doon us for to honge.   have us hanged
This tresour moste caried be by nighte

121

As wysly and as slely as it mighte.
Wherfore I rede, that cut among us alle — advise
We drawe, and let se wher the cut wil falle,
And he that hath the cut, with herte blithe, — blithe heart
Shal renne to the toun, and that ful swithe, — run, quickly
And bring us bred and wyn ful prively,
And tuo of us shal kepe subtilly
This tresour wel: and if he wol not tarie, — delay
Whan it is night, we wol this tresour carie,[186]
By oon assent, ther as us liketh best. — wither

That oon of hem the cut brought in his fest, — fist
And bad hem drawe and loke wher it wil falle, — look
And it fel on the yongest of hem alle,
And forth toward the toun he went anoon. — at once

And al so soone as that he was agoon,
That oon of hem spak thus unto that other:
Thou wost wel that thou art my sworne brother,
Thy profyt wol I telle the anoon. — directly
Thou wost wel that our felaw is agoon, — knowest
And her is gold, and that ful gret plente, — plenty
That schal departed be among us thre.
But natheles if I can schape it so
That it departed were betwix us tuo,
Hadde I not doon a frendes torn to the?

That other answerd, I not how that may be; — know not
He wot wel that the gold is with us twaye, — two
What schulde we than do? what schulde we saye? — say
Schal it be counsail?[187] sayd the ferste schrewe, — wicked person
And I schal telle thee in wordes fewe
What we schul doon, and bringe it wel aboute. — do
I graunte, quod that other, without doute,
That by my trouthe I wil thee nought bywraye. — betray

Now, quoth the first, thou wost wel we ben twaye, — knowest
And two of us schal strenger be than oon.
Loke, whanne he is sett, thou right anoon[188] — look
Arys, as though thou woldest with him pleye,[189] — wouldest
And I schal ryf him through the sydes tweye, — rip
Whils that thou strogelest with him as in game,
And with thi dagger, loke thou do the same.
And than schal al the gold departed be, — divided
My dere frend, bitwixe the and me: — thee
Than may we oure lustes al fulfille, — might
And pley at dees right at our owne wille. — dice

"Now, sirs," quoth he, "if you so eager be
To seek for Death, turn up this crooked way,
For in that grove I left him, by my fay,
Under a tree, and there he will abide,

122

Nor for your noise and boasting will he hide.
See ye that oak? close there his place you'll find,
God save you, sirs, that hath redeem'd mankind,
And mend you all"—thus said the aged man.

And thereupon each of the rioters ran
Until they reach'd the tree, and there they found
A heap of golden florins, bright and round,
Well-nigh seven bushels of them, as they thought.
And then no longer after Death they sought,
But each of them so glad was at the sight,
The florins were so beauteous and so bright,
That down they sat beside the precious hoard.
The worst one was the first to speak a word.
"Brothers," said he, "take heed of what I say,
For I am wise, although I jest and play,
This treasure makes our fortune, so that we
May lead our lives in mirth and jollity,
And lightly as it comes, we'll lightly spend.
By heaven! who would have thought that luck would send
Us three good friends to-day so fair a grace?
But could this gold be carried from this place
Home to my house, or else to one of yours
(For all this gold I well know is not ours)
Then were we in complete felicity.
But, truly, during day it cannot be,
People would call us thieves, and possibly
Hang us for our own treasure on a tree.
This treasure should be carried off by night,
As cleverly and slily as it might.
I counsel then, that we among us all
Draw lots, and see to whom the lot will fall,
And he that hath the lot shall cheerfully
Go back into the town, and speedily,
And bring us bread and wine full privily;
Meanwhile we two keep safe and secretly
This treasure here: and if he do not tarry,
When the night comes we will the treasure carry,
By one assent, where we think best, or list."

This man then held the lots within his fist,
And bade them draw and see where it would fall;
It fell upon the youngest of them all,
Who therefore toward the town went forth anon.

As soon as their companion was gone
The first one subtly spoke unto the other:
"Thou knowest well that thou art my sworn brother,
I'll tell thee what thy profit is to-day.
Thou seest that our fellow is away,
And here is gold, all heap'd up plenteously,
Which is to be divided 'mong us three.

But, nevertheless, if I can shape it so
That it might be divided 'mong us two,
Have I not done a friend's turn unto thee?"

"I know not," said the other, "how that may be;
He knows quite well the gold is with us two,
What should we say to him? what should we do?"
"Shall it be counsel?" said the first again—
"And in a few words I shall tell thee plain,
What we shall do to bring the thing about."
"I promise," said the other, "without doubt
That I, for one, will not be treacherous."

"Now," said the first one, "there are two of us,
And two of us will stronger be than one.
Look, thou, when he is sitting down, and soon
Rise up, as if to play with him, and I
Will stab him through the two sides suddenly,
While thou art struggling with him as in game,
And with thy dagger, look, thou do the same.
And then shall all this gold divided be,
My dearest friend, betwixt thyself and me:
Then all our wants and whims we can fulfil,
And play at dice according to our will."

THE RIOTER.

'For this witterly was his ful entente—
To slen hem bothe and never to repente.'

Thus these two ruffians made their compact to murder the third, as I have described.

This yongest, which that wente to the toun,	who
Full fast in hert he rollith up and doun	close

The beaute of these florins, newe and brighte.	
O Lord, quoth he, if so were that I mighte	
Have all this gold unto myself alloone,	
Ther is no man that lyveth under the troone	throne
Of God, that schulde lyve so mery as I.	
And atte last the feend, oure enemy,	
Put in his thought that he schulde poysoun beye,	buy
With which he mighte sle his felawes tweye.	slay
For why? the feend fond him in such lyvynge	
That he hadde leve to sorwe him to brynge:	sorrow
For this was outrely[190] his ful entente	
To slen hem bothe, and never to repente.	slay
And forth he goth, no lenger wold he tarye,	delay
Into the toun unto a potecarye,	apothecary
And prayde him that he him wolde selle	
Som poysoun, that he might his rattis quelle;	rats
And eek ther was a polkat in his hawe	farmyard
That, as he sayde, his capouns had i-slawe,	
And said he wold him wreke, if that he mighte,	avenge
Of vermyn, that destroyed hem by nighte.	
Thapotecary answerd,[191]Thou schalt have	the apothecary
A thing that, also God my soule save,	
In al this world ther nys no creature	
That ete or dronk hath of this confecture—	mixture
Nought but the mountaunce of a corn of whete—	amount
That he ne schuld his lif anoon for-lete;	quit
Ye, sterve he schal, and that in lasse while	die
Than thou wilt goon a paas not but a myle,	step
This poysoun is so strong and violent.	
This cursed man hath in his hond i-hent	caught or taken
This poysoun in a box, and sins he ran	then
Into the nexte stret unto a man	
And borwed of him large boteles thre,	
And in the two his poysoun poured he:	
The thrid he kepede clene for his drynke,	third, clean
For al the night he schop him for to swynke	prepared, labour
In carying of the gold out of that place.	
And whan this riotour, with sorry grace,	rioter
Hath fillid with wyn his grete botels thre,	
To his felaws ayein repaireth he.	again
What nedith it therof to sermoun more?	sermonize
For right as they hadde cast[192] his deth bifore,	arranged
Right so thay han him slayn, and that anoon.	have
And whan this was i-doon, thus spak that oon:	spake, one
Now let us drynke and sitte, and make us mery,	
And afterwards[193] we wil his body bery.	will
And with that word[193] it happed him par cas	by chance
To take the botel ther the poysoun was,	wherein
And drank, and yaf his felaw drink also,	gave

For which anon thay stervede bothe two.　　　　　soon, died
But certes I suppose that Avycen[194]　　　　　　certainly
Wrot never in canoun, ne in non fen,　　　　　　wrote
Mo wonder sorwes of empoisoning　　　　　　　wondrous pangs
Than hadde these wrecches tuo or here endyng.
Thus endid been these homicides tuo,　　　　　　be
And eek the fals empoysoner also.　　　　　　　also

The youngest, who had gone into the town,
Deep in his mind he turneth up and down
The beauty of these florins, new and bright.
"O Lord," quoth he, "if any-wise I might
Have all this treasure to myself alone,
There is no man that dwelleth under the throne
Of God, who then should live so merry as I."
And at the last the fiend, our enemy,
Put in his thought that he should poison buy,
With which to cause his comrades both to die.
For why? the fiend found this man's life so foul
That he had power now upon his soul:
For this was utterly his fix'd intent
To slay them both and never to repent
And forth he goes, no longer would he tarry,
Into the town to an apothecary,
And begged him plausibly that he would sell
Him poison strong enough the rats to quell;
Also, there was a polecat in his yard
Which had destroy'd his capons, he averr'd,
And he would gladly rid him if he might
Of vermin, which destroy'd them in the night.

The apothecary answered, "Thou shalt have
Something so strong, as God my soul shall save,
That in this world nothing that living is
Who in his food doth eat or drink of this—
Nay, but the greatness of a grain of wheat—
Shall fail to die, his life shall be forfeit;
Yea, he shall die, and that in lesser while
Than thou shalt walk a step beyond a mile,
This poison is so strong and violent."

This curséd man hath taken it and pent
The poison in a box, and forthwith ran
Hastily to the next street, to a man
And borrow'd of him some large bottles three,
And into two the poison pouréd he:
The third he kept untainted for himself,
Meaning to toil at carrying his pelf
From out that cursed place the whole night long.
And when this villain, bent on doing wrong,
Had filled his three great bottles up with wine,
Back to his mates he went, as if to dine.

127

What need is there of saying any more?
For as they had devised his death before,
E'en so they slew him, and with brief delay.
And when the deed was done, the first did say,
"Now let us sit and drink, and make us merry,
And afterwards we will his body bury."
And speaking thus, he chanced, upon the minute,
To take a bottle which had poison in it,
And drank, and gave his fellow drink beside,
Whereby within a little space they died.
But truly I suppose that Avicen
Did ne'er describe in canon or in fen
More frightful pains of deadly poisoning,
Than these two wretches felt in perishing.
Thus ended both the wicked homicides,
And that false-hearted poisoner besides.

Notes by the Way.

During the 12th, 13th, and 14th centuries the passion for gambling had spread from the highest to the very lowest class of the population. The practice of men drinking and playing themselves bare in the taverns, where both vices were encouraged by the taverners, was common enough to provoke numberless censures and caricatures, so much so that it is a mercy Sir Wilfrid Lawson was spared the spectacle. The Pardoner's Tale is one of the list.

The taverns were the resort of all the refuse of the people: the taverners found it suited them to act as pawnbrokers, advancing money on the clothes and property of the ne'er-do-wells who lacked cash to stake or to pay; and provided other attractions whereby men were tempted to various vices, and robbed during their drunken sleep. The language of these young rascals of both sexes is graphically condemned by the Pardoner; and gluttony is pointed out as the root of all evil, for which Adam fell.

Hazard was the game with which our rioters strove to 'drive away the day.' Mr. Wright, speaking of the use of dice, tells us, "In its simpler form, that of the game of hazard, in which the chance of each player rested on the mere throw of the dice, it was the common game of the low frequenters of the taverns—that class which lived upon the vices of society, and which was hardly looked upon as belonging to society itself." Men staked all they possessed, to the very clothes on their backs, on one cast.

Chaucer tells us contemptuously how the King of Parthia sent a pair of golden dice to King Demetrius in scorn, knowing he was a player, to express that he held his glory and renown at no value, being liable to disappear at any moment.

The three rioters were probably young men who had ruined themselves by folly and licence, and whose besetting sin, surviving all it throve on, urged them to any and every crime for the sake of renewed gratification. Their end is beyond measure frightful. For why?—The fiend found him in such living that he had leave to bring him to grief, says the severe old moralist.

The extreme beauty of this poem, even in a technical sense alone, is such that I lament the necessity of abridging it.

Complaint of Chaucer to his Purse.

To yow, my purse, and to noon other wight,   *no one else*
Complayn I, for ye be my lady dere;
I am so sorry now that ye been lyght,[195]
For certes, but-yf ye make me heavy cheer   *if*
Me were as leef be layde upon my bere,   *I were*
For whiche unto your mercy thus I crye—
Beeth hevy ageyne, or elles mote I dye!   *be thou*

Now voucheth sauf this day, or hyt be nyghte,   *vouchsafe before*
That I of yow the blissful soune may here,   *sound*
Or se your colour lyke the sunne bryghte,
That of yelownesse hadde never pere!   *rival*
Ye be my lyfe! ye be myn hertys stere!   *rudder*
Quene of comfort and goode companye,
Beth hevy ayeyne, or elles moote I die!

Now, purse, that ben to me my lyves lyghte,   *life's*
And saveour as doun in this worlde here,   *saviour*
Oute of this toune helpe me thurgh your myght,
Syn that ye wole nat bene my tresorere,[196]   *since, treasurer*
For I am shave[197] as nye as is a frere.   *nigh*
But I pray unto youre courtesye,
Bethe hevy ayeyn, or elles moote I dye!

To you, my purse, and to no other wight,
Complain I, for you are my lady dear;
I am so sorry now that you are light,
For truly if you make me heavy cheer
I would as lief be laid upon my bier.
Therefore unto your mercy thus I cry—
Be heavy again, or else I needs must die!

I prithee grant this day, ere it be night,
That I once more your merry voice may hear,
Or see your colour like the sunshine bright,
Whereof the yellowness had never peer!
You are my life, and you my heart shall steer;
Queen of all comfort and good company,
Be heavy again, or else I needs must die!

Now, purse, who are to me my life, my light,
And chief deliverer in this world here,
Out of this city help me, by your might,
If you no more will be my treasure dear,
For I am shaved as close as any frere.
But I beseech you of your courtesy,
Be heavy again, or else I needs must die!

Two Rondeaux.

Youre two eyn will sle me sodenly,   slay
I may the beauté of them not sustene,   sustain
So wendeth it thorow-out my herte kene.   goeth

And but your wordes will helen hastely
My hertis wound, while that it is grene,
Youre two eyn will sle me sodenly, &c.

Upon my trouth I say yow faithfully   tell
That ye ben of my liffe and deth the quene, are
For with my deth the trouth shal be i-sene
Youre two eyn, &c.

Your fair two eyes will slay me suddenly,
I know not how to bear their beauty's sheen,
It pierceth all my heart athrough so keen.

And if your words heal not full speedily
My heart's deep wound, while still the wound is green,
Your fair two eyes will slay me suddenly,
I know not how to bear their beauty's sheen,
It pierceth all my heart athrough so keen.

Upon my faith I tell you faithfully
Both of my life and death you are the queen,
For in my dying shall the truth be seen.
Your fair two eyes will slay me suddenly,
I know not how to bear their beauty's sheen
It pierceth all my heart athrough so keen.

Syn I, fro Love escaped, am so fat,
I nere thinke to ben in his prison lene:[198]   taken
Syn I am fre, I counte him not a bene.   since, free

He may answere and seye this and that:
I do no fors, I speak ryght as I mene: I care not
Syn I fro Love escaped am so fat.

Love hath my name i-strike out of his sclat, struck, slate
And he is strike out of my bokes clenebooks
For evermo, there is none other mene.   means
Syn I fro Love, &c.

Since I escaped from love, I am so fat,
No more I shall his captive be so lean:
Since I am free, I count him not a bean!

He may reply, and answer this and that:
I care not, for I speak but as I mean:

130

Since I from love escaped, I am so fat!

My name—out of his slate Love striketh that.
And he is struck out of my books as clean
For evermore, there is no way between!
Since I escaped, etc.

Virelai.

Alone walkyng,
In thought pleynyng   *mourning*
And sore syghyng,
Al desolate,
Me remembryng   *remembering*
Of my lyvyng,   *my way of living*
My deth wyshyng   *wishing*
Bothe erly and late.

Infortunate   *unfortunate*
Is soo my fate   *so*
That, wote ye whate?
Oute of mesure   *beyond measure*
My lyfe I hate,
Thus, desperate,
In suche pore estate   *poor*
Do I endure.   *remain*

Of other cure
Am I nat sure;   *not*
Thus to endure
Ys hard, certayn!
Suche ys my ure,   *use*
I yow ensure: *assure*
What creature
May have more payn?

My trouth so pleyn   *truth*
Ys take in veyn,   *taken*
And gret disdeyn
In remembraunce;   *remembrance*
Yet I ful feyngladly
Wolde me compleyn,
Me to absteyn to avoid
From thys penaunce.   *penance*

But, in substaunce,   *substance*
None allegeaunce   *alleviation*
Of my grevaunce grievance
Can I nat fynd;   *not*

Ryght so my chaunce
With displesaunce   *displeasure*

Doth me avaunce;   advance
And thus an end.

Alone walk I,
With many a sigh
In secrecy,
All desolate,
And still review
My life anew:
For death I sue
Both early and late.

My fate doth grow
So luckless now
That—do you know?
Beyond all telling
My life I hate:
Thus, desperate,
In woeful state
I still am dwelling.

I am not sure
Of any cure;
'Tis hard t' endure
With no relief!
But certain 'tis,
My state is this:
What thing that is
Could have more grief?

My story plain
Is taken in vain,
With great disdain
In recollection;
Yet I would fain
Alway complain,
To shun the pain
Of this correction!

For which find I,
Substantially,
No remedy,
My lot to mend;

So fate, I see,
Still draws on me
More enmity—
And there's an end!

Chaucer's 'Complaint to his Purse' was written, according to Mr. Furnivall, in September, 1399, when Chaucer was in distress for money, and sent to Henry IV. as a broad hint,—which was at once attended to.

It is a very clever piece of versification, like the 'Good Counsel,' &c., each line rhyming with the corresponding line in the other verses. He addresses his hapless purse as though it were his lady-love, and comically entreats her mercy, when he sees her inclined to be 'light.'

Mr. Furnivall's ingenious suggestion, that Chaucer's penury may possibly be due to his having dabbled in alchemy (an empirical branch of chemistry), is borne out by the technical knowledge displayed in the Canon's Yeoman's Tale.

We may add here—to defend our great man's character—that alchemy was believed in by many men of exceptional mental power. Roger Bacon, discoverer of gunpowder and the magnifying glass, is perhaps the greatest name among them; and vain as seemed much of their toil with crucibles and furnaces, alembics and aludels, we owe a great deal to the first meritorious alchemists, who really paved the way to modern chemistry.

There is no reason to suppose Chaucer had any vice likely to affect his pocket; but alchemy was the scientific mania of the day, and high and low were ready to risk fortune and health in pursuit of the philosopher's stone, the elixir of life, the way to manufacture gold. And, at the same time, there is no other sufficient reason for the extreme poverty which the poet had fallen into.

The two Roundels and the Virelai have been asserted and denied to be the work of Chaucer, but there is no clear evidence for either side. They may well be a portion of those many lost 'ditties and songs glad' with which Gower said 'the land fulfilled is over all,' written 'in the floures of his youth.' The second Roundel seems, on the other hand, to belong to his later life, when he so often alluded to his corpulence. As to the Virelai, this species of lyric was nery fashionable in Chaucer's time. It is skilful work, each stanza rhyming six lines together (which I have failed to follow in the translation).

Good Counsel of Chaucer.

Fle fro the pres, and duelle with sothfastnesse,	mob, honesty
Suffice the thy good, though hit be smale,	thee, it
For horde hath hate, and clymbyng tikelnesse,	hoards, uncertainty
Pres hath envye, and wele is blent over alle.	deceived everywhere
Savour no more then the behove shalle;	taste
Rede[199] well thy self, that other folke canst rede,	
And trouthe the shal delyver, hit ys no drede.	without fear

Peyne the not eche croked to redresse,	
In trust of hire that turneth as a balle,[200]	
Grete rest stant in lytel besynesse.	great peace lies, meddling
Bewar also to spurne ayein an nalle,[201]	awl
Stryve not as doth a croke[202] with a walle:	crock
Deme[203] thyselfe that demest others dede,	
And trouthe the shal delyver, hit ys no drede.	

That the ys sent receyve in buxomnesse,
The wrasteling of this world asketh a falle;
Her is no home, her is but wyldyrnesse.   here
Forth, pilgrime!—forth, best, out of thy stalle!   beast
Loke up on hye, and thonke God of alle!
Weyve thy lust, and let thy goste the lede,   give up, desire
And trouthe shal the delyver, hit ys no drede.

Fly from the crowd, and dwell with truthfulness
Contented with thy good, though it be small;
Treasure breeds hate, and climbing dizziness,
The world is envious, wealth beguiles us all.
Care not for loftier things than to thee fall;
Counsel thyself, who counsel'st others' need,
And truth thee shall deliver, without dread.

Pain thee not all the crooked to redress,
Trusting to her who turneth as a ball,
For little meddling wins much easiness.
Beware lest thou do kick against an awl,
Strive not as doth a clay pot with a wall:
Judge thou thyself, who judgest others' deed,
And truth thee shall deliver, without dread.

All that is given take with cheerfulness,
To wrestle in this world is to ask a fall;
Here is no home, here is but wilderness.
Forth, pilgrim, forth!—forth, beast, out of thy stall!
Look up on high, and thank thy God for all!
Cast by ambition, let thy soul thee led,
And truth thee shall deliver, without dread.

Notes by the Way.

We have Mr. F. J. Furnivall's authority, as well as internal evidence, for believing that this pathetic little poem expresses Chaucer's feelings at the time of his expulsion from the Customs offices, the beginning of his period of misfortunes, and was written immediately after the calamity. We seem to gather scattered hints of recent 'wrestlings' before the blow came—vain attempts to elevate, and purify, and carry out reforms, to make straight crooked paths. Lost labour—pain thee not all the crooked to redress!—trusting to fortune (money being requisite to reform): for those who value peace of mind should let sleeping dogs lie. We seem to catch the echoes of stormy times, of personal recrimination, envy, hatred, and malice, against a 'climbing' man, protected by Court favour for many prosperous years, but at length within the reach of foes when that protection waxed powerless. Chaucer may, like many another man, have made no enemies till he was high enough to stand in some one's light, prosperous enough to be dangerous; but his month of power in Parliament ruined him. It is pretty certain that some vote of his, while sitting for Kent, caused his dismissal from office. It was a case of win all or lose all, and he lost. To fight against such odds were as idle as undignified: surely, indeed, but courting worse injuries, 'kicking against an awl.' When the weak and the strong strive together, it is the weak who suffers. The criticism upon others, which had failed to do good, were now best turned philosophically upon himself. That which the fountain gave forth returns again to the fountain, as a poet 500 years later has said. It is impossible, in reading these melancholy and stately lines, not to feel that they ring true, and betray the half-sarcastic disappointment of a well-meaning man, the resignation of a religious man, and the faith in right-dealing bringing its own reward of a thoroughly honest man.

It is probable that the loss to Chaucer in a pecuniary sense was very severe; and the suddenness of the blow may account for much of his after poverty.[204] The loss may have come at a time when he had debts which it would be very hard to pay out of a diminished income—debts which may have hampered his whole after-life. His appointment of a deputy to the office of Clerk of the King's Works, in 1391, and his subsequent resignation of the office, appear to me to hint at ill-health, as may his death a year after getting his lease for fifty-three years of the tenement in Westminster, where he died.

The last verse of this poem is the most remarkable of the three. Full of just contempt for his enemies' aspersions, and of hearty trust in the power of truth to set things right, he rises suddenly into a passion of aspiration. Trying to be content with adversity, he is angry with himself for feeling it so deeply. To wrestle in this world is but courting an overthrow. But this is not our Home, this is but a desert leading to a higher state. Forth, pilgrim! gird up thy loins with fresh vigour to journey on. Forth, pilgrim! forth, beast, out of the stall of narrow hopes and interests! look higher, and thank thy God for all. To cast by all the soul's lets and hindrances—to be led by the higher self—that is the pilgrim's longing, and that is the sublimest hope of the human heart.

NOTES ON THE PICTURES.

I.—FRONTISPIECE.

THE costumes of the Knight, Squire, Prioress and Nun, Monk, Friar, Clerk (represented by Chaucer himself), Franklin, the Wife of Bath, the Summoner, and his friend the smart Pardoner, Mine Host and the boy, have been respectively studied from MSS. of the period. The attire of the Knight is open to criticism, for the amount of armour he wears is certainly more than he need wear on so peaceful an errand; but a portion of his well-used plate may be permitted him if only to distinguish the man of war from the numerous men of peace in the train.

The chain-mail, worn under the plate, would, I think, most probably have been retained by the Knight during his pilgrimage. The numerous miniatures of mailed knights journeying for no sinister purpose, appear to me to prove that it was very constantly worn. Unlike the mail which preceded it, the Asiatic kind which came into use in the twelfth century was comparatively light, being formed of slight rings interlaced, and not riveted upon leather. The hood of mail, which hangs on his shoulders, would have been no inconvenience at all. It joined the habergeon of mail, over which was his gipon, 'stained,' probably, by the rubbing of his mailed arms.

If, however, it be objected that the gipon was often an under garment (vide Meyrick, vol. ii. pp. 20 and 21), we may suppose him to have left a heavy hauberk of plate behind him in London 'till called for.'

Prioresses and nuns are often depicted in violet, in the contemporary MSS.; I therefore preferred that colour as more agreeable than black. Gloves such as the Nun's, were occasionally worn in the fourteenth century; the present example is taken from the effigy of William of Colchester, Abbot of Westminster, d. 1420. Gloves of fur, for winter wear, were common in the reign of Henry III.

The harness of the horses, bells and saddles, the Nun's chest, the Summoner's cake (probably ornamental gingerbread), and other details, have also been carefully studied from MSS. and tapestries of the time.

The boy's whip is taken from several fourteenth century and earlier drawings of horse-whips and whips for tops, and was therefore probably a common form.

The distant city is not necessarily London, as I failed to find a contemporary view of old London. The present sketch is borrowed from a fine MS. of Lydgate's poem, the 'Storie of Thebes' (MS. Reg. 18 D. ii.), and gives a good notion of the general look of a mediæval town.

Chaucer's portrait here was originally from the painting in the Harl. MS. 4866. I have no excuse to offer for changing the colour of Chaucer's gown from the grey or black in which Occleve always represented him to green, a very common colour at the time, except that it looked better in the picture, and we have no right to assume that Chaucer, even in his poorest days, had only one gown.

II.—DINNER IN THE OLDEN TIME.

The ordinary dinner-table or 'festive board' in a Franklin's or burgher's house has been taken from numerous fourteenth century illustrations. (Vide MS. Reg. 2 B. viii., and MS. Imp. Lib. Paris, No. 7210, &c.)

The carver, cupbearer, the fishbones left on the table in the absence of plates, the trenchers or slices of stale bread or buns used in lieu of them, and the other objects upon the table, are faithful copies from the MSS.

A minstrel was constantly employed to make music during the repast. The instrument here introduced is the cittern, played with or without a plectrum or quill. Behind are the servitors bringing in a pasty, some small birds on spits, and the nef or ship, containing salt, liqueurs, spices, or towel, &c., for washing the hands—or, if you like, it is a sotelté in the form of a ship. A subtlety was an ornamental dish that usually closed each course, made in some fanciful form, such as a castle, ship, or animal.

The dogs are munching the waste victuals under the table—such dogs being usually admitted during meals.

The pattern on the tablecloth is derived from a hunting-horn of the fourteenth century.

The peculiar folds at the sides of the tablecloth, which appear in many MSS., must, I think, have been purposely made for ornament, as we sometimes still see waiters crease cloths in various devices.

The sweet herbs strewn on the floor denote summer-time, in contradistinction to straw, which was used in the winter.

III.—LADY CROSSING STREET.

The background of shops and other buildings is borrowed mainly from the decapitation of G. de Pommiers at Bordeaux in 1377 (Froissart's Chronicle, No. 2644, Bibl. Imp. de Paris).

The costumes are those of middle-class persons. The clogs were in vogue with the long-toed boots.

Some of the streets were paved with large round stones, as in many French towns at the present day; others were not paved at all, and were, during wet weather, many feet deep with mud. An open channel or sewer ran along the midroad, which did not greatly add to the felicity of 'a walk down Fleet Street.'

IV.—FAIR EMELYE.

Emelye's garb is that common to the thirteenth and fourteenth centuries—a simple form with double sleeves. It will be remembered that Palamon mistook Emelye at first sight for a goddess; Arcite perceived her to be human. I have endeavoured to give the two men's views of her—each quite possible according to her position in the garden. Palamon may have caught sight of her just at a turn where the dazzle of sunrise behind the tree would be certain to lend a kind of halo to the outline of a head against it. An instant afterwards Emelye may have moved aside, the false halo disappearing, and she would seem what she truly was, simply an attractive maiden.

It is disappointing to find how very few were the flowers that adorned a mediæval garden. Our handsomest flowers were of course unknown—e.g., the immense catalogue of plants introduced from America and elsewhere. Many that 'have had their day and ceased to be' in fashion, were as yet unknown too; such as the sunflower, which was imported about the sixteenth century. The red and white may, the dogrose, primrose, and the flowers that we banish to the kitchen garden or admire only in the fields, formed the chief ornaments. We find nettles and nightshade reckoned among garden plants; the dandelion, which appears in the place of honour in many old tapestries, was then counted as a flower.

The big round tower is one of the chain of fortresses linked by a solid wall running around the domain, from one of which the captive knights saw Emelye, her garden being within the walls, and, as the castle was generally built on an eminence, on higher ground than the flat country beyond.

Shining yellow in the sun-rise light is a conventional view of a city—the city of Athens, which Palamon and Arcite could see from their prison window.

V.—GRISELDA'S MARRIAGE.

The huts where poor persons lived were, of course, very rude, and lacked windows, doors, or chimneys. Orifices in the roof or sides served these purposes. The dirt from the smoke upon walls and ceiling was consequently considerable. The draught beasts dwelt with their owners, much as the Hibernian pig resides with Pat and his family.

The hairy hat surmounting the hood came into use during the fourteenth century, and was made of skins, dressed fur outward.

Griselda's raggedness must not be construed into slovenliness. Needles were not as accessible to the mass of the poor as they are now; and moreover, the poor not being then compulsorily educated, an honest, industrious girl who could work in the fields and spin, was not always able to darn.

VI.—GRISELDA'S BEREAVEMENT.

It is expressly stated that when her child was taken from her Griselda controlled her feelings, and did not so much as sigh. The sergeant finds her in her chamber, or bower, more private than the hall, and more luxuriously furnished. She is sitting in one of the high-backed chairs which usually stood near the bed's head (vide various fourteenth century MSS.)—possibly a Prie-Dieu—raised on a dais.

Her dress is simple, but that of the upper classes in Edward III.'s reign, lined with vair, and having long tippets from the sleeves knotted for convenience; her hair adorned with 'bends' or silken straps, and a gold head-dress. Her distaff is still at hand, and the full basket betokens her continued industry. Floor-carpets or mats, embroidered or woven, were rare at this time, and could only have been in use in a wealthy house; but they are occasionally spoken of in early MSS. In 'Gautier d'Aupais' an old lady is described as sitting on a richly-worked counterpoint, by a coal fire; but this may have been a cloth flung over a chair; and in the romance of 'Queen Berthe' three persons are said to sit on carpets (sur les tapis).

It will be remembered that the dagger was frequently used with the left hand.

VII.—DORIGEN AND AURELIUS.

The parti-coloured dress worn by Aurelius, similar to the Squire's in the frontispiece, was common in Edward III.'s reign, and was peculiarly obnoxious to the satirists of the day. The cote-hardie or close-fitting tunic sometimes matched in colour one of the legs, sometimes was divided into halves of opposing colours; the shoes were very rich and of contrary hues also.

The ladies' gowns were long and of very rich materials, the arms bound with gold, and further adorned by fantastic streamers or tippets. Chess was the fashionable pastime of old and young. The pieces in this picture are from some ivory Icelandic chessmen of the twelfth century.

Behind is the lawn where Dorigen's meinie, or pages and household attendants, are amusing themselves with dancing and ball-playing among the enclosed flower-beds peculiar to the mediæval pleasure-garden.

The coat of arms repeated upon Aurelius' dress is that attributed to Chaucer. The instrument, on which he doubtless accompanied his mournful love-songs, is a form of cittern. The carved design upon the settle or seat is Anglo-Saxon; the fleur de lys on the curtain of the tent beside them was a common ornament.

I have not been able to discover at what precise date 'shot' materials came into use. There are many singular terms applied to the colours of dress throughout the middle ages, such as pourpre-gris, ecarlate-blanche, &c. In the 'Fabliau de Gautier d'Aupais' there is mention of 'un vert mantel porprine' (a mantle of green crimson). In my own mind I am persuaded that these terms, explicable easily in no other way, refer to shot materials. Mediæval miniatures and pictures also bear out this theory, dresses being depicted of certain colours shaded with certain others in strong contrast. The commonest is blue or red shaded with gold. There have been many conjectures with regard to the above terms. M. le Grand supposes that rare dyes, being chiefly used to dye rich cloths, gave at last their names to those cloths, irrespective of colour. The Saturday Review once accused the old masters of "sporting with pigments prismatically" when they used red as the shadow of green, &c., oblivious of the fact that if the early masters had a fault it was adhering too blindly to nature in their works. It is clear that in Quentin Matsys' day (fifteenth century) shot materials were quite common, for there is scarcely one of his pictures without a study of the kind. In his 'Dead Christ' at Antwerp several unmistakable examples occur; in his 'Virgin' at Amsterdam is introduced a curtain of green and brown shot. This being so, we have no reasonable ground for believing that shot silks, though not yet common, were unknown a century earlier.

I have therefore given two marked examples of similar silks, in the robes of Griselda and Dorigen, both wealthy enough to import such fabrics if in existence at all.

VIII.—THE RIOTER.

The ordinary cheap wine used in the middle ages was often carried in 'bottles' or pitchers of this form.

A longish gown was the dress of the commoner people in the fourteenth century. The Rioter is intended to represent a man of decent position, but not noble, who has come to the end of his tether, in a pecuniary sense, and whose slovenly hose and young but debauched and cruel face indicate with what facility he has been degraded by his elder companions.

PORTRAIT OF CHAUCER.

Chaucer's portrait is copied from a drawing by Occleve the poet (Brit. Mus. Harl. MS. 4866). Occleve made, or caused to be made, shortly after Chaucer's death, several portraits of him, of which two remain; and on these are founded the many now scattered over the country. The same features recur in all. The peculiar aquiline nose, mouth a little drooping, eyes downcast, the forked beard and fair complexion, the broad round jaw, are the same in all. Occleve always depicted Chaucer with a rosary in his hand, and his penner, containing his pen and inkhorn, hanging to his vest. His hands are small and well-shapen, his form is portly, his air calm, benevolent, almost pathetic.

These lines run beside the miniature in Occleve's MS.:—

Al thogh his lyfe be queynt, the resemblaunce	extinguished
Of him hath in me so fressh lyflynesse	liveliness
That to putte othir men in remembraunce	
Of his persone I have heere his lyknesse	likeness
Do make, to this end in sothfastnesse,	had made (faire faire), truth
That thei that have of him lest thought and mynde	lost
By this peynture may ageyn him fynde.	painting

Although his life be quench'd, so clear doth lie
Within my mind the living look of him,
That to put other men in memory
Of his appearance, here his face I limn,
That they to whom his image groweth dim,
And they that have of him lost thought and mind,
By this poor portrait may again him find.
The portraits by Occleve, his personal friend and disciple, whose deep affection for Chaucer is touchingly reiterated in his 'Lament' for him, maybe relied on as most conscientious pictures from memory of the great poet's habitual appearance.

The Tournament. (See Title-page.)—There must always have been, to some extent, a grotesque element in the Tournament. The desire to be conspicuous forced the combatants to assume the gayest and the biggest decoration. At a later date the tilting helmets sprouted into the most preposterous sizes and shapes. Figures and 'favours' assumed for the occasion, the gifts of enthusiastic lady-loves, as well as hereditary devices, surmounted the helm and glittered on coat-armour and harness. In Edward III.'s reign the beauty and éclat of the tourney was in its zenith; in Richard II.'s the beautiful began to be overpowered by the grotesque. I have tried to tone down the grotesque as much as may be, but a general dazzle and confusion of colour is inseparable from the scene, vivid, violent, and exciting as it was. Tents were often erected within the pale of the lists for the convenience of those awaiting or hors de combat. Shields or targets, for peace or war, were suspended in couples before them, emblazoned with the arms of each lord; and whoso sent to touch the targets was tilted with according to his wish—i.e., with sharp or blunt lances.

The end of Theseus' tourney was clearly a riot, but I have preferred to represent the orderly onset of the first combatants, guided by a MS. Froissart of the fifteenth century. It has been suggested to me that it would be impossible to tilt across the bar unless the spear-arm were next the bar, as the horse's neck would impede the stroke, and the rider's own spear would unhorse him: in tent-pegging and all sports with the lance the rider brings his spear-arm next the mark. But having found several early miniatures in which the spear is aimed as here given, I considered myself justified in trusting to contemporary MSS. in spite of modern theories.

The horses were the chief sufferers in these mimic frays. The heavy beasts, protected as they were by a great weight of armour, were often injured. The best-trained dreaded the shock of encounter, and, as we read in Froissart, their restiveness and swerving at the last moment frequently spoiled the 'course,' despite the most violent spurring, to their masters' deep chagrin and disappointment, and the disgust of the lady-loves.

The high saddles, sometimes locking the rider in his seat all round, were constructed to retain him on his horse, however violent the push; but they were the cause of many an unhappy accident. Death like Arcite's, from crushing against the saddle-bow, was by no means uncommon. So died William the Conqueror himself four hundred years before; when, riding down the steep street of Mantes, his horse stumbled among the embers he had kindled. (See Green's Short History of the English People, p. 85.)

Suffocation in the dust was a still more frequent cause of death; as thrown riders could not rise, nor rid themselves of their ponderous casques.

Skill rather than strength was needful in tilting. The spear, as in pig-sticking in India, was thrust rather by the weight of the horse than by the weight of the arm. Strength of back and arm were necessary to avoid being bent backwards or driven over the crupper; but extreme skill was requisite to hit one's slippery foe with anything like force. When both knights hit their mark so that fire flew from their helmets, without either falling, it was reckoned a 'handsome course.'

A word about the allans, as big as bullocks, which went leaping around Lycurgus' car. They were undoubtedly a kind of mastiff, large and powerful; they wore gold collars filled with torettz. This word is variously explained. Torete, ring-turret (Morris), ring or terret (Bell). 'Toret, a small wimble (or auger, big gimblet). Touret, a drill, &c.' (Cotgrave). 'Gros clou dont la tête arrondie est arrêtée dans une branche d'un mors' (Suppl. to Fr. Acad. Dict.).

I have ventured on translating 'toret' spike, after vainly seeking for authority for a collar filled with rings; though a single ring often hung beneath the throat. Contemporary illustrations of dogs' collars filled with long spikes are common enough—e.g. the fine fourteenth century tapestry now in the museum at Chartres, &c.

In India dogs are furnished with spiked collars in tiger and boar hunting: the allans were clearly hunting dogs, and such spiked collars would thus be almost indispensable.

John of Gaunt, Royal Coll. 20 B. 6. (See page 7.)—This portrait has an air of truth about it; in the MS. it is very carefully and delicately worked. The gown is of a reddish murrey colour, with ermine or miniver lining to skirt and sleeves, the under sleeves being blue. His hose are red, and he wears a golden circlet, necklace, and belt. One can trace some resemblance to Edward III., his father, in the long, narrow, but not unpleasing face. Other portraits of John of Gaunt have the same features. The hair and beard are grey. He appears to be respectfully lecturing the young King Richard, who is seated on his throne, receiving a book presented by a monk, in the presence of his three royal uncles.

Ship. (See page 8.)—How such ships could sail is a mystery, but this is the most usual anatomy for a man-of-war, or for a 'subtlety' at dinner in the form of a ship. I copied the present example from a MS. in the British Museum: it is one of a royal fleet. There is a Nef introduced in the famous 'Nancy' tapestry (fifteenth century) of precisely the same construction.

Stylus. (See page 10.)—The stylus was used for writing on waxen tablets. No doubt wax was cheaper and more easily procured than parchment or paper; paper made from rags being then quite a recent invention, and probably what was made was not white but brown, and imported from abroad. Wax could be dissolved and used again. Hence we find, in the romance of 'Flor and Blanchflor,' the king putting children to school, where they learned to write

Letres et vers d'amors en cire,
Lor greffes sont d'or et d'argent.

Letters and verses of love on the wax.
Their styles are of gold and silver.

The Yeoman. (See page 21.)—The term 'not-head' used by Chaucer may mean that he had his hair closely cropped—a head like a nut—as suggested by Tyrwhitt, &c.; but I think, on the contrary, it refers to his hood having the liripipe knotted around it, as there are numerous instances of such hoods worn by foresters, hunters, and others, to whom a long tail would be a nuisance, if not actually dangerous. The woodcut of a knotted hood, on p. 2, is that of a forester, in the Book of Gaston Phœbus, fourteenth century, in the National Library of Paris. Chaucer says the miller wore his 'typet ybounde about his heed' ('Reeve's Tale,' line 33).

The Prioress. (See page 22.)—Her costume (same as in Frontispiece) is borrowed from an Abbess or Prioress in a MS. of the History of the Emperors (Lib. of the Arsenal), fifteenth century.

The Monk. (See page 24.)—From Royal MS. 14 E. 4, temp. Ed. IV.: too late, indeed, but it appears that the clerical costume had suffered no great change.

The Clerk. (See page 27.)—The figure of the Clerk possesses peculiar interest, as it represents one of those ancient artists whose paintings in mediæval MSS. are so valuable to us now. His name is Alan Strayler, a designer and painter, and his dress is that of an ordinary middle-class man; it will be seen to be precisely similar to Chaucer's, who was himself a 'clerk.'

The Serjeant at Law. (See page 28.)—It is curious that the mantle of this figure, whose dress is taken from two effigies of Chief Justices of the King's Bench in the fourteenth century, should recall the Roman toga, being apparently fastened over the hood, on the right shoulder, so as to leave that arm completely free: an instance of the conservatism of official dress, which alters very little with the fluctuations of fashion, whilst those persons whose costume denotes no position are constantly undergoing protean changes.

The Doctor. (See page 29.)—The medical man is as much too early as the monk is too late, but it was the most characteristic one I could find, and I preferred thirteenth century to fifteenth century costume. The mantle recalls the Roman toga. (Copy from Sloane Coll. No. 1975.)

The Parson. (See page 30.)—See a brass of John Islyngton, vicar of Islington, in Norfolk, in 1393. The dress of a plain parish priest is not often represented: it will be seen to be not dissimilar to that of a modern French priest.

The Ploughman.—(See page 31.)—Studied from figures in a very ancient Anglo-Saxon MS. It appears to me that the liripipe (evidently then worn) is in this case twisted around the head.

The Pardoner. (See page 31.)—The Pardoner may have worn the ordinary clerkly gown, or, as in the Frontispiece, a close-fitting garb. Chaucer does not describe his attire, but says he thought himself 'al of the newe get' (i.e., fashion).

PRINCIPAL AUTHORITIES CONSULTED IN THIS BOOK.

Sir S. Meyrick, 'Antient Armour.'

Lacroix, 'Manners, Customs, and Dress during the Middle Ages,' &c., &c.

Skeat, 'Chaucer,' &c.

Morris, 'Chaucer' (Aldine edition), 1866, and 'Chaucer' (Clarendon Press), 1874.

Tyrwhitt's 'Chaucer.'

Bell's edition of 'Chaucer's Poetical Works.'

Fairholt, 'Costume in England.'

Wright, 'Domestic Manners during the Middle Ages,' and 'Womankind in Western Europe.'

Froissart's 'Chronicles.'

Planché, 'British Costume.'

Shaw, 'Dresses and Decorations,' 'Ornaments,' &c.

Furnivall, 'Babee's Book,' and 'Trial Forewords' (Chaucer Society), &c.

'Arthur of Britayn.'

Six-Text Edition of Chaucer's 'Canterbury Tales.'

Bonnard & Mercurj, 'Costumes des XIIIe, XIVe, et XVe Siècles,' 1840.

Le Grand, 'Fabliaux et Contes du XIIe et du XIIIe Siècle,' 1781.

Barbazan, 'Fabliaux et Contes,' 1808.

Footnotes:

[1] I use the word 'emphasis' in the same sense as one might speak of a crotchet in music, to which you count two, being more emphatic than a quaver, to which you count one.

[2] Those who wish to study systematically the grammar, and construction of the metre, I can only refer to the best authorities, Dr. R. Morris and Mr. Skeat, respectively. It would be superfluous to enter on these matters in the present volume.

[3] "No better MS. of the 'Canterbury Tales' could be found than the Harleian MS. 7334, which is far more uniform and accurate than any other I have examined; it has therefore been selected, and faithfully adhered to throughout, as the text of the present edition. Many clerical errors and corrupt readings have been corrected by collating it, line for line, with the Lansdowne MS. 851, which, notwithstanding its provincial peculiarities, contains many excellent readings, some of which have been adopted in preference to the Harleian MS." (Preface to Morris's Revised Ed. 1866.) This method I have followed when I have ventured to change a word or sentence, in which case I have, I believe, invariably given my authority.

[4] Roger Ascham.

[5] Mr. Furnivall, among some of his recent interesting researches anent Chaucer, has discovered with certainty his father's name and profession.

[6] The position of Chaucer, and his wife, in the King's service, and that of the latter in the service of Constance, Duchess of Lancaster, shared with two ladies of rank, be well as their lifelong interest at Court, prove, I think, that neither of them was of mean parentage, and that they occupied a very good social status.

[7] See also p. 19, note 34.

[8] It must not be forgotten, in reading praises of warm and sunny May, often now a bleak and chilly month, that the seasons were a fortnight later at that time, May-day coming therefore in the middle of the month, and May ending in the middle of June. The change in the almanac was made in Italy in 1582, in England in 1752.

[9] Dr. Morris writes—"The old supposition that the Philippa whom Chaucer married was the daughter of Sir Paon de Roet (a native of Hainault and King of Arms of Guienne), and sister to Katherine, widow of Sir Hugh Swynford, successively governess, mistress, and wife of John of Gaunt, Duke of Lancaster, was founded on heraldic grounds. The Roet arms were adopted by Thomas Chaucer. Then Thomas Chaucer was made (without the slightest evidence) Geoffrey's son, and Philippa Roet was then made Geoffrey's wife." And again, "It is possible that Philippa Chaucer was a relative or namesake of Geoffrey, and that he married her in the spring or early summer of 1374." It is, however, much less likely that there were so

many Chaucers about the Court, unconnected with each other, than that the common supposition is correct. At any rate, until there is any evidence to the contrary, this tradition may be fairly accepted. The recent discovery, in the Record Office, of Thomas Chaucer's deed, by Mr. Hunter, sealed with a seal bearing the legend, 'S Ghofrai Chaucer,' seems to support the tradition.

[10] A mark was 13s. 4d. of our money, but the buying power of money was eight or ten times greater than at present. So that, although ten marks was only £6 12s. of our currency, it was fully equal to £50.

[11] There are entries mentioning Philippa Chaucer in 1366, 1372, and 1374. The former names her as one of the ladies of the bedchamber to Queen Philippa, who conferred the annuity of ten marks in September, 1366. In 1372 John of Gaunt conferred on Philippa Chaucer an annuity of £10 (equal to £100). Her name is mentioned when the grant to Chaucer of a pitcher of wine daily is commuted into money payment, June 13, 1374, by John of Gaunt (again a pension of £10), for good services rendered by the Chaucers to the said Duke, his consort, and his mother the Queen.

[12] Green was the favourite colour of the time.

[13] Astrolabe: a machine used at sea to measure the distances of stars. The quadrant now in use has superseded the astrolabe.

[14] Thomas Chaucer was born in or about 1367, and died in 1434. Elizabeth Chaucer's noviciate was paid for by John of Gaunt in 1381. If Elizabeth Chaucer was about 16 in 1381 she would have been born about 1365; and, therefore, as far as dates are concerned, either Thomas or Elizabeth may well have been elder children of the poet: the chances being that he married in 1361-64. Moreover, John of Gaunt's interest in both of these persons, Thomas Chaucer and Elizabeth Chaucer, gives this a colour of probability. At the same time Chaucer seems to have been no uncommon name.

Chaucer's exceptional notice of his little son Lewis who must have been born in 1381, the year of Elizabeth's novitiate, since Chaucer describes him as being ten years old in his treatise on the astrolabe in 1391, may have been due to the appearance of a 'Benjamin' rather late in life.

[15] On the hypothesis, of course, that Chaucer married a Roet.

[16] For many new and curious facts about Chaucer, see my Chaucer for Schools, "Chaucer's Court Life and Position."

[17] In these cases, the sum received on the marriage of the ward was legally a fine on the marriage.

[18] See Chambers's Encyclopædia, 'Chaucer'.

[19] See Chaucer for Schools, p. 22, for further details.

[20] I have assumed that Thomas Chaucer was Geoffrey Chaucer's son, as there is no proof to the contrary, and a probability in point of dates that he was.

[21] See 'Notes by the Way,' p. 103.

[22] See Chaucer for Schools.

[23] Remembering the discussion raised as to the year of Chaucer's birth, coupled with the tradition of his venerable looks, we may suggest that in those days men were older at sixty than now. The average duration of life was shorter, and the paucity of comforts probably told on appearance.

[24] Author of the 'Testament of Love.'

[25] Alluding to the numerous dialects in use in England at the time.

[26] The mother should here read to the child some lines with the proper pronunciation: see Preface, pp. x., xi.

[27] Zephyrus, or Zephyr: the god of the west wind. It is become a name for the wind of summer.

[28] Pilgrims who have brought a palm branch from the Holy Land.

[29] Kouthe: past participle of the verb conne, to know, or to be able. It was used much as savoir is in French—to be able to do, to know how to do a thing. The verse means 'To serve the saints they could, or they knew of, or knew how to serve.'

[30] Thomas Beket, Chancellor of Henry II. He was Archbishop of Canterbury for eight years, and was murdered by servants of the King in 1170. He was canonized, or made a saint, by the Pope, after his death, and pilgrimages were then constantly made to his tomb in Canterbury Cathedral. In those days it was usual in sickness or peril to vow a pilgrimage to the shrine of some saint who was supposed to be able to help people by interceding with God, when pilgrims prayed him to. Erasmus alludes to the quantities of offerings on Thomas Beket's shrine, given by those who believed the saint had healed or helped them.

[31] A tabard was an outer coat without sleeves, worn by various classes, but best known as the coat worn over the armour (see p. 48), whereon there were signs and figures embroidered by which to recognize a man in war or tournament: for the face was hidden by the helmet, and it was easier to detect a pattern in bright colours than engraved in dark steel. So, of course, the pattern represented the arms used by him. And thus the tabard got to be called the coat of arms. Old families still possess what they call their coat of arms, representing the device chosen by their ancestors in the lists; but they do not wear it any more: it is only a copy of the pattern on paper. A crest was also fastened to the helmet for the same purpose of recognition, and there is usually a 'crest' still surmounting the modern 'coat of arms.' The inn where Chaucer slept was simply named after the popular garment. It, or at least a very ancient inn on its site, was recently standing, and known as the Talbot Inn, High Street, Borough: Talbot being an evident corruption of Tabard. We may notice here, that the Ploughman, described later on, wears a tabard, which may have been a kind of blouse or smock-frock, but was probably similar in form to the knight's tabard.

[32] People were glad to travel in parties for purposes of safety, the roads were so bad and robbers so numerous.

[33] Probably all or many occupied but one bedroom, and they became acquainted on retiring to rest, at the ordinary time—sunset.

[34] The word Knight (knecht) really means servant. The ancient knights attended on the higher nobles and were their servants, fighting under them in battle. For as there was no regular army, when a war broke out everybody who could bear arms engaged himself to fight under some king or lord, anywhere, abroad or in England, and was paid for his services. That was how hundreds of nobly born men got their living—the only way they could get it. This is what the knight Arviragus does in the 'Franklin's Tale;' leaving his bride, to win honour (and money) by fighting wherever he could.

The squire waited on the knight much as the knight did on the earl—much in the position of an aide-de-camp of the present day. The page served earl, knights, ladies. But knight, squire, and page were all honourable titles, and borne by noblemen's sons. The page was often quite a boy, and when he grew older changed his duties for those of squire, till he was permitted to enter the knighthood. The present knight is described as being in a lord's service, and fighting under him 'in his war,' but he was a man held in the highest honour.

[35] See p. 48 and Appendix, p. 107.

[36] "On nommait Bacheliers les chevaliers pauvres, les bas Chevaliers ... quand ceux-ci avaient reçu la chevalerie, on les appelait Chevaliers-Bacheliers ... quant à l'Ecuyer (Squire) c'était le prétendant à la Chevalerie."—Le Grand, Fabliaux & Contes.

[37] Chivachie: military expeditions.

[38] See page 45, note 96.

[39] Mr. Bell considers that these two lines refer to the squire's complexion of red and white. Speght thinks it means freckled. But there is little doubt that the material of his dress is what Chaucer means, for there is no other instance of Chaucer calling a complexion embroidered, and gorgeously flowered fabrics embroidered with the needle were peculiar to the period and in common use.

[40] As it was the custom for sons to do.

[41] Peacocks' feathers on them instead of swans'.

[42] It was a sign of the yeoman's carefulness in his business that they stuck out from the shaft instead of drooping.

[43] Bracer: a leathern defence for the arm: a similar shield is now worn in archery.

[44] Bokeler—buckler: a small shield—used chiefly for a warder to catch the blow of an adversary. Some pictures show the buckler to have been only the size of a plate, but it varied. In comparing the Wife of Bath's hat to a buckler, Chaucer could not have meant so small a one. It was usual for serving men of noble families to carry swords and bucklers when in attendance on them.

[45] Bawdrik—baldrick: ornamented strap to suspend the horn or dagger.

[46] Oaths were only too common among ladies as well as men. It was an exceptional refinement to use only a small oath. Tyrwhitt prints the name of the saint, Eloy, contraction of Eligius—a saint who, having been a worker in metals, was often invoked by smiths (see

146

'Friar's Tale'), &c.; but Dr. Morris says St. Loy is the old spelling of St. Louis of France, by whom the Prioress swore.

[47] Bell approves reading voice for nose, as Speght has actually done. It has not struck either of them that Chaucer is all the way through laughing at the fastidious and rather over-attractive nun!

[48] Knives and forks were not in use—people had to use their fingers; but some used them more agreeably than others.

[49] At meals one cup for drinking passed from guest to guest, instead of each having his own glass, as now. It was considered polite to wipe one's mouth well before drinking, so that the next drinker should find no grease in the wine. The great stress Chaucer lays on the pretty nun's courtesy seems to hint at very dirty habits among ordinary folk at meals!

[50] Mr. Bell naïvely points out the innocence and 'ignorance of the ways of the world,' which pervade the whole of the 'simple Prioress's character;' but you will notice that in laughing at the cheerful nun's affectation of court manners, Chaucer never once gives her credit for very high or noble character, though he does not speak ill-naturedly. I have ere now alluded to his dislike of the Church, friars, nuns, and all included: and here he shows that her charitableness and compassion were spent on wholly inadequate objects. She is extravagant to the last degree in feeding her dogs, and weeping for dead mice; but nothing is said of charity to the poor, or any good works at all. She is too intent on fascinating everybody, and dressing smartly. There is sharp sarcasm in all this.

[51] Wastel breed—a kind of cake—the most expensive of all bread.

[52] Wimple: a loose covering for the neck, close up to the chin, plaited daintily; worn especially by nuns.

[53] A rosary, the coral beads of which were divided by smaller ones, or gauds, of a green colour.

[54] 'Love conquers all things.' The Prioress might have twisted this device to refer to the text, 'The greatest of these is charity;' but the double entendre is apparent.

[55] From a French phrase, bone pur la maistrie = good to excel all others. The monk bids fair to excel all others or outstrip the rest in promotion, on account of his worldliness.

[56] "The custom of hanging small bells on the bridle and harness of horses is still observed on the Continent for the purpose of giving notice to foot-passengers to get out of the way; but it was no doubt often used for ostentation. So Wicliffe inveighs against the clergy in his Triologe for their 'fair hors, and jolly and gay sadels, and bridels ringing by the way.'"

[57] A bird more commonly eaten in those days than it is now, but expensive even then.

[58] Lymytour: a friar licensed to beg within a certain district or limit. This friar, no very pleasing character, is described as making such a good thing out of his begging, that he bribed his fellow friars not to come within his particular haunt, and interfere with his doings: an unprincipled dandy who is another instance of Chaucer's sarcasm against the Church.

[59] There were four orders of mendicant friars—Dominicans, Franciscans, Carmelites, and Augustins.

[60] Frankeleyns: a franklin was a rich landholder, free of feudal service, holding possessions immediately from the king. See p. 28.

[61] Confession, absolution, and penance: sacraments in the Roman Catholic Church.

[62] The rotta was an ancient instrument of the guitar tribe.

[63] Clerk: a scholar probably preparing for the priesthood. In many Roman Catholic countries it was the custom till very lately for poor scholars to ask and receive contributions from the people for the expenses of their education. They were often extremely indigent, coming from the labouring classes. The parson, for instance, spoken of later, is said to be brother of the ploughman travelling with him. The poor scholar and the good parson are 'birds of a feather.'

[64] Or, abounded: the O. E. snewe, like the Prov. Eng. snee, snie, snive, snew, signifies to swarm.

[65] The table dormant was a permanent table, not a board on trestles such as the ordinary one, mentioned on p. 2. It was only used by very rich people, for it was a new fashion, and expensive. See drawing of table dormant in 14th century, on page 28.

[66] Well-to-do.

[67] Chaucer speaks, you see, in very different terms of the poor and conscientious parish priest (who was supported only by his benefice and tithes of the people—a small income) from what he does of the monastic orders, corrupted by the wealth they had accumulated. Bell says—"It was quite natural that Chaucer, the friend of John of Gaunt, should praise the parochial clergy, who were poor, and therefore not formidable, at the expense of the rich monastic orders who formed the only barriers which then existed against the despotic power of the aristocracy." But, however that may be, there is no doubt that these parish parsons actually were a much better and more honest class of men than the monks, and the begging friars, and all the rest, were at this time. They were drawn, like the Roman Catholic secular clergy of the present day, from the labouring classes.

[68] No one of good position rode on a mare in the middle ages.

[69] Summoner: an officer employed by the ecclesiastical courts to summon any persons who broke the law to appear before the archdeacon, who imposed what penalty he thought fit. The Summoners found it to their interest to accept bribes not to report offences: therefore bad people who could afford to pay got off, whilst those who could not afford to pay were punished with rigour. Many Summoners extorted bribes by threatening to say people had transgressed the law who had not; and so they got to be detested by the masses, and Chaucer's hideous picture gives the popular notion of a Summoner.

[70] A face as red as the fiery cherubin: a rather profane simile! In many ancient pictures we find the cherubin painted wholly scarlet; and the term had become a proverb. 'Sawceflem' is from salsum flegma, a disease of the skin.

[71] See note, p. 92, note 175.

[72] Pardoner: Seller of the Pope's indulgences.

[73] A vernicle—diminutive of Veronike—was a small copy of the face of Christ, worn as a token that he had just returned from a pilgrimage to Rome.

[74] The Pardoner's eloquence and musical gifts account, perhaps, for the exquisite story he afterwards tells.

[75] Mr. Wright says this place was situated at the second milestone on the old Canterbury road.

[76] Tyrwhitt. Hyppolita, Smith's Dic.

[77] Feste in this place means rather festival than feast, as Theseus was only on his way to the city.

[78] At this period, the personal pronoun you was used only in the plural sense, or in formal address, as on the Continent now; whilst thou implied familiarity. The Deity, or any superior, was therefore addressed as you: intimates and inferiors as thou. Throughout Chaucer the distinction is noticeable: but as the present mode reverses the order, I have in my lines adhered to no strict principle, but have used the singular or plural personal pronoun according as it seemed most forcible.

[79] Thebes, in Greece.

[80] A garment worn over the armour, on which the armorial bearings were usually embroidered, for the purpose of recognition. See tabard, p. 48.

[81] The rites and ceremonies, observed on the approach of spring, from the earliest times in many countries, but which have now died out in England, are among the most natural and beautiful of all popular fêtes. I have already in the preface alluded lo the custom of riding out into the fields at daybreak to do honour to May, the month which was held to be the symbol of spring-time. Rich and poor, the court and the commoners, all rode out with one impulse. Boughs of hawthorn and laburnum were brought home to decorate all the streets, and dancing round the maypole, and feasting, and holiday-making, were observed almost like religious rites. It was a great privilege to be elected queen of May, and one which every young maiden coveted. At a later time we read of Henry VIII. and Queen Catherine of Aragon formally meeting the heads of the corporation of London, on Shooter's Hill, to 'go a maying.'

But one thing should be remembered when we see how many pleasures were referred to May, and how much more people seemed to count on the weather of a month nowadays proverbially disappointing. The seasons were not the same then as they are now. Not because the climate of the land has altered so much, though that may be fairly surmised; but because the seasons were actually arranged otherwise. In Chaucer's time, May began twelve days later than our May, and ended in the midst of June, and therefore there was a much better chance of settled weather than we have. This fact also accounts for the proverbial connection of Christmas and hard weather, snow, and ice, which we get as a rule in January, while December is foggy and wet. Twelfth Day was the old Christmas Day. (See page 4.)

[82] At point devise—with exactness.

[83] The love of the Anglo-Saxons and the early English for flowers is very remarkable. The wearing of garlands of fresh flowers was a common practice with both sexes: a beautiful custom, followed by the Romans, and previously by the Greeks.

[84] Formal compacts for the purpose of mutual counsel and assistance were common to the heroic and chivalrous ages.—B.

[85] The words court and royal, now applied only to the sovereign of the land, were applicable then to the domains of the great nobles, who were to all intents and purposes kings. Their pride, and wealth, and immense power, made them very formidable to the sovereign, as we constantly find in following the history of England or any other country. They often mustered as big an army as the king, because they could afford to pay the knights (see note, p. 19), and were invincible in their strongholds, surrounded by their serfs dependent on them.

[86] Tyrwhitt.

[87] Crop, the top of the wood; briars, the thorny brushwood and weeds growing on the ground. This pretty metaphor well expresses the fluctuating moods of an overwrought state of feeling.

[88] Tyrwhitt.

[89] Harness was a technical term for the complete armour or equipment, as opposed to portions, which were equally armour.

[90] Even these similes separate the two characters: the lion may be mad with rage; the tiger, which is a cat, is crafty as well as fierce.

[91] An exaggeration simply for picturesque effect, such as many have indulged in since Chaucer.

[92] The helmet entirely concealing the face.

[93] Ho was the word by which the heralds or the king commanded the cessation of any action.

[94] What were called the 'lists' were the places built and enclosed for combats on horseback, and tournaments. These combats got sometimes very serious, and many knights and horses were wounded, or even killed.

[95] A form of torture to extort confession. Theseus' grim humour at this juncture implies how far lightlier human life was held then than now. But he was naturally in a great rage when he knew who the knights were. Palamon's insolent address in the singular personal pronoun was not likely to mollify him, coming as it did from a captive, though an equal by birth.

[96] How idealized, and how idolized, the passion of love had crown to be with the new elevation of woman's condition in these times is well known. Love literally covered a multitude of sins: the malefactor was pardoned whose offences were caused by love; the rough was made smooth for the feet of love to tread upon. There was a reason for this. It is but too true that the morals of the people will not bear the light of modern times; but it would be unfair to judge them by that light. Those were rough days, when laws were often feeble, narrow, or ill-enforced. The want of legal organization placed a great refining and ennobling

power in the hands of woman. Many a knight, who was coarse or cowardly, was pricked to courteous ways and deeds of courage by his love of some fair woman, when without it he would have sunk lower and lower in vice and degradation. The arts were ofttimes cultivated to win a woman's ear or eye; knowledge itself was sought for her sake, for knowledge is power. Of course the love of courtesy, valour, and learning were deeply rooted in the age, or the woman's sympathy could not have existed. But her encouragement of all that was æsthetic, her influence over men, and therefore the impetus she gave to the higher life, must never be underrated, however we may reprove the errors of that day. The institution of actual 'Courts of Love'—tribunals for the judgment of love-matters, bearing a definite recognition, and which seem so strange, almost repulsive to us, presided over as they were by ladies only— was the result of the worship of physical beauty and the passion which it inspired, and the proof, however grotesque, of the real value seen to lie in it. This will be better understood when we observe that even children were encouraged to cultivate somewhat of this ideal love, and the childish education of boys and girls consisted to a very large extent in learning the art of writing love-letters. Thus Palamon's and Arcite's adoration of fresh Emelye are seen to be neither exaggerated nor futile.

[97] 'To pipe in an ivy leaf:' A proverbial expression, similar to 'go whistle'—meaning to be engaged in any useless employment.

[98] The tournament, great as the loss of life often was, seems to have been the greatest delight of the people in the middle ages. The ladies especially loved them, as they were often in homage to themselves. The victor in the mimic battle received a crown from the queen of the tournament. In this case, Emelye is not asked whether she likes to be disposed of thus coolly! but she could not fail to be touched by the great compliment paid her.

[99] There are no portraits, otherwise, of these two princes, whose characters are so clear and forcible all through that some physical description is sorely needed. The portraits of the two sovereigns fit singularly well the fierce, passionate nature of Palamon, and the cooler but equally noble one of Arcite.

[100] Kemped heres: Dr. Morris rejects the usual rendering of the word kemped as combed, and asserts that it means the very reverse, and, "instead of smoothly combed, means bent, curled, and hence rough, shaggy." A similar term occurs a few lines farther on, describing the hair 'kempt behind his back,' where Dr. Morris reads combed. It seems, however, contrary to the rule of courtesy observed by lovers, that a noble knight should appear at a festival like a wild man of the woods. If, on the other hand, the shaggy hairs were on the eyebrow, it certainly adds to the ferocity of his look. I prefer the former reading for Emelye's bridegroom.

[101] See page 42, note.

[102] Alauns. A species of dog used for hunting the boar, &c. Sp. alano. Speght says they were greyhounds, Tyrwhitt mastiffs, much esteemed in Italy in the 14th century. See Cotgrave—'Allan, a kind of big, strong, thick-headed, and short-snowted dog—the brood whereof came first out of Albania.'

[103] See Appendix, p. 111.

[104] A kind of rich silk.

[105] The 'mantelet' was at first devised to protect the burnished helmet from becoming inconveniently heated by the sun: it became afterwards fantastic in form, and is the origin of the 'mantling' seen in modern coats of arms.

[106] This fair countenance is oddly assigned to an Indian monarch: but some of the details of his appearance are poetic embellishments and must not be relied upon. The white eagle carried for his pleasure is probably one of the many exaggerations for picturesque effect, and is only a magnified falcon, a bird which was at this time the constant companion of the noble: hawking was in high favour, and the bird's tameness depended on its habituation to its owner's voice and touch. A little later on the hawks are mentioned as sitting on perches during the festival; such perches were in every room and hall in common life; so provision had to be made for their accommodation on the grandest occasions. In Wright's 'Womankind,' we read: "Different species of the hawk were allotted to persons of the different grades and ranks of society. Thus we are told that the eagle and the vulture belonged to the emperor, from which we must understand that the emperor was not expected to go often a-hawking." Evidently Chaucer was well read in his books on falconry.

[107] Carole (Tyrwhitt—the other editions have dance) was a round dance.

[108] The term for the whole panoply of knight or steed—armour and coat-armour included.

[109] A knight in armour was in very little danger from a cut of a broadsword, or even from the blow of a mace; but a thrusting sword might easily pierce through the joints of his armour.—Bell.

[110] Tyrwhitt's and Bell's editions read, 'Farwel, my swete, farwel, myn Emelye!'

[111] Tyrwhitt. Overnome is participle past of overnimen (Sax.), to overtake. The following, and the sixth line further on, are also Tyrwhitt's reading.

[112] See Chaucer for Schools, p. 86, for some curious details.

[113] The Summoners and the Friars were naturally always at variance, both deriving their money from the same Source: both belonged to the Church, but the Summoner was legally qualified to extort, whilst the Friar was only permitted to beg. Thus, if the Summoner had been to a house first, the Friar was likely to suffer.

[114] Houses of ill-fame were exempted from ecclesiastical interference on the ground that they were a necessary evil, and might be thus better surveillé.

[115] Gale—sing: it means here, 'If the Summoner likes to squeak when he feels the shoe pinch, let him!'

[116] "A dog trained for shooting with the bow, part of whose education consisted in following the stricken deer only, and separating it from the herd."—Bell.

[117] Ribibe: a shrill musical instrument—metaphorical for a shrill old woman.

[118] Tyrwhitt.

[119] The hell of the Teutonic race, before they were Christians, was in the north, and after their conversion, as their converters adopted their name, only giving the place a Christian

character, it was natural that the people should retain their original notion of its position.—Bell.

[120] Tyrwhitt.

[121] Money forced out of people by threats or ill-usage.

[122] A proverbial expression.

[123] Tyrwhitt.

[124] Tyrwhitt; more forcible.

[125] The first quarter of the artificial day: i.e. 9 o'clock.

[126] Tyrwhitt. Morris has 'nothing for to leere.'

[127] This verse means, 'You shall hereafter understand this subject so well, as to be able to give lectures on it, as a professor in his chair;' chayer being the term for pulpit or professor's chair; conne part of the verb conne, to know or be able; and rede, to counsel. The evil one is sarcastic on the special wickedness of the Summoner.

[128] Alluding to Eneas' visit to infernal regions (6th book of 'Eneid') and Dante's 'Inferno.'

[129] The text has 'Heit, Scot, heit, brok, what spare ye for the stones?' and it is singular that 'hayt' is still the word used by waggoners in Norfolk to make their horses go on; while Scot remains one of the commonest names for a horse in Norfolk and Suffolk. The Reeve's horse in the Prologue is called Scot also. Brock means a badger, hence applied to a grey horse. The carter presently calls this horse 'myn oughne lyard (grey) boy.'

[130] The value of twelve pence may be estimated by the relative value of food and labour. Bell says, "Twelve pence would have bought two dozen hens, or three gallons of red wine, or hired a dozen common labourers for twelve days," but surely he means a dozen labourers for one day, or one labourer for twelve days.

[131] There was then no means of conveyance for people who could not walk except horseback.

[132] A libel, a copy of the information or indictment. A libel is still the expression in the ecclesiastical courts.—Bell. The abuses, we see, have led to another interpretation of the word libel—as libellous.

[133] This singular (to us) term as applied to Christ, was of course borrowed from the popular notion of warfare, when each knight, inspired by some fair inciter, was the more valiant for her sake. The term is both picturesque and forcible as an appeal to the common understanding, in which the Friars were naturally adepts.

[134] Tyrwhitt.

[135] The Summoner's Tale (omitted) follows here.

[136] Students then entered the university at a far younger age than at the present day, almost indeed when boys now enter the public schools, so that the Clerk of Oxford may have been but a boy, which would account for his diffident demeanour: yet his education and knowledge might warrant mine host's fear of his being too learned for them.

[137] Table: a board upon trestles.

[138] These are the lines on which the supposition is based that Petrarch and Chaucer had met.

[139] "Joannes of Lignano, near Milan, a canonist and natural philosopher, who flourished about 1378."—B.

[140] Saluzzo, a marquisate near Mount Viso: Lat. Vesulus.

[141] Corage is used in several senses: impulse (as in the opening lines of the Prologue), feeling, or disposition may be implied. The word is derived from the Latin cor, the heart.

[142] See note 144 below.

[143] The courtsey of modern times is all that remains of the old custom of kneeling.

[144] The house without. In these early times, dwelling-places were usually built within a court. The court was, among the poor, a spot enclosed by a hedge or fence of sticks, and often a dry ditch; in the middle of this enclosure or house, the hall in which they lived stood— a mere covered room. The chamber or bower, for sleeping and privacy, was a second erection within the court; but, in the case of so poor a man as Janicula, probably there was but one covered room, hall or chamber, used for any purpose of shelter. So when the guests came into the house without, the enclosure is meant, within which a single hut stood, built of planks. Janicula's ox (used for draught, as now in Italy) inhabited the hut with them, and Griselda sets down her can in the stall when she enters the hut. In and around Naples we may still see the turkeys, pigs, and donkeys sharing the hovels with the peasants in this miserable way.

[145] On the Continent, even at the present day, the bride is expected to assent to the bridegroom chosen by her parents. Walter treated Griselda with especial consideration and respect by consulting her. Skeat quotes the legal formula of refusal, Le roy s'avisera, to show that Walter's question, "Wol ye assent, or elles yow avyse?" gave her the chance to refuse.

[146] In the 14th century it was the custom for everybody to go to bed with the sun. They rose in the morning at 4 or 5, had breakfast at 6, dinner at 10 or 11, and supper about 6.

[147] Sergeant and servant are doublets.—Skeat. Probably he was a cross between a highwayman and a soldier. Sergeant at one time meant squire to a prince or nobleman.

[148] Tyrwhitt.

[149] It was common, nay usual, in mediæval times for noble children to be put out to nurse in the family of some equal or dependent, for purposes of security. The removal of Walter's children from the mother was not an outrage: but concealing their fate from her was.

[150] Panico, Petrarch; Panigo, Boccace. I cannot be sure of the situation of this place, but there is a certain Paganico near Urbino, marked in old maps as a castle or fortress, which is not too far from Bologna to be possibly the place referred to. A river Panaro flows between Modena and Bologna.

[151] Tyrwhitt.

[152] It was not uncommon in olden times for girls to be married at twelve years of age.

[153] Skeat.

[154] The smock, or shift, was a high garment with long sleeves, often embroidered with black stitchery.

[155] "A jane is a small coin of Genoa (Janua); the meaning is, your praise is dear enough at a farthing."—B. Or the verse may be taken to mean, the smallest coin is dear enough to you when you are tired of better—for novelty's sake.

[156] Skeat; also second line beyond.

[157] Tyrwhitt and Skeat.

[158] Tyrwhitt.

[159] Skeat.

[160] Skeat and Tyrwhitt.

[161] For the analysis of these two remarkable and elaborately worked-out characters, see Chaucer for Schools, p. 111.

[162] Basse Bretaigne in France, called anciently Britannia Armorica.

[163] See Notes to this tale, p. 91, touching the homage paid to women during the middle ages.

[164] Penmark is placed on the maps on the western coast of Brittany, between Brest and Port l'Orient.

[165] The only means of subsistence a knight had was fighting—of course for hire.

[166] Backgammon.

[167] About the 20th of May by our almanac.

[168] Clerk at that time denoted a man of learning, and a student at the universities—generally in holy orders.

[169] Natural Magic, Chaucer.—All kinds of conjuring were very popular at this time. The minstrels or jougleurs added to their other accomplishments marvellous skill in sleight of hand (derived from the East): hence the modern signification of the word juggler. It is quite clear that many of their tricks were due to electro-biology, a science known to those mighty

cultivators and preservers of learning, the Arabs. For some knowledge of what we owe to the Arabs, and of their influence upon mediæval European literature, I refer the reader to the 'Literary Remains of Emanuel Deutsch' (published by John Murray), containing two articles on Arabic Poetry; and to Draper's popular 'History of the Conflict between Religion and Science.'

[170] This and the following line are not in Morris's edition.

[171] Bell's edition. This and the next six lines are not in Morris's edition.

[172] Equal to eight or ten times the amount now.

[173] Equivalent to 'What is done cannot be undone.'

[174] I could not resist inserting the vigorous old words.

[175] The ale-stake was a stake set up as a sign before the inn, generally adorned with a bush. This custom prevails in Normandy still, where you may see a goodly bunch of mistletoe hanging out wherever wine or cider is sold.

[176] "A small bell used formerly to be rung before the corpse as it was carried to the grave, to give notice to those who were charitably disposed that they might pray for the soul of the deceased. Our 'passing bell' has the same origin, though the reason for it has ceased."—Bell.

[177] "Perhaps an allusion to the great pestilence which devastated Europe during the 14th century. This pestilence means during this pestilence, as this year means during this year."—Bell.

[178] "This is still the ceremony used in taking an oath in courts of justice in Prussia."—Bell. Notice the emphasis laid on their close friendship, and their constant allusion to their being all 'one,' over and above the solemnity of the profane vow they make.

[179] The kindly custom of greeting passers-by, now rapidly going out even in our country districts, was more common in days when passers-by were infinitely rarer. Probably half a mile from the inn the road was lonesome enough, wherefore the old man's anticipation of rough treatment from three reckless and half-tipsy ruffians was not unreasonable. His calm and fearless answer was the wisest as well as the most dignified course to pursue with such assailants, being calculated to sober them as well as to save himself.

[180] Making a jest of the close coverings and wraps of old age.

[181] Caitif, wretch, wretched. Italian—cattivo, captive. Fr.-chétif, poor, wretched, paltry, pitiful, &c. Captive seems to give the most pathetic meaning, as though death were a looked-for freedom by a restless prisoner in the body. Fugitive is the next best for the sense, as the old man may be supposed to be flying to the gate for safety and comfort.

[182] Hair-shroud, sackcloth, the roughest cloth.

[183] Tyrwhitt's edition has the less bloody threat, 'Tell wher he is, or thou shalt it abie!'

[184] The old man probably saw that the young men were scarcely responsible for their actions, and determined to wreak violence on some one, and therefore he played on their mood to avert their violence from himself to some other object.

[185] Tyrwhitt.

[186] Probably in the vessels, &c., which had contained the food, thus avoiding the appearance of transporting treasure.

[187] Shall counsel he kept between us? literally, in schoolboys' language, 'Mum's the word—eh?'

[188] Bell's edition.

[189] Games which we now leave to children were formerly as popular with grown-up people. Hunt-the-slipper and blind-man's-buff were 200 years ago the common recreation of ladies and gentlemen, and wrestling and other romping was indulged in far more commonly than now by young men. Playing at ball was a favourite pastime.

[190] Tyrwhitt. Outrely, utterly, beyond all things. Vide the French—outre mesure, beyond measure. The common mediæval expressions, 'out of measure,' 'out of doubt,' were probably from the same word, outre = beyond.

[191] Tyrwhitt.

[192] Cast, as in 'cast a nativity,' means fix upon, arrange, discover.

[193] Tyrwhitt.

[194] Avicen, Ebn Sina, an Arabian physician of the 10th century. Fen, apparently an Arabic word, is the name given to the sections of Avicenna's great work on physic, entitled Canun.—Tyrwhitt.

[195] A play on the word: light meant also fickle or untrue.

[196] Tyrwhitt has treasure; Morris has tresorere, treasurer. The former seems the most appropriate to a lady-love. A similar expression is found in 'Li Congiés Adan d'Aras' (MS. de la Vallière, No. 2736 Bibl. Imp.), 'De mon cuer serós tresoriere.'

[197] Bereft of money as a friar's tonsure is of hair.

[198] Bell's edition reads tene, taken.

[199] Tyrwhitt's and Bell's editions. Morris has 'Do wel.'

[200] Fortune with her wheel.

[201] 'Kick against the pricks.'

[202] For the clay pot is the weaker of the two.

[203] Tyrwhitt. Morris has daunte and dauntest (Fr., dompter), meaning control.

[204] See 'Notes by the Way,' p. 103.

Note from the Editor

Odin's Library Classics strives to bring you unedited and unabridged works of classical literature. As such, this is the complete and unabridged version of the original English text unless noted. In some instances, obvious typographical errors have been corrected. This is done to preserve the original text as much as possible. The English language has evolved since the writing and some of the words appear in their original form, or at least the most commonly used form at the time. This is done to protect the original intent of the author. If at any time you are unsure of the meaning of a word, please do your research on the etymology of that word. It is important to preserve the history of the English language.

Taylor Anderson

Made in the USA
Columbia, SC
11 July 2024

38491016R00093